Blue Moon Bench

Second Edition

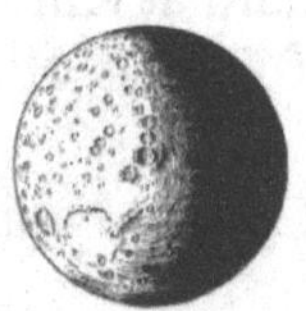

By D L Blanchard

First Edition
Published by D.L. Blanchard at Smashwords

ISBN: 97871301919307 - ePublish
ISBN: 978-1494209407 - Print Pub

Second Edition
Published by D.L. Blanchard at Kindle Digital Publishing

Library of Congress Control Number 2025917666

Hardcover ISBN: 978-1-969644-01-6
Paperback ISBN: 978-1-969644-02-3
ISBN-10: 19694401X
UNSPSC-Code: 55101500 (Printed Publications)

Table of Content

DEDICATION

This novel is dedicated to all pure teachers in the Nyingma Palyul Lineage who have brought great blessings to this student and help to end suffering.

To my sister Sue Alexander and her husband Kenny for all their kindness to me over the years. To my sister Helen Francisco for being a mom to me in the first half of my life, and a good friend the second half.

And last but not least to my beloved mother June and father Donald for all the protection and unconditional love they provided our family.

Cover design by D. L. Blanchard
Cover artwork by D.L. Blanchard

https://bluemoonbench.com/

ACKNOWLEDGMENTS

A special thank you to my ex-husband, Greg Senter, who stood by me many years ago when his job stole me away from northern Arizona and the land I loved, and caused me to write this novel filled with the longing and desire to return to that magical land that had become such a part of me forever. And to all the authors I respected and read over the years, including Daphne DuMaurier and her incomparable 'Rebecca,' which has fascinated so many for so many years including this writer.

To Peter Blystone, that rascal of a dear friend who inspired my adventurous nature, who made me hike impossible trails and find stunning rock art and ruins, and who still embodies the magic of the southwest. Thank you for your efforts in helping me to get it 'right' in the last edits.

And most important, to those readers who may have been raised as I was, a sometimes Christian with a good heart. May this novel open your hearts to a new way of seeing a spiritual path as something that cannot be labeled: truth is truth. All paths of faith are precious: including the Buddha Dharma.

Chapter 1: And It's Murder

Summer, northern Arizona Hopi Reservation, Hotevilla

The three of them stood in silence as an expectant hush came over the village, and in the distance a gentle tinkling sound floated on the summer breeze to mix with the lone buzz of a fly. High in the sky, a hazy Arizona sun gave the pueblos an almost buttery hue. Both observers standing with Jessica on the roof looked in anticipation to the east, and she shifted her gaze in the same direction.

"They'll come to the plaza through the alley to your right," her husband Alex whispered into her ear. His eclectic accent came from the many languages he spoke, and it gave an artistic twist to his words. He stood behind her, tall and shading her from the summer heat. He always allowed his dark hair to grow too long and it now tangled in the breeze while he looked down at her with a smile, his teeth white against his tanned skin.

It was a tradition in the small Hopi village they were visiting, for those attending the dances to stand on the flat pueblo roofs of the village. Today's dance was well attended so the three of them were surrounded by other observers who had made the long trip to this remote village to observe this ancient dance.

"Rachel never came to the Kachina Dances," Mac, a longtime friend of her husband's said suddenly, "she was far too much of a lady." He swiped under his eye and Jessica wasn't certain if it was a tear or sweat. Whatever it was, the comment met with silence from herself and Alex.

Jessica realized she felt the usual companion of jealousy standing just behind her, a cold hand on her shoulder, horrible and mean. It always visited her when anyone mentioned Rachel, her husband's dead first wife. She stayed brave and glanced up at her husband now, seeing the usual reaction on his handsome face; pale and tight-lipped silence.

Rachel had died over a year ago, but in the six months Jessica had known her husband, she'd come to discover that he still loved his achingly beautiful first wife, who died long before she'd met him. His reaction was always the same; he hated anyone bringing up the past. She felt certain it was her job to help him forget, or their marriage of three months would not survive.

After a bit, she began to wonder if she should have brought a hat to protect her from the Arizona desert sun. Almost everyone around her was Hopi, and she was sure none of them felt the heat like she did with her light hair and pale skin.

Mac, standing opposite of her husband, touched her shoulder just where the jealousy and fear had a moment earlier. She felt a shiver go down her spine.

"I saw someone I need to talk to," he said quietly. "I'll come back up and join the two of you at the end of this dance. Do you mind?"

He was an anthropologist, like her husband, and had tagged along with them for the day. Now they bargained to meet him at their truck on a break, and Jessica caught a glimpse of his blonde head as he climbed off the roof and down the ancient ladder. He soon disappeared into the crowd.

They were on the Hopi Reservation in northern Arizona, attending the Home Dance in the village of Hotevilla on Second Mesa. It was an annual religious dance where the Native American people of the village said good-bye to the Kachinas; the Hopi's spiritual beings that they believed took physical appearance during the growing season. Today's dance was giving them a sendoff after the long winter and spring months. The Hopi believed that the Kachinas were on a trip back to their home on the thirteen-thousand-foot San Francisco Peaks that rose out of the Arizona desert over a hundred miles away.

Jessica's eye caught a blaze of color coming through the crowd in the street below. Holding her breath, she watched from her perch on the roof as a line of at least fifteen Kachinas came into the village plaza just below them. The gentle tinkling she'd heard earlier came from bells that were attached to their knee-high leggings. This was her first glimpse of the famous Kachinas and she wasn't disappointed. Each dancer wore a large wooden mask that completely covered the head. The masks were artistically painted white, accented with brilliant turquoise, black and red. From the top sprouted feathers and pine twigs, and a bushy, pine-bough collar graced each of the dancers' shoulders.

After entering the small plaza, which was nothing more than a dirt-floored space between four different mud buildings, all of the dancers formed a circle and stood in silent expectation. An elder white-haired man, dressed in jeans and a plaid shirt, sprinkled each Kachina and spoke so quietly that Jessica found herself leaning dangerously over the edge of the roof, trying to catch his words.

"He's blessing them with corn," Alex told her softly in explanation. Both of them were Buddhists and very interested in other religions in the world because they believed all spiritual paths are sacred.

Looking back into the square, she saw that the Kachinas stood motionless for a few moments as the elder's voice spoke on, dusting each dancer.

Alex spoke to her quietly, his attention on the dancers, "I'm thirsty. I'm going to the truck to get some water. You don't mind, do you?"

She smiled up at him and admired his dark hair tangling in the light breeze. "That's ok, I can wait. You should hurry though."

Without another comment, he gave her a quick kiss, then left her and followed Mac's route off the roof with a brief wave and a quick "I'll be right back."

She watched his head with dark, shiny hair as it bobbed along through the crowd below her. He stood heads taller than all the natives lining the way, so she was able to watch his progress until he disappeared around a corner.

After Alex's departure, she stood for several minutes watching the activity in the plaza, shifting from foot to foot. She was totally clueless as to what the dancers were doing, and without Alex to explain the intricate ceremony, she felt lost.

With a sudden decision made, she turned and made her way to the ladder, deciding to follow Alex to the truck. She wanted a hat to shade her head from the sun anyway, and she knew she'd rather see the dance with him there.

On the ground, she began her walk to the truck, suddenly a little uncertain of her route. She remembered the blue screen door and a pile of juniper wood stacked against a mud covered stone wall with a plastic truck in the dirt next to it. Hadn't Alex made a joke about the truck on their way down this same alley earlier that morning?

As she turned the corner of a pueblo that had been sheared up with chicken wire and mud, she noticed a rangy man leaning against the wall of an adjacent alley. He was looking directly at her from beneath the rim of a bright red ball cap. As soon as she'd looked his way, he'd stood away from the wall, taking his hands from his pockets. He looked Native American, but his features were more elongated than a Hopi, and because of that she thought that he didn't look as if he belonged.

Walking in the deserted dirt alley, keeping in the buildings' shadow, she moved toward the south side of the village. Glancing instinctively behind her, Jessica saw that the stranger had begun following her. His hands were jammed back in his pockets, and his long, stringy hair flopped in a breeze that made its way between the buildings.

Uncertain if the stranger's path just happened to match her own, Jessica casually turned down another back alley, the thought of meeting Alex forgotten. The man followed her route, and she then knew that he had singled her out as a target. He had picked up his pace, and was gaining ground, directly meeting her eye as she looked nervously over her shoulder. She felt a little snap of fear, but thought she must be wrong. Why would anyone follow her?

Deciding that her immediate need was to get back to the crowd, she picked up her pace. She tried to judge where the plaza was from the sound of the chanting and drums that came to her from a distance. She could hear the dancers' chants rise up and fall, the sound bouncing off the pueblo walls and confusing her sense of direction. The song would build to a peak, hesitate, almost dwindle and then suddenly begin to gain momentum, the volume creating echoes all around her.

She was beginning to realize that she was very alone in a village where she knew no one, and the vulnerability it gave her was not welcomed. She wasn't sure why the man was following her, but he had left an impression of acne scars and greasy hair. She began to sweat from her rapid walk, and her breathing became labored. Now she was pissed-off and gave a brief thought to turning on the man and challenging him outright.

She gave a darted look behind her once more before turning another corner toward what she hoped was the plaza, and saw that her stalker was almost upon her. Not only that, but she had seen something glint in his right hand, now low at his side. She had this terrifying thought that it might be a knife, and the image of the cold steel in her ribs caused her to almost stumble in her hurry.

She told herself that she was being ridiculous, but she still broke into a trot, skidding a little in the dirt as she took a left turn down another small alley. Just as she rounded the corner, the sound of the chanting came full force, and she realized she'd made it to the plaza with the dancers and a crowd of onlookers.

Pushing her way into the throng, she didn't hesitate to begin a path to the other side of the plaza. She quickly turned to see that her follower had slowed, but the crowd had not stopped his progress. The chanting and the beat of the drums had risen to a feverish pitch, much louder now that she was right in the mix.

The rhythm played in Jessica's chest, along with her racing heart, still accelerated from her run. She clenched her teeth, feeling the grittiness left by the dust that rose from the dancers as they stamped in a circle around the plaza. They were so close that she could hear the grunts and overworked breathing as they labored around her under the tremendous weight of the masks. She had an intense impression of large, sweating bodies covered in rusty red grease paint, decorated with white markings. The sound of the rattles and the vibration of each foot tromping with the sharp tinkle of the bells sounded loud in her ears. The dancers' aura filled the square, their strength and presence was striking. Jessica felt small and jarringly out of place, and she knew the man following her was close and in pursuit behind her.

The pueblo walls facing the plaza each had a line of onlookers—one and two deep. As she moved between them and the Kachinas, her shoulders stiff with discomfort, she shot sharp glances around her. Each man, woman and child watched her progress, silent and staring as she moved among them, her fair skin and hair color setting her apart from the others.

The dancers' circle had spread to meet the line of onlookers, effectively blocking her route of escape. She noticed a space along a wall left opcn by someone and quickly claimed it, and then turned to look back the way she'd come. She saw that the man had stopped following her. She wondered if she'd imagined it and sighed in frustration. When the Hopi woman next to her gave her a smile, she felt safer for the moment and trying to set aside what happened, she took a deep breath and leaned against the warm mudded wall to collect herself.

Slowly, through a dreamlike haze, the faint thump of the drum and the hum of the dancers' voices hung in the quiet air of the village and rose up around Jessica. Each Kachina wore a kilt that came to mid-thigh and a woven belt tied around the waist. She caught a glimpse of a small figure dressed like a woman wearing a black wig and painted face mask standing in the middle of the huge Kachina gods. Carrying a large drum face-up and suspended from around her neck, she was beating out a steady rhythm, like a mother leading her children.

As if on cue, what appeared to be the leader of the dancers began to build the chanting by shaking his brightly painted rattle more rapidly, while the woman with the drum picked up the rhythm. The leader's bare, powerful legs lifted and pounded as the other dancers joined him. Low, strong voices broke back into song, compelling, with infinite variations that Jessica had failed to recognize earlier from the roof.

The line of Kachinas started picking up momentum, moving slowly around the plaza in a circle, following the leader in a counter-clockwise direction. Dust again rose up around them as they stamped and shuffled their feet, and Jessica was mesmerized by the sound of their chant, the rattles and the drum.

She closed her eyes for a moment and just listened to the ancient sounds of the Hopi Kachinas singing to their village. She felt a little dizzy and, for that space in time, she lived in another reality—her thirst, her pursuer, and her husband—all forgotten. Opening her eyes, she skimmed the old pueblo buildings that stood around the plaza holding onlookers on the roofs as they had for centuries. All the homes in the village maze were constructed from hand-trimmed sandstone blocks finished with mud plaster making them blend in with the surrounding desert landscape.

By choice there were no telephone poles, no streetlights, and no hum of air conditioners. She could smell the ancient scent of the village and the wood smoke that came from the many cooking fires. She felt connected with the ancient mesa on which the little village was resting, the waving heat of summer rising off the desert around them. As the song of the dancers rose and fell, she found herself a part of this world where magic floated around her. Licking the salty sweat from above her upper lip, she tasted the dirt as if it might be an elixir that could keep her captured in the past. She swayed on her feet, feeling a little high, and a little elated and one with all the colors, smells and sounds.

A blur of red caught her peripheral vision, and Jessica was brought back to the present with a jolt. She wiped under her sweaty eyes and glanced to the spot where the man following her had chosen to stand and saw that he was still watching her, leaning indolently against the wall once more.

The dancers' chanting stopped and they turned as a group and each picked up heavy burlap sacks and baskets that had been left earlier in the center of the plaza. Now, they began pulling items out to throw into the crowd, and Jessica remembered Alex telling her there would be gifts made from corn, a holy food to the Hopi. Candied popcorn balls, and pikki bread, an onion skin thin cornbread, both yellow and blue, delicately rolled and placed into small zip-lock bags. Jessica watched as they also threw apples and oranges, causing a flurry of laughter from onlookers who dodged the fruit, trying to catch it as it whizzed by.

The north side of the plaza was filled with a few rows of folding chairs where, Alex told her, the honored family members sit. The Kachinas walked among the children and young people and handed out items such as small, hand-carved Kachina Dolls, beautiful woven baskets and toy-hunting bows with colorful arrows. The children's giggles and chatter bubbled up as they showed their gifts to their parents, probably just as the parents had when they were children.

Jessica used this activity and confusion to slip out the opposite side of the plaza, thinking to escape the watchful eye of her follower. Trying to get her sense of direction back, she wondered if she'd ever find her way to the roof where she and Alex were supposed to meet. She moved between the buildings, quickly glancing behind her to see if the red baseball cap was still in pursuit. She felt great relief when he was nowhere to be seen.

To her surprise, after only a few minutes, she came out of the crowd of small pueblos and saw Mac sitting on a large, flat rock in the shade of a cottonwood tree. He was tying one of his hiking boots, bent over and intent.

"Mac!" she called, waving over her head so he'd see her among the few other people walking around. His head came up at the sound of her voice and as soon as he recognized her, he stood and waved back, smiling.

"I was just getting ready to re-join you on the roof," Mac told Jessica as she walked toward him. He sat back down and patted the rock, indicating that she should join him. He seemed in no hurry to return.

As she sat next to him, the shade of the tree was a welcome relief from the sun. Closing her eyes, she took a deep breath and slowly let it out. She briefly thought of telling Mac about the man in the red cap, but she realized that she was a little embarrassed. She decided it was better to be silent, and now that she felt safe, it felt unimportant.

Mac took his old felt hat off his head and began to fan her. "Jeez, you look as if you could use some shade, luv," he said with concern. "Your face is flushed." She wasn't hot, just a little frustrated. She let it go as his imagination.

Like her husband, he also had an accent, but it was obviously Australian. It was in that country where he and Alex first met. Mac was now living in northern Arizona and studying the learning styles of native people all over the world, including those on the reservation in Arizona. He was a man of high intelligence, medium height, and gave the impression of stature simply because of his perfectly erect posture.

Jessica smiled her thanks at him and explained how she'd tried to follow Alex to the truck and gotten lost in the confusion of pueblos.

With a chuckle in response to her deliberately woeful expression, Mac swung a sloshing canteen from his side, removed the lid and offered it to her. At that moment she gave no thought to anything but the cool canteen that she grasped with both hands like an eager child and tilted her head back, allowing the water to dribble a little in her haste. It was only a little cool, but sweet and wet.

He gently took the canteen from her and dampened his handkerchief before placing the cap back on. Jessica was surprised by his solicitation. She knew he was being overprotective and she wondered why.

"It's such a shame that these dances might soon be closed to the public," Mac commented, looking off over her shoulder toward the village.

"Really?" Jessica asked with surprise, "Why would they do that?"

"Because most outsiders just don't understand the importance of the dances. Too many people come, but don't take the time to learn even a little about the culture." He saw Jessica's puzzled look and continued. "Well, take for example, a visitor I saw today from Japan. He went over to a Kiva and climbed up its ladder to photograph the street. The Kiva is a very sacred building to the Hopi, and no one is allowed to touch it or stand by it when the Kachinas are in residence. Not to mention that photos are not allowed." Mac ran his fingers through his short, blonde hair. "Sometimes I'm embarrassed when I'm here."

Jessica noticed that his cropped hair barely moved in the breeze. He was a fit man of solid muscle, tanned and lean, and wore a mustache and beard. He favored the expected khaki shorts, a light tan tee shirt and sturdy brown hiking boots. Jessica had thought from the beginning that his face was mild and gentle. They sat there a few more moments and just when Jessica was about to suggest they rejoin Alex, Mac shocked her with a question.

"Jessica," he said in a quiet tone, "How much do you know about Rachel's death?"

Jessica blinked her surprise. "Not much, actually," she admitted to Mac, "Alex is reluctant to speak of it and, I don't know, I guess I respect his privacy." She watched as he dropped his eyes and realized that his mood had grown very serious.

He stood up and turned away from her, looking out across the desert plain. "I know this must be hard for you," he said, shifting his gaze to his feet, not speaking for several moments. Then he turned and lifted his intense blue eyes to look straight at her. While she'd thought him mild-looking, she now realized that his blue eyes gave away a quick and clever mind. His Australian accent became more pronounced as he said, "Jessica, I have a real concern for your safety. I believe you're in danger."

She just sat there staring into his face, feeling different emotions rise inside of her in response to his comment. He seemed sincere and her next thought was of the man in the red ball cap and his pursuit.

"I have two things to tell you," Mac went on, stepping so close to her she had to lean back. "One, Rachel's death was not accidental, and two, she was not alone that night on Blue Moon Bench where her deserted auto was found." Jessica stared at him, too surprised to say anything.

"When she was found dead at the bottom of the Grand Canyon," he continued, fiddling with the canteen now strung back over his shoulder. "The FBI was called in and the blokes claimed there was nothing that would lead them to believe there was any 'foul play'," Mac told her. "I, on the other hand, think differently."

Jessica sat very still, afraid to look away from his intense eyes. She wanted to know. A breeze rustled the leaves of the tree high above her and the dappled shadows danced nervously across his face. The drums and chanting in the distance sounded surrealistic.

"I won't say any more now," Mac said. "Just ask yourself this. If Rachel was one of the most loved women alive, how could she end up dead at the bottom of a desolate canyon? She was beautiful, accomplished, and happy. Ask yourself why she'd drive out alone so late to the Navajo Reservation, leaving her guests on the night of a big party in her own home?" He stood in front of her looking down into her upturned face. "I really like you, Jessica. I would hate to see you hurt. Take care of yourself. I'm here if you need a friend."

Jessica searched his face once again and saw that his eyes were filled with concern and he seemed sincere. She took a breath as if being awakened, his words echoing in her ears. How do you process a comment like that?

She thought for a moment and then asked, "What are you saying?" She leaned forward to rise, her motion forcing him to step back, giving her room to stand.

Looking around as if he were worried someone might hear them, he moved closer toward her and placed his hand on her back, whispering into her ear, "Alex had an alibi for the night she died. I'd check it out if I were you, mate. I think it's a lie." His Australian accent had grown so thick she wasn't sure she'd heard right. His breath was hot on her neck. Jessica jerked away and met his eyes, his hand now resting on her shoulder.

"Jessica! Mac! Where did you both go?" Alex's voice came to them from a short distance and they both jumped, as if guilty, and turned toward him.

Jessica worked at keeping calm, while she had a tangle of reaction inside. She threw Mac one swift glance and then put it aside for the moment. What else could she do? She moved toward her husband. "I decided to follow you to the truck and lost my way," she told him in explanation. "I came upon Mac, and he acted as rescuer, giving me some of his water."

Alex put his arm protectively around her and his attention helped calm her emotions; she gave him a small smile, searching his face and saw no duplicity. Mac was getting busy with his canteen, obviously shifting his own mood to accommodate Alex's arrival. Mac must be confused Jessica thought, he has to be confused.

"I insisted she sit here in the shade and cool off," Mac volunteered. Jessica was impressed with how ordinary he looked now. His smile small and tight, his complexion a little paler, but his hat was back on his head at a cocky angle.

Alex fussed over her a bit, and after she insisted she was fine, he said, "The first set is over and the dancers have gone back to rest. I brought the water and my pack with some goodies from the truck, thinking we could grab a little lunch while we waited for the next dance to start."

"That was a great idea, darling," Jessica said, taking his pack and laying it on the large flat rock where Mac sat. She wasn't sure she could eat, but anything that could distract her from the memory of Mac's comment was welcomed.

While she and Alex began unwrapping the lunch, Mac began making jokes in a light, almost normal tone. They all sat on the flat rocks in the shade, eating a lunch well packed by their housekeeper, waiting for the dancers' rest to end. Jessica found she could act casual and ordinary on a day that had turned a little odd.

They exchanged comments about the dancers, but after a bit it became evident that Mac had grown decidedly quiet. Alex, noticing his mood, asked if he was okay. He gave a ghost of a smile and without prompting began telling them a strange story that started almost as if he were revealing a secret folktale.

"Long ago, deep in winter," he began, "The Bean Dance, another celebration open to outsiders, had begun with its usual colorful parade of Kachinas through the village streets. While waiting for the dancers to pass by, two women tourists unwittingly leaned against the Kiva they stood next to. Almost immediately, a Whipper Kachina came out of the crowd and approached them."

"What's a Whipper Kachina?" Jessica asked when Mac paused.

"A kind of police, or peacekeeper, if you will," Mac told her. His eyes darted to Alex as he continued his story. Jessica followed his gaze and saw that Alex stood watching Mac, his expression unreadable.

"The Whipper saw the two women touching the Kiva and gestured for them to move away. But they smiled; they didn't understand. So, the Kachina lunged toward them, and struck them with his whip. The whip is a symbol of his office, a staff the Whipper must carry." Jessica shifted on her hard rock and watched Mac, becoming fascinated. As he spoke, his voice had gotten quieter with each word until she had to lean forward to catch the last sentence. "The Whipper gestured one more time for them to move, but the women started laughing."

Suddenly, his voice became loud and forceful. "Like a snake striking, the Whipper began beating these women with the whips. They ducked and cringed, but he was relentless, hitting their shoulders and their heads. Everyone grew silent in the crowd." He dropped his arms before letting out a breath, and turning his gaze toward Alex. "In the crowd was a man, an outsider. He leaped forward and tore the whips out of the Kachina's hand, bringing them to a halt—a discipline that has been around for centuries! He interfered in the ritual of religious belief that should never be tampered with!" His voice hinted at disgust.

"And what he hasn't told you yet," Alex suddenly interjected in a quiet voice, "but I'm certain he will eventually, is that the man was me."

Jessica turned toward Alex in surprise as he continued, "And he also failed to tell you that the whips don't really hurt. They are designed to create more noise and theatrics than harm. With my help, the women finally realized what they needed to do, and moved away from the Kiva." Alex gave a careless shrug. "Really Mac, you've become dramatic in your old age."

All three of them sat in silence. Jessica caught Mac casting a dark look toward Alex, and saw that Alex wore a mildly tolerant expression. She wondered over the encounter, especially after the brief conversation she'd had with Mac before. Maybe he was just a man who loved the attention and liked center stage. She'd look at that later when she was alone.

A sudden quickening of the crowd told them the dancers were done resting and were headed back to the plaza. Alex gathered the leftovers and zipped them back into his pack. He removed an ugly fishing hat from another compartment and, smiling, put it on Jessica's head.

"There, that will protect that fair skin of yours," he said, giving her a quick kiss before swinging his pack over his shoulder. The three of them headed for the ladder that would lead them back onto the roof.

The rest of the day was a blur, dampened by her conversation with Mac, and the ugliness of the fishing hat. Jessica wanted to dismiss what Mac had said to her and thought that a true friend would have never handled it that way. And was he serious when he said that Alex's alibi might be a lie? *The thought carried a lot of karma,* she thought. Was she brave enough to delve deeper?

When the last dance was finished and the Kachinas began to disperse, Mac decided to head back to town. Before walking away, he gave Jessica a meaningful look and a quick hug, while she stood a little rigid and unresponsive. He then threw Alex a quick wave and turned to walk to his car. Alex looked after him, puzzled. "I wonder what's bothering Mac. He seemed rather moody," Alex said. "Oh well," he shrugged, "Guess the old boy has got things on his mind."

"*I guess he does*," Jessica thought, "*Murder*!"

Chapter 2: The Wind, and the Cold

Three months earlier, Northern Arizona

The late March storm had come in from California, bringing with it snow in the higher elevations of Arizona and rain to the lower plains. A solid wall of dark clouds made a cold ceiling, under which lived lower, lighter gray clouds, swirling against the dark backdrop. The winds gusted, cold and chilling, bringing the smell of ice and dampness to the air.

Jessica stood in the freezing wind, glad she had Alex's jacket on. She'd volunteered to get out of the Rover and open the gate to the ranch so Alex could drive the car through. The entrance to the Monte Vista Ranch was an impressive affair of stone and metal with an arching sign spanning over the road with the name Monte Vista Ranch welded into it. Alex told her a friend of his dad's had created the sign in the 1950s. Jessica could see, even through the rain, that the iron was red with rust from years of being in the weather, giving it the feeling of an artistic sculpture.

As she hurried back to the warmth of the Rover, she thought about how surrealistic it all was. Three months ago, she'd been thirty-two years old, single, and living on her own in San Francisco. An independent woman, free to make her own choices, she had been in the middle of a successful career as a professional illustrator. She had been living a quiet life in her inherited condo that looked down from the eighth floor to the Golden Gate Bridge. Then she'd gone on assignment in Arizona and one day while meditating in a large Buddhist temple while visiting Scottsdale, she met the handsome, wealthy, widowed anthropologist, Alex Dawson.

Now she was a woman coming home from her honeymoon to a ranch in the middle of northern Arizona, newly married to a man she had known only three months. Something she would have never believed of herself. She'd heard it said when love strikes, you become its prisoner. Jessica was finding out from personal experience that the saying hit directly home.

As Alex drove the Rover through the gate, Jessica glanced at him in the dimness of the car. His face was unique and rugged, with a sensitive look in his eyes, something she'd noticed about him right away. With his exotic charm and quiet manner, she'd had no choice but to surrender to love. While he'd teased her about the numerous men in her past that she'd turned down, in truth, none of those men had struck a cord deep within her as Alex had. A telling connection that made her believe there was truth to the belief in past lives.

From the first, it was true that she'd felt lust for his tall, broad-shouldered body, his dark, unruly hair that he always forgot to get cut until it hit his shoulders. But it was his intelligent indifference that challenged her feminine instincts to conquer. It started out as a harmless flirtation, but quickly turned into an obsession on Jessica's part. She wanted to storm the citadel of his emotional fortress, and find the man behind the face. In the early weeks she thought of it as a schoolgirl crush, but watched almost from the sidelines as her heart betrayed her and camped out on his doorstep. She wasn't as surprised at his proposal of marriage as she was at her own acceptance. She, the woman who gave in to no one, was excited about spending her life with a dark-eyed man she could not quite find.

Just after the wedding, they had arrived in Phoenix and drove up to the ranch in the Rover. The day had started sunny, but as the storm moved across the state, the wind had picked up and buffeted them the whole two hundred miles. Jessica had felt a cold coming on earlier, but now was in full fever, chilled and tired, even though she sat in the car with Alex's coat on and the heater on its highest setting. They'd made a few stops, taking the time to eat lunch in a small town along the interstate, and then got back on the road, only to hit snow just outside Flagstaff. It was slow going through the higher elevations, but when they started to drop down to the ranch, the snow had turned to rain. The long drive had left some time for Jessica to think more about the reality of what she had done.

Coming to Monte Vista Ranch as Mrs. Dawson, she found herself wishing she could be back in Lake Tahoe, carefree and playing the newlyweds. Or she wished they could live in San Francisco in her little townhouse, as a professional couple with no more worries than when to pay the mortgage. The idea of being married to a man as wealthy and politically powerful as Alex seemed a little daunting. The thought of her role in his life was only now fully coming to light in her mind as they drove up the road to the ranch house.

The road itself seemed to curve endlessly before them, muddy and indistinct in the rain. At times, it would take a jog around a juniper or pinyon pine tree, dipping and carving its way through the hills. A couple of times Jessica wasn't sure the Rover would make it through some of the deeper rivers that seemed to cover the road. She took a package of tissues from the glove box at Alex's recommendation, and blew her nose. Her head was pounding and she felt pretty crappy. It was late enough that Alex had turned on his headlights, and the eerie shadows that jabbed around them gave the drive a sinister look. Jessica didn't remember the road being so long on the one visit to the ranch that she'd made before they were married.

"Oh, I forgot," Alex said to her over the sound of the heater of the car, "I wouldn't be surprised if Mother and Dotty have put together a big homecoming." Jessica grimaced. Dotty was the kindly housekeeper who was almost part of the family. She and her husband Ralph had worked on the ranch for over twenty years and both loved Alex like their own.

"I told Mother that we'd probably be too tired to see guests on our first night back, but I know how they are. There's probably a crowd waiting to surprise us." He gave her another quick glance and said, "I know with that cold you're probably not up to it, but we'll just have a couple of drinks, and then leave them to their partying." He reached over and squeezed her hand in apology.

A stab of panic suddenly overcame her. Her earlier thoughts of the responsibility that came with being Alex's wife reappeared, and with it came a feeling of uncertainty. Any measure of self-possession seemed to disappear, as if rattled by the storm outside of the car.

Dreading the thought of meeting all of Alex's friends and family, she cursed him for not telling her that morning so she could have dressed accordingly. She was tired from the flight and the ride up from the valley, and felt awful from her nasty head cold. Her auburn hair was frizzy from the storm, and she thought her make-up was probably non-existent by now. As she pulled down the visor to peer into the mirror at her blue eyes, rimmed with dark smudges, she couldn't imagine being more miserable.

"Only a couple minutes now," Alex told her, "This storm should let up any time. It's rare for it to storm for so long. I guess this isn't much of a homecoming is it?" He reached over and tucked a strand of wild hair behind her ear.

She forced a smile his way, and did not answer him. Pulling her head deeper into the collar of his coat, she closed her eyes and sniffed while stubborn thoughts came up.

"Here we are," he said, a note of excitement in his voice. Jessica leaned forward, trying to see the house through the rain. "That's odd. There aren't any lights," Alex said even before Jessica had seen the house. When it came looming out of the dark, she realized he was right. It was gloomy and seemed to be unoccupied. She let out a deep breath of relief that she hadn't known she'd been holding.

The house was a two-story rambling adobe with a flat roof and a long portico on the front. She couldn't see it all in the dark, but she remembered its stately beauty from an earlier visit and was suddenly excited about moving in with Alex as his new bride.

He parked the truck right in front, and opened her door so she could run for the covered portico. Huddled in the darkness she watched as he fumbled around for the lock, finally throwing open the door with a curse. "Damn, the heat isn't even on. Here, stand just inside the door so I can get some lights and heat on. Don't move. I don't want you to hurt yourself."

Soon he had the lights on, and she could hear the rumble of the heater starting up somewhere in the cold house. He quickly brought in the luggage, dripping all over the flagstone in the foyer, all smiles and happy. He came over to her and wrapped his arms around her. "At least we don't have to deal with a crowd. We can turn on the hot tub after we have some dinner."

After disposing of their wet coats, they went into the great room and she wrapped herself in a soft Navajo blanket and plopped on the couch. As he started a fire in the fireplace, she watched as he worked from a small stack of wood to a huge pile that soon roared with orange flames.

The warmth seemed to wake Jessica from a distant kind of trance, and she sat up and said. "Can I go into the kitchen and find something to heat up?"

"Nope," he said, placing a palm on her forehead to check her fever, "sick as a dog and still so kind. You just sit right there. I'll take care of you." She couldn't raise the energy to say that she wasn't that sick. So, he kissed her red nose and got up from the couch. His cell phone rang suddenly and he answered it while walking into the kitchen. She could hear his voice indistinctly through the door as she watched the flames leaping in the fireplace.

After a few minutes, she idly looked around her at the grandeur of the house she would now live in. The great stone fireplace in front of her reached up to the high-beamed ceiling and stretched at least twelve feet wide. Alex had told her that it was made of what was known as cream flagstone, taken from the ground near the ranch. The rest of the room was white, smooth stucco covered with expensive artwork. The room was filled with beautiful hand-built furniture of leather and hardwood, built in a rustic Santa Fe style. Huge, colorful Navajo rugs graced the red Saltillo tiled floor and a wall of display cabinets was filled with priceless pots and other artifacts found on the private property of the ranch over the years. The way Jessica saw it was that Alex came from wealth and lived a stable, secure life on his family's land. While she was an orphaned misfit who was fated to chase her destiny much like a tail, and never quite getting it. She was sure that his stability and sense of family had been part of her attraction to him.

When Alex came back from the kitchen sometime later, Jessica had almost dozed off on the couch. He'd heated some stew Dotty had left in the refrigerator.

"Here," he said, handing a steaming mug of hot cocoa to her, "I'll put the bowl of stew right here on the table. Let it cool a little."

Jessica curled both hands around the mug of chocolate and sipped with her eyes closed in pleasure. "Mmmm," she said, "you're so sweet. Thanks." She smiled over at him. The warm, rich chocolate soothed her sore throat. "Who was on the phone?" she asked absently.

"It was Mom. Dotty and Ralph are in Flagstaff helping her with a fund-raising dinner. Because of the storm, they'd decided to stay there for the night. Everyone had been sure that we would wait it out in Phoenix, and not drive up until tomorrow so they didn't think to call." He shrugged before he took a bite of stew, tearing a piece of bread from a chunk he'd brought with him. "It's definitely for the best, we could both use a good night's sleep." Jessica couldn't have agreed with him more.

They sat in silence, Alex eating his stew, Jessica draining her mug of chocolate. She picked up the stew, but poked at it until Alex took it away from her, cold and unappetizing.

"I should have remembered your addiction to sugar," he commented. "Next time I'll only bring you the stew." Jessica made a face at him and stuck out her tongue.

Coming back from the kitchen, Alex banked the fire in the living room and they wrapped an arm around each other, walking into the bedroom. They even forgot to crank up the hot tub, both too tired to care. Jessica allowed herself to be tucked in like a child, warm under the down quilt, while Alex bumped around in the house, securing everything for the night.

She had to smile, thinking of how far she had come over the years. Orphaned when she was twelve, divorced when she was nineteen, and once again orphaned by her guardian Aunt when she was twenty, Jessica had been forced to find inner strength early in life. She'd sworn to herself that she'd never marry again, that she'd stay free as a mustang, independent as a wild cat, loose as a goose. And here she was, in love to her teeth with a man who was almost too good to be true. She found herself clenching those same teeth with the tension of childhood fear and the memory of Mac's comments to her. Closing her eyes, she began quietly reciting a favorite mantra, "Om mani padme hung," and she felt her body begin to relax. She would not give in to her childish nightmares. Alex was a good man and would not desert her, they belonged together and together they would stay until death parted them, and maybe not even then.

Alex turned off the lights and climbed under the down quilt, his body warm and solid. They curled up together, comforted by each other's closeness. Jessica's last thought was, so this was it, a pretty quiet welcome to her new life.

Chapter 3: The All American Princess

Out at the Ranch

The next morning the storm had cleared away, and Jessica got up with a head cold that left her feeling drained and lightheaded. But she didn't let that discourage her because she and Alex made love before he got up to make them breakfast. She dressed warmly in jeans and layered a sweater with a turtle-necked tee shirt, looking outside at the snow covering the desert. She and Alex ate the small breakfast of fruit and coffee, but she also made herself a piece of cinnamon toast with plenty of sugar and watched as he lit up his cigar. "So we both have our vices," she said, smiling at him. He gave her a wink with no comment.

She was disappointed at first when she learned he smoked, but relieved when she saw that he preferred small, slender cigars that had an interesting spicy odor. He had them delivered monthly to the ranch from Honduras, and had told her in apology that he began the habit on a trip to that country in his early thirties. She eventually decided it looked rather sexy on Alex and decided not to complain.

"I have a special surprise for you," he said when they were done with their breakfast. He grabbed her hand and began pulling her outside and through the gate of their courtyard. The patio and walkway had been shoveled, and the snow smelled fresh and chilly-cold. He led her down the path with a trail of cigar smoke behind them, and out to the old adobe house on the rise. It was the original house where his parents once homesteaded when they first moved onto the ranch. It was left empty when they moved into the current rambling ranch house where she and Alex now lived. His parents were now living in a house in town, preferring the convenience of doctors and shopping, leaving the main house for Alex and his new wife.

Over the years the charming old adobe had become the gardening house, a place for the storage of pots, old gloves, pruning shears and rakes. Now, Alex led her up to the door and opened it with a flourish. She stepped in, giving him a puzzled look and came to a dead stop. The house had been converted into an artist's studio! Jessica was stunned by what she saw.

"Oh, my God, Alex. I can't believe you did this!" Jessica exclaimed. She began to tour the little building, astonished by the enormity of the project.

The living area of the house had been cleared of its gardening table and planting debris, and had been replaced with a huge professional drawing board. Two walls of built-in bookshelves awaited her reference books, and two overstuffed chairs sat in the corner with a small table between them and a reading lamp. The terracotta tile floors had been polished to their original sheen, and the walls painted bright colors.

Jessica was so overwhelmed and touched that she felt tears blur her eyes. She couldn't believe that Alex had come up with such a wonderful idea, or that he had completed it before she'd moved out here. There was almost nothing more sacred than a spacious studio to an artist.

She was now seeing just how wonderful the man was that she was married to. She couldn't begin to express her gratitude enough, but she threw her arms around his neck and planted a sloppy kiss on his lips anyway.

Alex smiled and pulled away to look down into her face, "Now, I've been away a long time, and I have some work to do." He put his arm around her and they both began walking toward the door. "Dotty and Ralph arrived back this morning. Why don't you get with Dotty in the kitchen, and you can tell her your housekeeping preferences. I think there's a dinner coming up in a couple of weeks. She can clue you in on what's expected." He paused at the door and turned back to her. "It's a social thing. It'll be the usual dull, boring, influential people of the political scene," he smiled with dry humor. "Dotty takes care of everything, so you won't have to do much, but I'm sure she would welcome your input."

He left the studio with a wave and went off to his office, while Jessica gave a deep sigh before heading for the kitchen. She'd prefer staying in her studio instead of talking to the housekeeper about a dull dinner party, but she supposed her role as wife meant she needed to also involve herself in Alex's social world.

She was having trouble thinking of the housekeeper as 'Dotty,' so she decided to use the more formal name for her, Dorothea. Jessica found her sitting at a kitchen nook snapping peas, and stripping them from their shells, her long graceful hands working rapidly. When Jessica came into the room, she glanced up with a mild smile on her broad face, and bent back to her work.

"Good morning, Dorothea," Jessica started. "Alex tells me there's a dinner party coming up." She noticed Dorothea was wearing the same uniform she always wore, capris, flat shoes and a matching blouse with decorations on the bottom. This one today was lime green with a white, curling trellis pattern.

"Oh, yes, there is." She put her peas aside and gave Jessica her complete attention. "Would you like to see the menu?" Her German accent was light and hardly noticeable, her words a little formal.

They went over the dinner plans and then talked about the care of the house. Dorothea was her usual efficient self, and seemed helpful and friendly. She was a big-boned woman, and not very graceful in her movements. Jessica noticed that she was masculine in many ways, except for those unusual hands. Her hands were delicate and seemed in contrast with the rest of her body. And if she felt awkward at having another Mrs. Dawson arrive in her domain, she hadn't given Jessica any indication.

"Look, Dorothea," Jessica told her with a little hesitation. "This kind of life is new to me, and I know very little about running a household like this. I hope we can be friends and work together. I'll depend a lot on your experience."

"Of course," Dorothea said, "I'll be happy to help in any way I can." Her face remained unchanged, leaving a question about her sincerity. But then she gave a strange little smile that Jessica would learn well. It was made with just the corners and looked slightly distressed. "The first Mrs. Dawson always had her coffee in her office, where she would answer her email and make her calls first thing. I'd be happy to email the next day's menu every morning for your review if you'd like."

"Oh," Jessica said, feeling awkward. "I didn't know there was an office." The few times she'd been to the ranch before marrying Alex, she'd only seen the main part of the house. The very idea of sitting in Rachel's office answering emails seemed completely creepy.

"It's upstairs above the master suite," Dorothea went on to say. Did Jessica see a small glint of satisfaction in her eye as she watched Jessica fidget? "It was made into an office and a sort of sitting room a few years ago. I know the computer is still there. We each have one, and Mrs. Dawson networked them throughout the ranch. She says it's the best way to communicate, since everyone is always coming and going." Again came the suffering smile. "Can I get you some coffee?" She rose when Jessica said yes, putting her peas aside for the moment.

As Dorothea prepared her coffee, Jessica felt a little shiver up her spine. Had Dorothea realized that she'd used Rachel's title as Alex's wife in the present tense, as if she were still alive? It left her unsettled. When the cup of steaming coffee was set before her, she noticed it was black and she had the guilty thought that perhaps that was how the first Mrs. Dawson had taken it. Jessica preferred it light with sugar and Dorothea hadn't even asked.

As she left the kitchen when they were finished, she realized that there was no choice but to rely on Dorothea's ability and willingness to help her winningly host a dinner for ten. Apparently its successful accomplishment could influence Alex's attainment of State Representative, a nomination his friends were supporting him in. She suddenly felt a real fear. What if she really wasn't able to fill Rachel's shoes?

Two days later, Alex drove off to a dig on the rim of the Grand Canyon that he was currently excavating, and Jessica stood shivering in the driveway, waving to him as he drove away. They both had known he'd have to get back to work and would be gone a week to meet his deadline, but it had been planned that Jessica would go with him. Her cold wasn't better, however, and after a lengthy discussion, they both agreed that she needed to stay home and get well. As she stood in the driveway watching Alex leave, she was faced with a sudden feeling of loneliness.

She began to have a sense of displacement. Only months ago she'd been living happily alone in San Francisco. What was she doing in Arizona, married and under pressure to perform? She had never seen this path for herself before she met Alex. Even though they had both agreed that she should continue her illustration career as long as she still enjoyed it, she wondered if she would ever feel at home here in this rambling house filled with beautiful things, performing like the dutiful wife of a politician.

Earlier, before Alex had left, she asked about the office and computer. He'd told her there was one set up for her in the studio, and like the others, she was wired into the ranch's private network so she could receive private e-mail, as well as be connected to the regular internet. He also told her the information about guests with their preferences was already loaded in the database that she had access to, so she could help with parties and visitors. She made the assumption that it was a database the ever-efficient Rachel, his first wife, had compiled.

After Alex drove away, she wasn't sure what she'd do with herself for the rest of the day and supposed that she should get back into bed with a good book and sleep. That was why she had been left behind after all, and she knew she needed rest. But right at that moment, she felt a little at loose ends.

She wandered back into the bedroom and looked around her. It was a tasteful room done in navy blue and rust. A small beehive fireplace graced one corner, and the south wall was made up of four French doors, which opened onto the beautifully landscaped courtyard.

After some exploration, she found the sitting room that Dorothea had mentioned earlier. It was up a small flight of stairs that twisted behind the fireplace, hidden behind a tall, tri-fold screen. The room upstairs was very feminine and she saw that it looked ready for use. When she first went up the stairs and entered the room, she distinctly smelled an expensive French perfume mixed with the affluent surroundings. She suspected that the perfume must have been the scent everyone still identified with Rachel.

The room was decorated in a costly floral fabric that looked suspiciously like the designer Ralph Lauren, one of her timeless favorites. There was a set of overstuffed couches facing each other with a huge hassock in between. Pillows abounded, with ruffles and fluff, not Jessica's style. A small antique desk sat in the corner with a laptop resting on it, closed and shiny black. Jessica threw open the long drapes at the windows, and from the looks of the rest of the room, it felt as if someone had been keeping it clean and tidy, ready for Rachel's return. She almost went back down the stairs to the safe bedroom below, feeling like an intruder.

But, before she could leave, she noticed an expensive dressing table in a small alcove that sported a large, round mirror, and it dangerously caught her attention. Walking toward it, Jessica saw that there were several bottles of the same perfume, a pricey electric curling iron and a carved crystal bowl with a few pieces of elegant jewelry thrown into it. Jessica imagined Rachel taking off the bright red earrings and tossing them into the bowl before taking a shower prior to the party Mac said was at the ranch the night she died.

Two framed photos sat on the tabletop facing her, one was of a black horse with Rachel on its back, and the other was of Rachel and Alex dressed for a party. Jessica picked up the one of her riding, afraid to look closely at the other photo. In the picture she picked up, Rachel was wearing an expensive looking white shirt, tan riding pants, high boots and a jaunty ponytail. She also had on a sunny, beautiful smile lighting her suntanned face. The woman had been spectacularly beautiful, with the winning looks of a classic model. Jessica felt ill when she looked at her own reflection in the mirror. Her own red hair lacked Rachel's bright color, and was in its usual disarray, plus her nose was pink from her cold. She felt awkward and homely compared to the All-American princess in the picture. She carefully replaced the frame and stepped away from the table, hugging her arms to her sides.

Beyond the dressing table were large double doors that she hadn't noticed earlier. Jessica slowly stepped up to slide them open, the squealing sound of sliding wheels on metal tracks eerie in the quiet of the room. She stood in terrible expectation, almost as if she would discover Rachel standing on the other side, all blond and smiling, but somehow gruesome in death. Certainly, her ghost did lurk just beyond.

It was a huge walk-in closet filled with Rachel's clothes, one of a woman's most personal possessions. It suddenly gave her a perverse feeling of emotional satisfaction to think that she would finally get this intimate glimpse into the dead Mrs. Dawson.

The clothes hung, each on its own hanger, like soldiers ready to march into a lost battle. It was obvious that Rachel's taste had been exquisite. The clothes were expensive designer pieces, custom-made with tailor labels in each one of them. There were riding outfits, incredible ski clothes, sexy little red jeans that surely must have fit extremely tight, evening clothes, cocktails dresses, and suits.

A wall of the closet had been painstakingly built of custom shoe racks, and on those racks was an amazing array of shoes. Cowboy boots, high heel pumps, evening sandals, tennis shoes, slides, riding boots with fringe, every kind of expensive shoe style one could imagine. Jessica saw right away that Rachel's feet had been tiny, feminine and at least a size smaller than her own. The more she looked, the more depressed she became.

Turning to leave, she couldn't resist first opening one of the built-in drawers. Inside were some of the most beautiful undergarments Jessica had ever imagined. She pulled out a black French-styled bra. Low-slung, sheer and exquisite, she could never imagine herself wearing such a sophisticated piece of underwear and wondered if Alex missed seeing his wife in this kind of garment. She was more the cotton bikini kind of woman. When she found herself holding up the bra for size, she realized that this room was very dangerous.

She dropped the soft garment as if it burned her fingers and quickly left the room with its expensive French boudoir smell. She was shaking from the tension of it, and when she reached the downstairs bedroom, she had to sit and force herself to breathe slowly.

She realized at that moment that she carried a deep fear that Alex was still deeply in love with his dead wife. Having her things so close was something she could change. The question was would Alex have a problem with removing Rachel's things from the house? She was hoping it was an oversight that someone hadn't done it before this, but had her doubts. Looking at the spotless state of the room, it seemed as if someone had been keeping it pristine and ready for who knew what.

Alex would call that evening and she decided to talk to him about it then, her determination over-riding her fears. It was better to face the subject straight on and now before it became an issue for her.

Jessica let out a deep sigh that caused her to cough roughly. Taking a tissue from the nightstand, she knew it was important for her to remove Rachel's ghost from their life in whatever way she could. While she respected Alex's grief, she still knew if her marriage was going to be a success, she would have to help them both move-on. A vague idea started to form in her mind about making the upstairs their own small family room with a TV and stereo. Then if they had guests in the house, they could still have a quiet evening in privacy. She could use that idea as a motive for giving Alex a reason to agree.

She felt exhausted and spent from the tension and attributed some of her stress to the cold. The rest of the day she stayed in bed reading and napping, setting aside the images of the frilly room just one floor away from her. She asked that her dinner be sent to their bedroom, and tried to enjoy the peace and quiet. After a soak in the hot tub, she slept deeply until the phone rang. It was Alex calling from the site on his cell phone, wishing her a goodnight.

She tried to bring up the dressing room delicately, fearing his usual withdrawal and anger whenever someone spoke of Rachel. Instead, to her surprise, he seemed in an especially cheerful mood and simply said he'd completely forgotten her things were even there. He agreed with her decision about the items being donated to charity, and even acted very embarrassed about it being overlooked. It wasn't even five minutes after they hung up before she fell back asleep, thinking of Alex and their new life, the ghost of Rachel temporarily forgotten.

The next day it dawned partly cloudy and chilly. Jessica awoke confused at first as to where she was, and then remembered it was Arizona. Her cold was better, but she still felt achy and a little feverish. As she lay in bed, missing Alex, and the sounds of the boats in the bay back home, she decided it was time to see a little more of the ranch.

Chapter 4: The Blessedness of Forgetting

The Rim of the Grand Canyon

The large, long-horned sheep stood perfectly still on the ledge above Mac. The two stared at each other for several seconds before the wild animal spurted up the impossibly sheer wall to disappear behind an outcropping of boulders.

It was beginning to turn dusk in the Grand Canyon and Mac wanted to make it to the rim before dark. After his stare-down with the sheep, he again gave his attention to the trail and began his own rapid climb out. His plan was to meet Alex at his base camp above the cave that was receiving Alex's research group's undivided attention.

The cave Alex and his team were working on was located high up on a steep wall where it was hidden over the centuries from hikers and explorers. It was a yawning cavern where a large extended family of early natives had made their home deep in the canyon wall. When Mac had last visited the site with Alex, erosion and probably earthquakes over the centuries had sheared off the path into the cave, making it impossible to enter except by repelling down from the top. That was why it had never been found before now.

Mac knew that Alex was now trying to beat a deadline that had been set for him by the Smithsonian Institute. Mac was jealous that the Institute had gotten wind of Alex's project. Although Mac also had been researching a cave for over a year with much more importance, he was reluctant to reveal it yet to the public. His site needed to be handled with much more delicacy than Alex's, but he knew he'd one day get more attention for his own find.

In his native homeland, there were thousands of sites that hadn't been discovered yet, and he hoped to one day return to Australia for that reason. He had little to stay for in the United States anymore.

As Mac negotiated the darkening trail, his mind found a familiar notch of anger. It was a place where Mac got comfort, a place that was easy and safe. He knew how to feel jealousy; oh yes, he knew. He wondered again why the bloody hell Alex always seemed to have everything he always wanted. The bloke had been born with the damn silver spoon in his mouth, and good things just gravitated his way. While Mac always had to fight and claw for everything he had. He felt the familiar flush of temper in his face. But he wasn't hopeless anymore. No, Mac had a plan.

Stopping on the trail, he zipped open a pocket on his pack and removed a small, high-intensity light with a thick elastic band attached. He quickly slipped the band around his head, centering the light in the middle of his forehead, and clicked it on. The light flooded the trail so he could see his way out of the canyon. He was almost to the top and the glow of light from Alex's camp glimmered on the ridge above him.

His thoughts of Alex led him to a further thought. After Rachel's death, he'd noticed that Alex had wanted to be alone more and more. That's why it had surprised him when he'd come home with a new bride. While Jessica was a beautiful woman, Mac couldn't imagine how anyone who had been married to Rachel could even think of trying to replace her. Rachel had been blond and spectacularly beautiful. Jessica seemed nice, but she sure as bloody hell didn't measure up to Rachel in his mind. Still, Mac thought to himself, *that blond-haired, gray-eyed witch had been filled with betrayal.*

Mac swallowed his anger as he came to the canyon's rim. He knew that he had to forget the past, to move on. To pretend like everything was normal until he could wind things up and leave. Then he didn't care what the bloomin' lot of them thought, he'd be free.

As Mac came out of the gloom of the evening dusk and into the campfire's light, Alex turned from something he was packing in the back of his Rover.

"Well, I'm so glad you decided to stay 'ere tonight to feed an old bloke." Mac's Australian accent sounded even more pronounced as it often did after he was away from other people for several days.

"Old, my ass," Alex said. They both knew Mac had just hiked around fifty of the hardest miles of the country anywhere and he knew he looked damned fit.

As darkness settled in, all four of the researchers sat around the campfire and ate the meal that had been prepared for them. The students Alex was working with and Mac conversed about what he had found on his hike, and they told him about the newest findings in the cave.

Soon, Alex joined the discussion, and Mac sat back watching him. In the course of their conversation, he mentioned his parents, and Mac thought they would have enjoyed being there in the mix of the conversation, listening to the theories and discoveries. They had always enjoyed stimulating discussions, and no matter how detailed they got, they loved learning more about Alex's field of study. Mac's own parents had died when he was only a tike, and he'd come to America to study anthropology in Albuquerque. He'd always thought Alex's parents were exactly what his parents would have been like, if they'd lived.

Alex's father had been a cattle rancher for many years here on the plains of northern Arizona. With his private land and agreements with the BLM for grazing rights, his fortune was made early in life, and he married a sweet cowgirl from Winslow. Mac's own mom and dad started out with a small three-room billabong house, and little land, but still they raised cattle from when Mac was an infant.

By the time Alex was born, Mac knew that Alex's family had

moved into the two thousand, six hundred square-foot ranch house where Alex & Jessica now lived. The ranch was named "The Monte Vista" after the hotel in Flagstaff, where his father won the small original homestead in a private poker game. The name meant "Mountain Vista" in Spanish, and there was no doubt that the view of the San Francisco Peaks from the ranch was spectacular. In comparison, Mac's own home in Flagstaff was close to the university, and by most standards, not modest. But it still wasn't a ranch.

Mac stretched out his legs and leaned against a rock, staring at the fire. He remembered when he was a young man and he and Alex used to visit his ranch on summer break. Alex's father used to talk about how the Navajo people would drive the old dirt road to Flagstaff once a month across his ranch. With their wagons full of woven blankets and Yeis' (the Navajo Kachina dolls) ready for trade, the Navajo families went to trade for flour, sugar and fresh fruits and vegetables—things they couldn't get out on the reservation. Even today, Mac could still see the line of lava rocks used to mark the road's track, which still ran parallel with the new highway that still makes its way into today's modern Flagstaff.

He often saw Navajo families driving into town, but now it was on the paved road, and their transportation was a pickup truck instead of a wagon. Few had blankets to trade, and they were usually on the way to K-Mart for odds and ends, or a quick stop at the local hamburger joint for fried zucchini and a cheeseburger. Life on the reservation was hard, and most families had either moved into town, or struggled to live on the reservation in small hogans, without electricity or running water. Mac knew that Navajos often chose that way of life, however, because the possession of material items went against their religious beliefs. It seemed that life, as a Navajo today, was a tug-of-war between being a good Christian and not giving up the cultural beliefs of the Navajo rituals.

Mac looked up from his pondering and saw that the two students had finished their coffee and gone off to their respective sleeping bags. He watched as one of them came out of his tent and shook his bedding to check for scorpions or other desert visitors in the folds of the blanket.

As Mac and Alex shared the dying campfire, a group of coyotes could be heard off in the distance, and Mac was reminded of when he used to camp out in the desert of New Mexico. He had been working on his master's degree in Albuquerque and Alex joined him in the program late. The two would go on long expeditions into the desert, the best of friends, looking for lost cultures and listening to the serenade of the local coyote families at night as they sat around a campfire.

Alex had then taken three years abroad to work with some of the most noted anthropologists in the world, working on digs in South America, Asia, and Egypt, while Mac had stayed in the U.S., struggling to make ends meet. Alex had learned to scale steep cliffs from some of the best rock climbers in the world, and Mac would hear stories at home of how he'd won competitions involving some of the most technical climbs outside the U.S.

By that time, Mac was in Arizona, happily publishing book after book on Navajo & Hopi cultural differences, and gaining tenure at the University of Arizona. The two had kept in touch over the years and even worked together on a couple of projects that involved ancient sites in New Mexico.

During all of Alex's travels, however, Mac knew that he never stopped thinking about his home. He told Mac that he knew he would eventually return to use his knowledge to help research and save the history of native cultures right in his own backyard just as Mac would. And that's exactly what he had done.

Now, Mac knew that Alex had been flirting with the idea of running for state representative, something a group of local businessmen were supporting. They both knew it would give him the opportunity to do even more for the preservation of Arizona's history. Alex being nominated seemed like one more morsel served on the

Alex Dawson plate. It was something Mac was having trouble getting behind.

Mac now remembered that eleven years before, Alex had finally traveled home to stay, bringing with him a new wife, the beautiful Rachel. Alex had told Mac that he'd met her on a ski trip he'd taken with friends in Europe, on a break from work. Rachel was there, training with her team for the Olympics and he had immediately been floored by her beauty and intelligence, which to Mac was completely understandable.

Mac understood how two weeks together in such a romantic spot could spell trouble for a couple. Alex had failed to return to his research in South America, and Rachel had failed to make the team because of her absence at the trials. Somehow, they decided marriage was the only solution for such negligence. Mac supposed that it made sense at the time. He felt the usual black regret in the pit of his stomach. What a mistake it had all been. He felt the familiar anger rise up inside of him, dark and uncontrollable.

Alex suddenly rose, throwing the stub of his cigar into the fire and walking up to the edge of the canyon. Mac watched him as he looked out into the blackness. Looking up at the sky himself, he saw that stars and a small sliver of a moon had come out to give slight illumination to the landscape, sculpting the shapes of the different pinnacles like huge spirits, standing still and quiet in the Grand Canyon's vast darkness.

Mac wondered if Alex speculated on how it had felt for Rachel, falling into that canyon. The moment before she hit the first abutment must have been breathtaking. To know you were about to meet your fate, to feel like you were flying, free from any entanglement here on the mortal plane. Alex himself leaned over the edge and Mac knew he was dangerously close to going over. He held his breath and thought that Alex following Rachel in her death seemed appropriate. *But not yet,* Mac thought, he had other plans for his friend. He quietly stood up and walked toward Alex, seeing him outlined against the canyon lit by the small moon.

The sound of Mac's footsteps behind him seemed to bring Alex back to reality. He turned slightly to acknowledge Mac's presence, and then rotated back around to face the canyon's maw.

"A little too near the edge there, eh, Alex," Mac said as he came carefully closer. "You mustn't allow a slip of the foot to end your life. You have far too much to live for now, with your new wife." There were just enough sarcastic twists to the tone of his voice to make him regret having said it. When Alex turned away from the edge, he frowned, but didn't comment. Mac hesitated before stepping away so he could pass by, the two of them walking back to the campfire. As soon as they reached the fire's warmth, Alex said goodnight and headed for his tent. Mac stared down at the flames in the fire pit, mesmerized by their dance. He knew one thing for sure. Alex was a man who was surrounded by luck. And that luck was about to change.

Chapter 5: What Wasn't There to Love?

Out at the Barn

Will had just finished giving orders to one of the ranch hands when he noticed a woman with light auburn hair coming over the rise from the main house. He turned and headed for his office, sure that she was the boss's new wife, and he wondered why she was headed his way so early. He'd heard about her from one of his hands, Ralph, whose wife was the head housekeeper on the ranch. There had already been rumblings about the changes the new Mrs. Dawson was making in the kitchen.

Will was a lonely man with deep and quiet thoughts. He'd been working at the Monte Vista Ranch since he was a boy, and his first loyalty was to the Dawson's. He had no second loyalty. Ten years before, his wife left him for a richer life and took his only son. For reasons he shared with no one, he'd agreed to the divorce and stayed on at the ranch. Few noticed that Rachel's death had left another scar on his secretly tender heart.

As he continued toward the main barn, he noticed that the clouds had cleared off. The day had started so cold it almost hurt to inhale. But now the sun glistened off the hoarfrost that covered most everything, and it had risen high enough to warm some of the rain puddles just enough to make them mud.

Will stripped off his coat as soon as he felt the warmth of the barn. He'd just finished hanging the heavy thing on a hook when he heard the side door open. The new Mrs. Dawson entered and stamped her thick-soled hiking boots to rid them of as much mud as possible. It gave Will a few seconds to size her up.

His first impression was of her small-boned, delicate build, and the aura of femininity that emanated from her. Her hair wasn't really red, but the color of cedar wood, and it was in wild disarray from the wind outside. While she didn't have the stellar beauty of Rachel, Alex's new wife was certainly in the same class. As she reached up to brush her hair away from her face, Will thought that, in fact, there was a graceful sensuality about her that had been missing in Rachel.

He watched as she closed the door behind her, raised her head and smiled as if she enjoyed the whiff of fresh hay and the sound of the horses snorting in their stalls. Will started toward her just as a little caramel-colored filly bobbed its head playfully over the stall gate, catching her attention. She walked over to pet its soft nose, talking to it in a quiet, husky voice.

"I'd be a little careful there," Will said from behind her. She turned wide blue eyes on him in surprise. They were a light turquoise actually, and rimmed in black lashes. "She's a nipper," he went on to say as he continued toward her. "She'll get yer sleeve before ya know it."

"Oh," was all she said, pulling her hand away. She stepped back and looked at the horse as it shook its head and snorted, wanting her attention back.

"Hi, my name is Will Schnebly, the ranch's foreman," he held out his hand in greeting. "You must be the boss's new wife."

She shook hands with him and smiled. "I hope I'm not disrupting anything. Just thought I'd see a little more of the ranch." She sniffed and he could tell by her voice that she was nursing a cold.

"Not at all," Will answered her. "Glad you came to visit while I was in the office." he pointed toward a glassed-in area of the barn.

She looked as if she was surprised that he had an office. He knew that the operations on the Monte Vista Ranch had to be pretty impressive, even to a woman who must have known she'd married into one of the richest families in the state.

The office Will had referred to had tack and photographs of horses hanging on the walls, and his flat-screened monitor was visible through the large window that allowed him to keep an eye on the horses while he did his paperwork.

"A Macintosh? I had no idea ranching had come so far into the technology age," she said, putting her hands in her back pockets. "Do you keep spreadsheets?"

She was joking, but Will gave a quirky smile and said, "As a matter of fact, I was just working on my budget. How much do you know about spreadsheet programs?"

"Oh, no!" She held up her hands in defense. "Not me. I hate budgets."

His smile turned to a grin, something that didn't happen often these days, and he decided he liked her. Because of that, he generously offered to take her on a tour of the ranch and she accepted with equal grace. As they began the rounds, Will felt her slide him a curious glance and he felt his face grow a little red.

He knew that he was a burly-looking man, but he'd been told a time or two that he had a kind and intelligent face. He was shorter than Jessica, and physical work had left him with wide shoulders that showed under his heavy canvas jacket. His hair was a warm brown and thinning on top, and on a cold day like today, he kept it covered with a worn cowboy hat. He picked up his pace and began pointing out the different buildings, hoping to divert her attention from him.

The sun rose higher as they walked, warming them and the rest of the day. Will kept up a steady stream of conversation, explaining how the ranch worked and the role all the different buildings and people played. He told her several interesting stories about the animals, answering all her questions amiably, and by the time they returned to the original building where they had started, they were calling each other by first names as if they were old friends.

As they walked toward the barn doors, they passed a paddock with a prize horse pacing the perimeter of the fence. "That's an incredible-looking animal," Jessica commented, standing still in obvious awe, staring at the black beast.

"Yep. That's Salt & Pepper. He used to be Rachel's mount. I keep him outside most times, 'cause if he's in the barn with the other horses, he just raises cane until the whole barn gets in an uproar." Will gave a brief smile as they walked up to the fence. He draped his arms over the top rung and clicked his tongue. Salt & Pepper took his time coming over and sniffed his gloved hands, searching out and finding a piece of sugar. When the horse was close, it was obvious where he had gotten the name, from the sprinkle of white spots on his black muzzle.

"Was Rachel a good rider?" Jessica asked with hesitation, as if she wasn't sure how her question would be received.

"Ohhh ho. Rachel." He thought for a moment, looking down at his boots. "Yep. She was a very good rider." Will took a moment to look at his feelings and as usual the deep feeling of loss swept over him.

"Will," Jessica asked in a quiet voice. Again she hesitated, perhaps unsure of his silence, "What was Rachel like? I mean, what was she really like?"

He was surprised by the question. First, he would've thought Alex had already told her about Rachel. And second, he was caught off guard by how honest she was being. He thought for a long moment, propping his boot on the bottom rung of the fence and collected himself. He looked out at the black horse, restless and pacing. Then he squinted into the sun and said, "Well. I guess she was the most beautiful creature I'd ever seen," he told her sadly. "She rode like the wind, and I don't believe she was ever afraid of anythin'."

"I hope you don't think I'm strange for asking." She looked down at her dirty hiking boots. "It's just that I'm reluctant to ask Alex. He still seems, well, so sad. I guess he loved her terribly."

Will picked up a rock from the ground and juggled it from hand to hand, watching its dance intently, his bitter thoughts warring inside. "When he first brought her home, I'd never seen him happier. Folks said their marriage was a fairy tale made in heaven. She made the place a showcase, and had parties that couldn't be matched in the county. She could ride, and ski and spit with the best of the bunch. What wasn't there ta love?" He threw the rock as hard and as far as he could.

They were both silent as they stood watching Salt & Pepper prance around the corral, showing off for his audience. Will felt the day had darkened a little. He wondered how a sweet, little girl like her was going to take Rachel's place in Alex's life.

Wanting to change the subject, Will asked if she would like him to teach her how to ride. They started back toward the main barn as they talked about it, and Will felt relieved at having escaped from a dangerous subject.

"All right," he told her. "We'll do lessons twice a week, if yer fanny can stand it." They agreed on the day and time, and when she asked what she should wear, Will gave her some suggestions.

"Jeans and a tee shirt outta do it, and bring a jacket of some kind. Gloves to protect those perty hands, and a hat. Plus, you'll have to get some kinda ridin' boots," he said looking pointedly at her muddy shoes. "Circle Q in Flagstaff is havin' a sale this week. You should stop by. Tell 'em who you are, and you'll be treated real nice," he teased.

She gave him her small smile once again before thanking him for the tour of the buildings. They shook hands saying their farewells, but just as she turned to head out of the barn, Will decided to call her back.

"Don't know if you like animals, but I was wonderin' if you'd do a favor." He let out a sharp whistle, and around the corner came a young female dog, black with white markings. She still hadn't grown into her feet, and her ears flopped as she trotted toward Will. “Hey, Chili,” Will said, slapping his thighs. Chili galloped up to him and jumped up to lick his face. Will was too tall, but Chili gave it her best shot anyway, leaping and trying to bite his nose. “She got her name because she just loves eatin’ green chilies.” Will grinned while dodging the dog’s nips. “She’s a puppy from a liter dropped by our best cow dog. She’s got a paw that’s hurt, and needs ta be somewhere where she won’t be tempted ta run with the other dogs ‘till she’s healed.”

Before he could say any more, Jessica squatted down and called Chili over to her. She seemed shy at first, hanging next to Will and looking at her hesitantly. Will reached down and petted her head, giving her a hand command to go to Jessica. After just a brief hesitation, she walked slowly over to Jessica, head down wagging her long tail. Jessica now noticed a bandaged foot that she had at first thought was a part of the dog’s markings.

“Can I take her to the house?” she asked Will, thinking of Dorothea.

“Mrs. Dawson, you can have ’er sit at the dinner table if ya got a mind to. I reckon it’s your house now.” She looked up and saw that he was smiling with amusement.

“Then she’s mine. At least for the time being.”

Will got a leash and attached it to Chili’s collar, giving the handle to Jessica. “You probably need ta keep ’er confined for a couple of days so she won’t take off back to the barns. Feed her some steak with chili, that’ll earn ’er love forever.” He petted Chili’s black head. “I’ll send someone around ta the house once a day ta check on the bandage on ’er leg. She tangled with a coyote two days ago, and it’ll take a few days ta heal real good. She’s had ’er rabies shots, and the vet dipped ’er for fleas. She’s in good shape, just needs the gentle hand of a woman.” He said he’d send some dog chow that they fed the other dogs, up to the house.

Will shook his head as he watched them walk away, the tall,

slender woman with the cap of auburn hair, and the long-legged puppy barking and dancing around, tangling both their legs in the leash. Jessica bent down to gently untangle them both while having an earnest talk with the dog. It seemed to work, because when she straightened up and again began walking away, Chili behaved herself and walked quietly alongside. However, the dog's excitement was ill-disguised because of the wagging tail and happy glances she kept throwing at her new master. Will was satisfied that he'd thought of the arrangement. It would take the burden of keeping the dog in the barn off of him, and give Jessica a new friend. A friend he believed she would no doubt need.

Chapter 6: More Than Good Friends

Macy's Coffeehouse, Flagstaff

The sun glistened off the snow around her and did nothing to improve her mood. Even with sunglasses, Emma's head began to ache from the glare. She had completed her errand and was trying to make her way through downtown, back to the university, but had to struggle like a fish pushing against the current. She planned on picking up a quick sandwich at the cafeteria, and if she didn't hurry, she'd have to eat it at her desk.

She stopped on another corner, waiting for the light to change, when a man who was obviously a tourist in town to ski, approached her with a camera and a goofy smile.

"Excuse me," he said to Emma, a noticeable midwestern accent curdling his words. "Would you mind posing with my son? He wants to tell everyone back home he met an Indian."

She felt her headache getting worse as she stood where she was and the man's overweight son leaned next to her. Flipping her long, dark hair back just before he snapped the picture, she concealed that she flipped the bird under her coat. The traffic light finally changed and she escaped, pissed that she hadn't given them a piece of her mind. In reality, she was only one-quarter Native American and half Hispanic, and if she'd had the time and energy, she would have most definitely expressed herself.

As she crossed the railroad tracks and avoided ice that had collected in shadows on the sidewalk, movement down the street caught her attention.

A tall, slender woman with a fall of reddish hair was tying a black and white dog up to a post outside Macy's, a local coffee house. Emma immediately recognized the woman as Jessica, Alex Dawson's new wife. She felt a pang of jealousy stab through her. All the years she had befriended Rachel, it had been with the hope of getting closer to Alex. From the first moment he had found her when she was only fifteen and hiding from her abusive uncle, he'd been the only man for her. She thought that perhaps her feelings came from a girlish crush, but it was true that you never forgot your first love. The news of his marriage to this new woman had coldly come to her through gossip in the halls of her office.

Emma had already seen Alex and his new wife from afar before hearing the gossip, and before they were married. They were with Alex's parents and all four of them had been laughing and on the way into one of Flagstaff's better restaurants. She'd been careful they didn't see her because she had felt so insecure and embarrassed. A few days before that, she'd left a couple of casual messages for Alex at his office, but he had never returned her calls.

Now, as she watched Alex's wife go into Macy's, she wondered what she was like. How was it that this woman had won Alex's heart? Emma came to a dead stop on the sidewalk and felt tears prick her eyes. She had been so alone most of her life, and she was so tired of it all. She was starting to believe that it was most definitely her that had nothing to offer, even though she had been trying so hard to improve her life. She continued down the sidewalk lost in her thoughts.

As she came even with the dog, she reached down indifferently and gave the animal a pat on the head. Then with a quick decision, she turned and entered the restaurant. As usual, there was a line, but Emma didn't care. She decided to get a sandwich here instead of the cafeteria, even though it would be much more expensive. That would give her more time to observe the new Mrs. Dawson.

She fished a pill out of her purse while she waited, hoping it would improve her disposition. Swallowing it without water, she knew her tension headache would soon disappear. Not all that long ago, the pill might have been something much more than aspirin, but today, she was rid of her habit and felt good about it. Even if she sometimes still felt that tension of need, it certainly made her life less complicated to be clean.

She watched as the woman with the light hair found a place to sit at the window. Emma smiled as she saw her wave to the dog outside. She had always liked people who really liked their pets, not just tolerated them like so many of her family on the reservation.

She ordered her sandwich to go, and then stood aside, waiting for her lunch to arrive from the kitchen. Looking toward the window, she shrugged and made her way through the mismatched tables of the café.

"Excuse me, but aren't you Alex Dawson's new wife?" she asked. The woman looked up in surprise.

"Yes I am. I'm sorry, do I know you?" she asked politely with a smile.

"Well, no. Actually, I'm a friend of Alex, Mrs. Dawson. You and I have never met, but I saw the two of you downtown back several months ago. My name is Emma Begay."

As soon as she said her name, she saw a flash of recognition cross the woman's face and she immediately wondered if Alex might have mentioned her.

"Oh, yes," his wife said, inviting her with a motion of her hand to have a seat at the counter next to her. "Alex told me you've been friends for years. It's a pleasure to meet you. Please call me Jessica."

Emma sat down, trying to decide if she was pleased that Alex had indeed said something about her to his new wife, or disappointed. But she supposed he had nothing to hide when it came to his feelings for her.

She was glad she'd dressed all in black and wore her favorite bright red wool coat. It gave her confidence, something she needed before this attractive woman with bright blue eyes. "I just love Macy's," Emma said, trying to sound sophisticated. "You always get a real show coming here just for the price of a cup of coffee."

"A show?" Jessica asked.

"Oh, yeah. See those three guys in line with the weird stocking caps?" She was careful not to point. "They're river runners working in town for the winter, some of the best rafters around. And that fellow over at the next table?" she bobbed her head at a rugged, tough-looking older man. "That's Colorado Bob. He's an old miner from Colorado who believes he can find gold Incan artifacts here in Arizona. That nice blond, longhaired, hippy-looking chick is a midwife. She's better than some of our full fledged doctors when it comes to delivering babies the natural way."

Jessica gave her a grin and Emma was disappointed that she liked how it looked. She had been hoping to hate Jessica. "And are you some of that local color?" Jessica asked her, the question appearing between them out of thin air. It surprised Emma, but she felt pleased that she'd met someone who could be just as outspoken as she was at times.

Emma smiled and gave a little snort in response to Jessica's question. "Not likely. I'm just an L.A. girl, misplaced in the woods of the Arizona Mountains."

"You're from L.A.? I didn't realize that. I guess… I mean…"

"I know. Because I look Native American you figured I was from Arizona. Nope," Emma said while looking at her watch, wondering where her lunch was. "I'm only part Navajo. My Mom was Hispanic, my Dad half white, and half Navajo. That makes me only one-quarter Native American. Mom moved us back to her family in California when I was only four."

Emma knew she only had a trace of a Navajo accent, a roll from her Spanish, and the rest was pure Californian. She watched as Jessica took a sip of her mocha, and then glanced out the window at the dog. The puppy was getting plenty of attention from people passing by, her tail wagging with enthusiasm.

"What brought you back to Arizona?" Jessica asked, turning back to Emma.

"Ohhh. I don't know. My father died when I was only seven, and my mother and three brothers raised me. I guess when I was fifteen, I got tired of the L.A. scene. It was killing me. All play and no sleep makes Emma a dull girl," she smiled, looking at her nails, which were painted black and had little white moon decals on each one. "So, I moved in with my uncle and his wife when I first got here. But after a couple of years on the reservation, I just couldn't take it any longer. "

"So you moved to Flagstaff?" Jessica asked, pushing her cup away.

"Yeah. And then when I turned eighteen, Alex helped me get a job at Northern Arizona University, and the rest is history."

Jessica smiled at her and Emma felt herself drop the last barrier. This lady was nice, and it never hurt to have another friend. Jessica's next question diverted her thoughts. "So…do you work at the university now? I mean, what do you do?"

"Oh, I work in the admissions office. Data input. Very boring, but it pays well, and the benefits are terrific." She looked once again toward the counter for her sandwich, and watched as Jessica took another sip of her coffee. "I'm hoping to finally get my degree in Computer Science, and as an employee, I get a break on my tuition. Of course, I have no idea what I'll do with a degree on the rez."

"Are you planning on going back?" Jessica asked.

"Actually, I'm not sure yet," Emma told her, "I'll probably just wait until after I graduate to decide."

"You're very lucky to have such a great job. I hear the market in

Flagstaff is very competitive because so many want to live here." Jessica told her.

As they continued to talk, Emma realized that her old insecurities were creeping back. Watching Jessica, light-skinned and beautiful, self-assured and educated, she felt herself shrinking in comparison. She knew she was a young woman in the middle of a real identity crisis.

Before she knew how it happened, she was telling Jessica her story. She told her that from the moment she'd returned to Arizona, she knew she was living with one foot on the Reservation, and the other in the modern world of the white man. Her uncle had tried to encourage her to become a traditional Navajo, to follow the old ways. It was difficult because her Hispanic mother and family in L.A. had brought her up Catholic. She found herself telling Jessica that, while she never attended church anymore, she had become unsure that she wanted to believe all the superstition and ritual that went with her Navajo roots.

Emma's sandwich arrived, and getting back to work on time had become unimportant. It had been a long time since she'd felt as if she had a sympathetic ear from someone. As Jessica went out to give her dog some water, Emma removed her lunch from its brown bag and began to eat. When Jessica returned, she asked Emma to continue her story, so she talked around her mouth full of her sandwich, grabbing a sip or two of her iced tea as she continued.

"That was when I finally left the Reservation to take up residence in Flagstaff." Emma knew she was leaving out the fact that Alex had found her a family to stay with, but what the heck, she had to keep something sacred. "I wanted to get to know who I was without my family shoving me in different directions."

Suddenly Emma felt like she was talking too much about herself, and she turned the conversation to Jessica's work as an artist. Emma was impressed when she discovered just how professional Jessica's career was. She admitted that she had never known any artist who had really made a living at it.

"Once, when I was in high school, I won a competition with a drawing I did of my aunt," Emma admitted shyly.

"Do you still draw?" Jessica asked her.

"No. I quit years ago," Emma told her. "I'm not sure if I really have enough talent to make any money at it. It was sorta just a hobby, and then, I don't know, I just haven't drawn in years."

"You should draw again," Jessica told her. "I always believe being an artist is never learned. You have to be born with talent. And if you're born with the ability to create, you should always find that outlet in your life."

"So, are you living out at the ranch now?" Emma asked her, looking up from her lunch. She was embarrassed that she had even mentioned that stupid drawing.

"Yeah. We just returned from our honeymoon about a week ago. Alex had a deadline on an excavation that he couldn't ignore, and my cold was too bad to go with him. I came into town to buy some boots. Will's teaching me how to ride."

"Good'ol Will. Always willing to teach a girl to ride," Emma said a little sarcastically.

"Excuse me?" Jessica asked, surprised at the insinuation in Emma's voice. She had definitely caught the innuendo.

"Sorry. It's just that he always had it bad for… Alex's wife. I got tired of all the slobbering whenever she was around him." Emma knew that there was some jealousy in her tone of voice. "He is a terrific horseman though," she went on to say, "have you ever ridden a horse before?"

"No," Jessica replied, "Actually I'm hoping he'll make me into a good enough rider to keep up with Alex. Of course, I'll never be as good as Rachel."

Emma just smiled down at the crumbs from her sandwich, a little shocked to hear Rachel's name from Alex's new wife. She raised her head and looked back at Jessica, rattling the ice in her glass. "You do know that she and I were good friends," Emma asked, referring to Rachel. "Actually, Alex and Rachel kind of adopted me." When her eyes met Jessica's, there was a kind of steel in them.

"I believe Alex did mention that."

"Yeah," she said quietly, suddenly still. "For a while, I almost lived on the ranch. Alex loved having me visit. He'd take me on the coolest adventures on the ranch. And Will taught me how to ride back then."

Jessica just sat there looking uncomfortable and didn't reply. She glanced out the window and Emma followed her gaze. They both saw that her dog had wound her leash around the post she was tied up to. She struggled, trying to get out of her collar, and looking purposeful in her gyrations.

"Oh! Excuse me. I have to rescue my dog," Jessica said as she leaped from her chair, ready to run out the door. Emma was guessing that Jessica was probably glad to have a reason to change the subject. "I'll be right back." Emma watched as she went outside and untangled the puppy from the post, petting her head and removing the spilled water she set out earlier. She came back inside the restaurant and started collecting her things.

"I really need to go untie her. I think she's getting tired. It's been nice meeting you," Jessica said as she held her hand out to shake with Emma.

"Oh, that's OK. I'll walk outside with you. I'm done with my lunch anyway." Emma stood and swung her big purse over one shoulder, and followed Jessica to the door. The two of them stood on the sidewalk, looking toward the dog.

A man was unfastening Chili from her post, and they watched as he turned toward them, leash in hand.

"Ron!" Jessica said with a big smile. "How are you?"

The man threw his arms around Jessica, giving her a big hug while

Emma stood aside and watched.

"Hey," Ron said, "I saw you the first time you came out to untangle this little dude. I was right across the street," he said, motioning toward a couple of tables sitting in the sun. "She looked like she needed a tree stop."

Jessica thought of how she had first met Ron on her first assignment in Arizona. She had been staying at the historic El Tovar Hotel and Ron, a river runner waiting for the rafting season to begin, had been working in the restaurant as a waiter. It wasn't unusual for a river runner to find other employment during the off-season, and that year he had chosen waiting tables.

He was one of those likeable blond men with blue eyes that crinkled when he smiled. He wore his hair in a casual ponytail and his clothes reflected his love of the outdoors. Ron was the only man she knew who hadn't loved Rachel. In fact, he'd seemed rather indifferent.

"I can't believe you're here!" Jessica said, giving him a quick hug. Then she remembered she wasn't alone. "Oh, Ron, this is Emma Begay. Emma, this is a good buddy of mine from the El Tovar Hotel," she looked back at Ron as she said that. "Yeah. Why are you here in town?"

"Well, as a matter of fact, I broke my arm. And after you left, the restaurant held no charm for me." He gave Jessica a disarming smile that made his dimples poke out of his beard stubble. He extended his left hand to Emma in greeting, and Jessica noticed the cast on his right arm for the first time. "Actually Emma and I know each other," he said casually. "Hi, it's good to see you again." He and Emma bobbed their heads at each other in greeting, awkwardly shaking hands.

"So, you're here in Flagstaff now?" Jessica asked him.

"Yeah, I'm working over at The Edge, the Babbitt family sports store on San Francisco Street downtown?" he said, looking back at Jessica.

"Will you get to do the river at all this year?" Jessica asked him.

"It doesn't look like it. But, hey, that's OK, there'll be next year," he said, reaching down to pet Chili's head. He straightened up and looked at Jessica grimly, "I heard you got married. Congratulations." She thought he looked carefully indifferent.

"Yeah. Thanks," she said, remembering the night at the El Tovar when Ron had made too many champagne toasts and revealed his true feelings for Jessica. She later had to tell him gently that she was in love with Alex, a hard thing to do. She'd hated hurting his feelings.

"Well, I guess I need to run," Emma said, looking at her huge black watch, "I've got to be back to the office in ten minutes." She bent toward Jessica and gave her a little hug. "It's really been great talking with you. I hope we can be friends."

"I'd like that," Jessica said, pleased with the prospect of having a female friend in town. Emma said goodbye to Ron and after giving Chili a hug too, she headed off down the street.

"So, how long have you known her?" Ron asked after Emma was out of earshot.

"We just met. We've been talking for a long time though. She seems nice," Jessica told him.

"Yeah, well, I'd be careful around her," Ron told her.

"Oh, really? How so?" Jessica asked as she took Chili's leash from Ron and started walking the puppy to find a grassy spot behind the building.

"I don't know. I heard she was pretty into drugs at one point."

"I also hear she was really good friends with Rachel."

"Good friends with Alex, you mean?" Ron said. "Everyone knows she's had a terrible crush on him for years."

Jessica smiled, "I know. I could tell when she was talking about him." Jessica could understand how a young woman could have a crush on Alex. He was a man who was easy to love.

Chili was busy smelling every bush and blade of grass along the ground. "Ron, was there anything about Rachel anyone disliked?" She had no qualms talking to Ron about Rachel. After all, he was the one who originally told her about how Rachel's car was found deserted out on Blue Moon Bench.

"I mean, everyone paints this picture of perfection," Jessica went on to say. "It's getting rather irritating." She tugged on the puppy's leash when she became too interested in an old flat fishing hat the wind had probably blown into the bushes.

"I don't know," Ron replied as he sat on a cement step at the back of Macy's building. "She wasn't perfect, I suppose, but she was pretty special… to a lot of people. I heard rumors that weren't very nice, but I guess I never really listened to any of them."

"Mmmmm," was all Jessica replied. She wondered if there were complete strangers talking about her and Alex. They'd probably compare her to Rachel, and even more likely find her sadly lacking. It'd only been a year since Rachel's death, not enough time to fade the memory of her beauty and accomplishments. The thought just added to Jessica's feeling of inadequacy.

She squatted down and pulled Chili closer to untangle her leg from her leash and gave her a good hug, ruffling her floppy ears. The dog leaned into her thigh and gazed up at her with thanks for the attention. Jessica stood up and shaded her eyes from the sun.

"Still," she told Ron candidly, "sometimes I really feel intimidated by her memory. She seemed so perfect."

Ron stood up and dusted off his pants. "You have nothing to worry about, sweetheart," Ron said. "You're just as cute, and twice as nice. Now… come on. I'll buy you a piece of pizza and a salad for lunch, and right across the street is the only art supply store in Flagstaff."

Changing the subject didn't remove the concern from Jessica's mind. It only put it on hold for a while. She knew she might never escape the feeling that everyone was comparing her to Rachel and that she didn't quite make the grade. Still, the thought of looking at art supplies definitely took the sting out of the thought of her husband's paragon first wife.

Ron bought the pizza and salads, and they ate on a deck in front of the local pizza place. Jessica did her usual thing of drinking her entire large Coke, but this time, she finished her salad. She decided living in the high altitude was improving her appetite, even if Alex didn't think so.

Chili was allowed to roam around the walled-in area, and was even indulged with some pizza herself. She needed to be walked again because she drank a good bit of water after the pepperoni. Jessica grabbed a handful of complimentary mints from the counter before walking with Ron to the art store across the street.

Ron stood outside with Chili while Jessica went in to see what the small store had to offer. She saw that they stocked most of the wonderful paints, brushes and paper that she would need for her work. She briefly talked to the owner and then walked out happy with her discovery. She and Ron walked back out to the sidewalk, and Ron told her he needed to head back to work.

"The Edge is a terrific store. They have everything you'll ever need for adventures. Stop in sometime and say hi." He gave her a last hug and then took hold of her shoulders and turned her to face him. "And, Jessica? I'm glad we can be friends. I just want you to know that if you ever need someone to talk to, or to give you support, or just take you to lunch, I'm always here." Earlier he had written down his phone number and given it to her with great ceremony. Now, he smiled at her with a touch of sadness. "You know I'd do anything for you, Jessica. Just say the word and I'll be there."

"Thank you, Ron. I really appreciate you being so sweet," Jessica told him, feeling a little awkward. It was obvious he still carried feelings for her and she wanted nothing but friendship from him. "Perhaps you can come out to the ranch one weekend for dinner with Alex and me." She felt like a stinker, but she wanted to make sure he understood where they stood.

He seemed to accept her insinuation, and even said he'd take her up on the invitation. They tentatively arranged for a weekend two weeks down the road, and he said he'd call her beforehand to confirm. Before releasing her, he bent down and gave her a gentle kiss that Jessica was careful not to respond to. His eyes seemed a darker blue than usual, and she wondered if they showed the intensity of his feelings. Her own were mixed. She knew if Alex weren't in the picture, Ron would have definitely been in her life as more than a friend.

He turned and walked off, waving to her before he turned the corner and headed toward downtown. Jessica watched as he disappeared. She decided it would be interesting to see if he followed up on the visit to the ranch.

As she headed toward home, she thought about Rachel and Alex. To her, it was obvious that Alex still loved Rachel. Every time someone said her name, or if something on the ranch reminded him of her, he became quiet and saddened.

Wherever she looked, whoever she talked to, wherever she went, waking and sleeping, she constantly ran into the ghost of Rachel. She knew what a nice figure Rachel had cut from the clothes in the closet. The long, slim legs, the small, narrow feet, her slender waist. Jessica knew what she'd looked like from the photo she'd found in the upstairs sitting room. The long, straight, natural blond hair, the heart-shaped face, the stunning grey eyes framed with dark lashes and brows. She knew the perfume she preferred to wear, the food she preferred to eat, and she could imagine her laughter and her smile. Everyone had loved Rachel; everyone missed Rachel. Everyone respected Rachel. She had been a capable horsewoman, a successful hostess, and an exemplary wife. How could Jessica ever expect to follow in those footsteps? When she had agreed to Alex's marriage proposal, she thought it was just the two of them. Had she known it would include a third, she would have thought more carefully before saying yes.

She decided to go home and meditate. It was the only thing that could give her peace of mind when she felt worried or stressed. In fact, today might take more than her usual hour.

Chapter 7: The Coyote's Breath was Hot

Utah border, northern Arizona

The dark, silent night seemed to be closing in on the truck like a black scourge. Holding her hand up before her face, close enough that she could feel the warmth from her palm, Jessica realized she couldn't even see it and that really unnerved her.

She was lying on her back, fully dressed and trussed-up in a sleeping bag. Next to her, Alex was breathing the slow, easy in-and-out of someone asleep. They were camping out on the Navajo Reservation and after finishing the dinner dishes from their meager meal, Alex casually turned off the lantern. They climbed into the back of the truck's camper shell to lay on a soft futon designed for just such an occasion as this, and he promptly fell asleep.

Jessica, on the other hand, laid stiff, holding her breath. From the first moment they'd arrived in this isolated place, Jessica had felt uncomfortable. It was like sensory deprivation for her. There was absolutely no sound except the light breeze blowing through the small bushes speckling the ground. No traffic, no people, no engines, no nothing. At one point, it was so quiet she could hear the sound of her own blood in her ears, like when you put a seashell up to your ear. She was a city girl in a place she could not comprehend. All around her was spooky silence and it made Jessica feel displaced and nervous.

The more she tried to relax, the tenser she became.

She held her breath and tried to listen for sound outside the truck but could only hear Alex's steady breathing. Damn, why couldn't she sleep like that? She tried to relax her body, but the more she tried to let go, the more she tensed up. Her eyes were becoming adjusted to the dark, and indistinct shapes showed in her peripheral sight. *All right. Think it through. What are you afraid of? The only large animals around are coyotes, and they're actually afraid of man. Alex says they'll run if they see you.*

Ahhhhh..., another thought rose up in her mind, *...but what if the coyote was rabid?*

She looked to her right at what looked like the camper window, half opened, leaving only a screen between her and the outside. She began to get dizzy with holding her breath.

Oh, my, God, Jessica thought, *I have to get my fear under control. This is awful.*

She began to apply a technique she'd learned in Buddhism. Calming the mind, keeping it focused on one thing—her breathing. The idea was to get her breathing to slow, her mind to relax, and the fear to dissolve.

Suddenly, to her utter astonishment, a real coyote lunged through the screen of the window and was attempting to surge into the interior of the camper shell. The coyote wasn't able to get his whole body through the window on his first leap, but it was obvious that he was determined to get at his victims in the truck. He was hanging awkwardly over her, riotously yelping and barking, all the time slinging flecks of rabid foam all over her hair and face. She could hear the sound of his back claws frantically scratching on the metal of the truck's body. She knew he was trying to get a good foothold so he could make it the rest of the way into the camper to attack them. Jessica was frozen with fear. The coyote's breath was hot and stank of something wild and foul, and his sharp teeth seemed to get closer to her exposed head with each jerk.

Jessica sat straight up, jerking away from the animal. She couldn't stop the scream that billowed up out of her chest. She could feel when it woke Alex with a start and he also sat up..

"What?" he asked, bleary-eyed. "What happened? Are you OK?"

She was sitting up in the dark, gasping for breath. He turned on the overhead light in the camper and reached to pull her close. In the glare of the light she saw there was no coyote, there was no hole in the screen, and she had been having a nightmare!

He didn't say anything for a minute, just held her close, cradling her head under his chin. When she was calm, she sat up, coming away from his arms and told him what her nightmare had been about. He laughed a warm laugh and gave her a kiss. It put the whole thing in perspective and brought her back to reality.

She clenched her teeth to stop the chattering and tried to regroup. Then she said, "Alex, I rrrealy nnneeed to go pee."

"Will you be OK alone...?" he asked while opening up the camper's back tailgate.

"Yeah, that's OK," she answered, wanting to appear brave after her lapse into being a typical girl. "I'll just take the flashlight."

He hid his smile from her, eyes sparkling, and said, "Brave girl."

She suddenly matched his mood and smiled while snatching the flashlight out of his hand. She climbed out and shrugged into her sweater, her shoes loose with untied laces. "I'll just go out in the front of the truck," she mumbled. Once there, she carefully squatted, being concerned that she might get her fanny too low to the ground.

"Can scorpions jump?" she hollered up to Alex in the night. She felt silly when she heard his "No," laced with a snicker.

When she was finished, she quickly ran back to the camper shell, barely giving enough time to pull up her jeans. Alex was standing with his hands in his pockets, gazing out across the night valley before them. She sank into his welcoming embrace and they stood together in the quiet night. Looking up, she noticed the millions of stars that glinted in the sky. The Milky Way was a white stripe of star clusters that softly illuminated the land around them. To her surprise, her eyes had adjusted to the dark, and now it seemed she could see for miles in a night that had seemed dense and black earlier. It gave her a feeling of comfort that he was warm and safe next to her.

"I'm sorry, Jess. I didn't realize you were so nervous about camping out. You should have told me. Are you OK now?" He kissed the top of her head.

"Yeah, I'm OK. Actually, I never realized I was so nervous before now. I've never camped out before."

"Never?" he said incredulously.

"Nope," she said in answer. "Unless Girl Scouts count. There were 130 other girls, and twenty Moms. It was nothing like this."

"Come here," Alex said, taking her hand and leading her to the top of the hill behind their campsite.

He stopped walking when they arrived on a ridge of flat flagstone chilled from the night air and high above the valley. Turning her around he said, "Look around you, Jessica. Do you see the ridge over on the other side of the river?" When she nodded, he went on. "A small indigenous tribe used to live at the base of that cliff. This was their home. They farmed this valley, planting corn and irrigating the crops from the river. See that grove of trees over there?" He pointed downriver at an outcropping of ghostly cottonwoods. "Behind those trees is a cliff full of ancient rock art. It was probably where the young braves would meet before going on a hunt. They participated in ceremonies that they believed would give them strength and cunning as they rode off, intending to bring meat to their families. It's believed by some that the village Shaman, or medicine-man, was the one to carve the images into the cliff, pictures of a small hunter with a bow aimed at a group of long-horned sheep. Some think they believed what was carved into Mother Earth would make the magic stronger. Tomorrow, I'll take you there and you can see the ancient pictures for yourself." He turned to Jessica and kissed her forehead.

"This land was home to those people, Jessica," Alex continued. "They knew every rock and every tree for miles. They lived, and loved and bore their children here for centuries. Look over there," he said as he pointed off in the distance. She realized she could see a faint light, flickering way over by some dark hills in the distance. "And there, and there." He pointed in two different directions. He was right; there were several dim lights all around them. "Those are small hogans, Navajo houses out here on the reservation. Those are homes, families and friends living close to each other. They have sheep, dogs and children, and they probably had mutton stew for dinner tonight."

Jessica felt her shoulders relax, and she had to smile to herself. This was someone's backyard, not some wilderness in the middle of nowhere. She felt ridiculous after her nightmare, but she was glad Alex had explained how he saw this land. Indeed, it helped her to look at it differently.

Alex stood up and took off his coat, laying it out on top of the rock. He drew her down on the coat next to him and folded her in his arms. "See the stars overhead? Those are the same stars our friends saw hundreds of years ago. They looked up at the heavens just like we are, and then they made love," he kissed her deeply and started to remove her jacket. "How about it? Are you up for the adventure?" he asked softly, smiling. Sometimes, Alex was so charming, she'd find herself doing things she'd never do for anyone else. This night was no exception. She sank down with him onto the jacket and allowed herself to be carried away by his romantic mood.

They made love under the stars just like the ancients of long ago, with Jessica's thoughts of scorpions and coyotes gone.

She was pleased to realize that she was beginning to feel as if she had become part of the land. She knew it would take time to get over the fear of being so far from what she considered civilization, but she also knew that she was beginning to see the Arizona wilderness in a different light. No matter how quiet or dark it became, now she understood it wasn't hostile land; it was home. To someone, sometime over the years, it had been a place someone had been familiar with. Just as she knew the streets of San Francisco, these people who lived out here knew the curve and dip of the river. Just as she loved the smell of coffee in the morning, they probably loved the smell of the earth as they farmed it.

The next morning, Alex and Jessica visited the cliff that Alex had talked about the night before, and Jessica was charmed by the beauty of the rock art. The images had been pecked into the rock wall, making the little hunter and his sheep stand out against the stones' darker color. Simple in line, it was expressive and so sweet it touched her in a place that was deep and secret. She wanted to learn more about this form of art. Alex told her that the scientific name for the work was petroglyph, or pictograph, depending on how the images were sketched onto the rock. He said there were sites all over Arizona that would take her breath away. He explained that they were holy sites, respected by Native Americans of today, and Alex stressed how important it was not to touch or in any way deface the panels.

"There have been cases of people using sites like this for shooting practice, and others have taken broken pieces home to use for door stops." It broke Jessica's heart to think of such a horrible fate as that for this beautiful art form.

As they climbed over the cliffs to view the different panels, Alex taught Jessica some rudimentary techniques of rock climbing. He'd brought extra equipment, and he said he enjoyed watching her natural athletic ability mold itself into a sport he'd always loved.

When they were done, they hiked across the river to the pueblo ruins, and ate lunch under the large cottonwoods, bare of leaves. Green buds had started coming out on the branches, but only a few had sprouted. It was too early for spring to visit the valley, but it wouldn't be long.

Jessica looked down between her feet and saw three kernels of Indian corn and she wondered if it was a good luck omen. She knew that corn was a symbol of abundance and prosperity to Native

Americans. She quietly picked up the brightly colored kernels and put them in her pocket, rubbing them with her thumb as she did so. She would always keep them so she could remember this trip, and of finding her place in this beautiful land.

They climbed into the truck at about 3:00 in the afternoon and headed down the reservation road that would eventually take them to the Cameron Trading Post. The plan was to have dinner at the restaurant there with Alex's friend.

The road they were on led them to an intersection with three other dirt roads, taking off in what appeared to be random directions. Alex took a left without hesitation, driving with confidence on the graded washboard route. They came to another intersection, this time with only two other choices. "How in the world do you know where you're going? There aren't any signs," Jessica asked as he once again made a confident turn.

"Well," Alex said, "You just have to know your way. Did you see that car muffler sticking out of the ground back there at the intersection?" Jessica looked back and sure enough, there was the muffler sitting straight up like a signpost.

"Yeah, so?"

"So, that's where you turn east. The roads have numbers, but they just don't post them. The Navajo feel more comfortable with their own form of signage," Alex said with a smile.

The dirt road intersected with the main highway, and with a left turn, they almost immediately arrived in the small community of Cameron with enough time to look around the famous Trading Post. It was a large affair filled with 'stuff'. Jessica couldn't think of what else to call it. Some would consider many of the things she saw junk, but judging by the number of people buying them, it was obvious the things were quite popular with the tourist crowd.

Alex led her over to the south side of the store, and that was where the real works of art created by Native Americans were carefully displayed. Beautiful pots and sculptures resided next to animal fetishes carved from stone. One small area of the store had been corralled off with a fence, and inside was a spectacular selection of true Navajo blankets woven by local artisans. The fine weave and colors of the wool felt soft under Jessica's fingers. She was amazed at the variety and detail of the designs that graced each weaving. Alex explained the different regions that dictated the names of the designs, such as Two Grey Hills and Ganado Red. He showed her how she could tell Navajo blankets from Mexican knock-offs. And she learned what the difference was between hand-dyed, homespun wool, and manufactured wool.

She and Alex continued to explore the store, admiring the Hopi Kachinas. They were carvings made from cottonwood branches, which depicted the different Hopi gods. Centuries ago and still today, this type of doll was used by the Hopi to teach their children to recognize the different Kachinas and to learn the role each of the over 200 characters played in their annual religious ceremonies. Each doll was beautifully painted and carved in detail from a single cottonwood root, down to the kernels on an ear of corn that one doll carried in a clenched fist.

Glass cases filled with delicately crafted silver and turquoise jewelry flanked the center of the store, and Native American employees went about their work of showing the pieces to interested customers. The abundance of talent and craft was almost too much for Jessica to take in all at once and as an artist, she was awed by the display.

"Jessica, I'd like you to meet an old friend," Alex said as he led her toward a Native American man headed their way. "This is Johnson Longname. Johnson, this is Jessica, my new wife."

Johnson Longname was a small-boned man about the same height as Jessica with a wiry build. His face was round and sported a thin, black mustache. His high cheekbones were shiny, and his alert dark brown eyes glanced at her with interest.

He wore a white tee shirt under a gray and brown plaid flannel shirt. His bowed legs were cased in stiff, dark blue jeans, and he wore light-tan work boots that bore the marks of being most loved. Jessica saw that he was carrying a well-worn, sweat brimmed cowboy hat, which had a simple leather band and one black feather stuck in it. When Alex introduced him to her, he did a slight bow in her direction, and then looked shyly away before looking back at Alex.

Jessica reached out to shake his hand and said, "It's nice to meet you Mr. Longname." Alex had already asked her to be very respectful when meeting any Native American on the reservation. Most of the more traditional ones put a lot of importance on formality. He also told her that when they shook hands, their grip was intentionally light. A centuries-old Navajo fable said that shaking the hand of a stranger might hex them, because the stranger might be a witch. It was believed that this fable developed because when the Spanish first arrived on this continent, they had brought with them diseases that the Natives had no immunity for, and many of them died of the 'white man curse'. Alex believed that some clever Medicine Man probably began the fable to help save his people.

Jessica accepted his gentle squeeze of her hand, and waited respectfully for him to speak to her. He seemed shy and hesitant. Alex was the one to pick up the conversation. "How's your family?" he asked politely. Johnson shuffled and smiled, looking across the room.

"They are good. Miranda had a baby last month, and Mother finally decided to let me get a generator for the hogan." Johnson's speech was clipped and choppy, and carried an accent Jessica would later learn to recognize as Navajo. "She wanted to play Monopoly, but the lantern light was too dim to see the board."

Both Alex and Jessica laughed and the conversation became a little easier. He began to address Jessica directly as they talked, and she was happy to be included in his glances. When they parted ways, Johnson Longname had asked Jessica to call him by his first name, and he promised to show her the rug room on her next visit, intending to tell her the story of his family's weavings.

"I'm ready to eat," she told Alex with enthusiasm as they left Johnson. They walked into the restaurant, looking forward to their first real meal after roughing it for two days camping on the rez. Mac had not arrived yet, so a young Navajo woman seated them at one of the tables, which was next to a window with a view into the Little Colorado River Canyon. Alex pulled out her chair, and gave the top of her head a lingering kiss after pushing the chair in behind her. She was looking forward to her meeting with Mac McInnerney. She had only met him once at Alex's, early in the relationship, but she remembered him being a rugged man with a blond mustache and beard, intelligent, very clever and fun to be around.

Mac arrived as they were studying the menu, bringing with him a real gusto, filling the room. He gave Jessica a friendly hug and Alex a slap on the back. He seemed suntanned, smiling and up for anything. Tonight, he wore blue jeans, hiking boots and a turtleneck tee shirt under a black fuzzy that sported electric blue trim. He carried his trusty old bush hat, tossing it on the extra chair at the table as he sat down.

Although he was medium in build and just a smidgen under six feet, he seemed to fill up a lot of space with his personality. His Aussie-accented voice, confident and full of enthusiasm, took up most of the conversation and added a festive feel to the evening.

As the evening progressed, she retreated a little to watch Alex and Mac talk about a cave project, and could see from their familiarity that they had been friends for many years.

Before long she was drawn back into the conversation by Mac, and everything seemed light and happy. He asked several questions about her illustration career and her home in San Francisco. He showed great interest in a Forbes cover project, and found the duck pond job she was working on humorous.

"My grandfather had ducks at his home in Australia, and I can tell you, mate, don't draw the decking completely around the pond if you want to be practical. They'll do their duty all over the deck and make it inhabitable. They're some of the dirtiest creatures I know," Mac told her. "On the other hand, make the deck high enough to keep them in the water, mate, and you will have a deck and pond that'll make the neighbors jealous." He gestured expansively with both hands.

Jessica laughed. "I'll make sure the architect that's designing the project gets your advice. I'm afraid I just get to draw his ideas. But I'm sure he'll appreciate your experienced input."

They ordered dinner, with Jessica going first, ordering the Navajo Stew. Alex recommended it even though it wasn't on the menu.

"They've served it for years, but only the locals know to still ask for it. Try it." Alex encouraged her. When Mac was done with his order and flirting with the waitress, who seemed to know him well, she asked what they would like to drink in her clipped Navajo accent. It was Coke for Jessica, and iced tea for the other two and when the waitress left with their order, Mac entertained them with stories of a Navajo family with whom he'd just spent the whole week. He was an excellent storyteller, and a good observer. His descriptions were colorful and full of life, and Jessica enjoyed learning more about the Navajo people.

When the meal arrived, she was determined to eat all of her stew even though it was a large bowl filled to the rim, rich with chunks of vegetables and tender meat. The Navajo fry bread was unleavened, as big around as the plate and flat. She knew it was probably terrible for her diet, but so amazingly delicious when dipped in the stew juices, she enjoyed every bite.

As the evening came to a close, the three of them trailed up to the cashier. Mac and Alex fought over who should pay the bill, each insisting it was the others' turn. Alex ended up with the ticket and as he paid the cashier, Mac turned to Jessica and looked at her appraisingly.

"Well, as usual, Alex has done it again," he said in his Australian accent. "He has always had a taste for beautiful, intelligent women. Just like Rachel, you are very charming, and a man cannot help loving you. Eh, Alex?" he rotated toward Alex at the register.

Jessica turned to see Alex's reaction and saw the same cold, quiet look he always assumed whenever Rachel came up in conversations. She immediately felt compassion for him and wanted to change the subject. However, Mac was faster than she was.

"Well mate, I certainly hope you appreciate this one more than you did the last one," Mac said, and with that cryptic remark he strolled into the store-part of the Trading Post, and picked up an expensive piece of pottery, peering at the bottom as if to look for a signature.

Jessica was shocked at Mac's insensitivity toward Alex's loss. The only indication that Alex had even heard Mac's comment, besides the grim expression on his face, was the way his knuckles turned white as he gripped the pen to sign the charge receipt.

Jessica, desperate to change the subject, turned and grabbed an Indian Country map off the rack next to the register. "Oh, Alex, I wanted to get this map. You said it showed all the roads on the rez that weren't marked. May I get it?"

As Alex took the map, his expression relaxing a bit, she wondered at Mac's comment. It seemed to Jessica that there was a strange twist to Mac's voice as he'd made the remark without any remorse, almost as if he deliberately wanted to hurt Alex. And what had he meant by saying Alex hadn't appreciated Rachel? Alex had loved Rachel and still mourned her death more than was healthy.

Turning to watch the man who was supposed to be Alex's best friend, she wondered if she hadn't seen just a little jealousy in his eyes.

Chapter 8: Isn't That Where Rachel Died?

Desert View Tower, Grand Canyon

The Watchtower on Desert View Point along the Grand Canyon was originally built as a rest stop and observation point back in the 1940s. It was a seventy-foot structure, built from local stone, rising on the highest point of the South Rim, modeled by the architect from towers found in Native American ruins. A few visitors were milling around out on a flagstone overlook, which sat next to the tower and the rim of the canyon. Ron watched as Jessica turned her face to the sun, eyes closed. It was certain winter was on the way out and spring was already showing its warmth.

He had been on his way to visit a friend out in the Grand Canyon Village when he'd seen Jessica's green Discovery ahead of him on the two-lane highway that twisted its way into the Park. Earlier, he'd called Lucy and asked her to lunch for two reasons, first because he was pretty sure she'd sleep with him, and second she was a good friend of Jessica's, and he was using her to get information about what was going on at Dawson's ranch. He knew he was living a dangerous life by feeding his obsession over Jessica, but he just couldn't help himself.

Therefore, when he'd seen her Discovery on the road, he'd simply followed her to the Tower, quickly calling Lucy on his cell phone to cancel on her once again, and approached Jessica in the parking lot. She'd been surprised to see him, and he felt some hope rise up in his heart when he saw a small spark of pleasure on her face.

While Jessica explained that she was there to do some preliminary sketches for a Forest Service project, he watched her beautiful face light up as she talked about her work. He felt his heart swell with the love he could not turn off.

He was certain that she was his soul mate. The one woman meant specifically for him. Coming out of a disastrous relationship, he had written all the things down that he was looking for in a woman only months before he'd met Jessica for the first time. Like a spell, or a wish list, he'd worked on it for days, and then there she was, sitting at a table in his station at the El Tovar Hotel restaurant. She had taken his breath away with her light auburn hair and electric turquoise eyes. As he'd served her dinner, he skillfully learned as much as he could without being indiscreet. He'd been cautiously delighted to discover that she had everything on his list, right down to her great body and the fact that she was an artist. The only problem was that later, she'd married Alex Dawson instead of him. He felt like it was his fault that she'd strayed down the wrong path, and he intended to help her see that.

"Oh, God, isn't it beautiful?" Jessica was saying breathlessly. She was gazing up at the Desert View Tower with awe in her eyes. "I swear that I have a feeling of connection and empathy with the artist who designed this building for the Harvey Company. She was so amazing. I wish I knew more about her." She started moving toward the tower, skirting the tourists that were around her, snapping photos, and talking in a rush.

"That I can help you with," Ron told her, following her along the walkway. "I did tour guides through this building one summer. I'll bore you with the whole treatment if you're interested." He hadn't really been a tour guide, but he'd dated a woman who was, and he remembered a lot because he helped her to memorize the facts while he'd been trying to get her to bed.

"Yes!" Jessica told him. "Tell me everything while I shoot more pictures from down here." Ron sat on a bench that looked solid, handmade, and rustic, and began to tell her what he knew.

He told her that Mary Jane Colter was an artist originally from St. Paul, Minnesota, who attended San Francisco's California School of Design. "There she was taught the arts-and-crafts philosophy of Architecture," Ron told her. "And designed her first building for the Fred Harvey Company in… 1902. The first building she designed for the Grand Canyon was the Hopi House, which you already drew." He paused as he got up and followed her around to the side of the building. "Let's see. In 1910, Ms. Colter was hired full-time by the Harvey Company to become the company's architect and designer. The Officials of the Forest Service liked Ms. Colter's work so much that other architects working on other projects for the National Parks were urged to emulate her style. I guess it kind of pissed them off because she was a woman and they were men." He stopped talking as they headed into the old building's front door.

The circular room, now a gift shop, was lined with windows that showed close to a two-hundred-degree view of the Canyon, which was so spectacular, everyone who first entered usually stopped in surprise. There was something totally breathtaking in seeing the Canyon framed by the large windows, giving a better feeling for its immensity than when you stood outside and saw it with no comparison for size. The shop was filled with trinkets and some nicer pieces of artwork, and Native American flute music was coming from some unknown origin.

Jessica and Ron dropped the required quarter in the old-fashioned turnstile, and had to wait their turn while a couple came down the narrow and worn stairway that led to the top of the tower. As they climbed the circular set of steps, they looked out each window that had been built intermittently along the stairwell, Jessica like a child, nose pressed up against the glass. The tower was four stories high, and the walk-up took their breath away and not just because of the elevation. Each floor was decorated with images done by a Native American artist named Fred Kabotie, who used Hopi legends and sand paintings to inspire his work.

But nothing could match the magnificence of the view from the top of the tower. Ron was surprised that it always had the ability to impact him anew each time he saw it. It was a birds-eye view, looking down on the mighty Grand Canyon. It was a bright winter day, and far below the land, sat so far away you lost the texture.

"You can see only the color and shadows from the sun," Jessica said with reverence in her voice. "It makes an abstract painting of reality."

Coming directly toward them from the north was the Canyon, making its curving turn to the left, passing by the tower on the rim, to continue on to the west.

"Look, there," Ron told Jessica, coming right up behind her and pointing over her shoulder. "See that other canyon coming from the east?" Jessica looked where he was pointing and nodded when she saw the second canyon, deep and dark, but not as wide; join the Grand Canyon right before the bend. "That's the Little Colorado River, or the LCR. Where they come together is called the confluence of the two rivers."

Ron paused for a moment. The landscape reminded him of another beauty who'd left so many hearts spurned, just like Jessica would probably do to him. He only allowed himself a moment of regret, then he turned to Jessica. "See the point on the northeast side?" he said in a quiet voice. When Jessica indicated that she saw what he was talking about, he said, "That's Blue Moon Bench." As soon as the words came out, he regretted saying them. He dropped his arm and turned, heading back down the stairs without another word. He hadn't meant to bring up Blue Moon Bench, because he was afraid that it might embarrass or hurt her. He hoped that she'd just forget he'd said it.

Ron heard her footsteps as she followed him back down the stairs to the observation deck that was over the gift shop. He hoped the past wouldn't darken this special day. He didn't often get Jessica to himself, and he wasn't about to let bad memories take that away.

The gift shop's circular building was separate from the Tower and its roof, built as an observation deck, could be accessed from the small door that opened from the Tower's second floor. The gift shop building had been built to emulate the Hopi Kivas, holy buildings where religious ceremonies were performed. Jessica caught up with Ron on the roof and he stayed busy with photographing the building with her camera, hoping she wouldn't mention his slip. When he quickly threw a glance her way, he saw that she had taken her sketching things from her daypack and had begun to make sketches for her drawings. The early morning light reflected softly off the stones of the round tower that rose before them.

"I read that one day, when the stone layers were being placed," Ron told her, "Some of the hand-picked stones went on in the wrong order. Colter made them take over four feet of wall apart to fix the mistake." Jessica had paused in her sketch, watching as he continued to photograph. He turned suddenly and took a quick shot of her perched on the wall, the sketchbook in her lap forgotten for the moment. Her light hair danced in the updrafts coming out of the canyon, and the sun glanced off her sunglasses into the lens. Ron thought that she was a dramatic picture of a beautiful woman.

They worked until around 11:00, when Jessica stopped to stretch her cramped muscles. "What a view from up here," she said while standing and arching her back, arms in the air. "I guess you really know this country."

"Like the back of my hand," was Ron's reply. After she told him that she was ready for lunch, he began to help her pack up her collapsible stool, while she boxed her charcoals back into a side pocket of her pack.

"Ron," Jessica said, not looking at him while keeping busy with stowing her gear. "That name you mentioned earlier, Blue Moon Bench. What is it?"

Ron tried to hide his disappointment. He'd been hoping she'd forget. "It's a flat bench of land that stretches along the east side of the Colorado River on the Navajo Indian Reservation," Ron answered.

Jessica stopped what she was doing and turned toward him. "Isn't that where Rachel died?" she asked.

Ron started messing with the camera, putting on the lens cap and clipping the strap back on. "Yeah," he answered her reluctantly. "It was."

Jessica just stood there, staring at the stab of land he had pointed out earlier from the top of the tower. He wondered if she imagined Rachel's tiny speck of a body falling over that edge into the canyon. God knew, he had thought of it enough times. Ron stopped what he was doing and blinked a couple of times, angry that his eyes were watering.

"Did you know her well?" Jessica asked him, sounding casual. She turned and looked at him with a clear face.

"Yeah," he looked down and let out a big huff of air. "Yeah, I did." He turned away from her.

"Ron?" she said, and when he didn't answer her, she added, "Are you okay?"

"Look, not everyone finds it easy to share their feelings." Ron heard himself say with a twist of sarcasm. Then he felt regretful that he'd been rude. "I'm sorry," he added quickly, turning back to face her. "I shouldn't have said that."

They stared at each other for a few moments. Then Jessica said quietly, "You too. I had no idea. I wondered why you were the only guy who escaped from her. Now I understand."

"I didn't love her, if that's what you're getting at." Ron felt ugly inside. "But if you want to know about her, I'll tell you. She was really special. She had been a blonde woman full of life, and friendly with everyone. She was an athlete, a downhill skier. She was up for the Olympic team when she met Alex. I guess it was love at first sight and she blew off the team to move to Arizona so they could be together."

"How did it happen? Did she fall?" He quickly looked at her face and wasn't surprised to see that she had turned pale. After some thought, he decided to answer her question, but he wondered why her husband hadn't already told her. As he began the story, he watched her turn her gaze back to Blue Moon Bench in the distance.

"That's the weird thing about it," Ron said. "They never figured it out. The ranch is about fifty miles from there, and to get to Blue Moon Bench, you have to skirt the Little Colorado River, probably some forty-five minutes. She would have had to drive all the way out there on a dark dirt road. They found her car deserted on the edge of the canyon on Blue Moon Bench." He turned and followed her gaze, still holding the camera, forgotten in his hand. "It's a very remote area and no one really knows what happened or why she was out there."

Jessica walked to the wall that skirted the roof lookout and stopped just at the edge, her small hands grasping the rail. "Where was Alex when this happened?"

Now Ron knew for sure that Alex hadn't told her anything about it. In some twisted way it pleased him that their marriage wasn't tight enough for that kind of honesty. Maybe he had a chance with her after all. "I guess he was at an Anthropology Conference up at Lake Powell that night," Ron told her. "I heard he didn't know she was missing until he got home the next day. Two days later they found her body at the bottom of the Grand Canyon."

Jessica was quiet. He suddenly felt guilty for allowing the

conversation to head in this direction. He knew she was sensitive and he should have been more careful. "Look, forget it. It's the past. The day is beautiful, so let's enjoy it. Why don't I go get the food you said you brought and we can eat lunch?" He moved to where she was standing and gave her a gentle hug and was pleased when she allowed him. He smiled a little over her head, where she couldn't see.

When Ron returned quickly from her truck carrying the cooler he'd found in the back, he was relieved to see her color had returned. Together they went behind the tower and found a large flat rock that was worn from years of human feet coming and going, to collect firewood. The pile of wood was stacked behind a beautiful wall, standing in a half circle that had the artistic touch of the architect. It reached eight feet high and tapered off like an old ruin wall. Blocking the wind and the noise from the growing number of visitors to the tower, it felt private.

He suddenly wished he could tell her the truth about his relationship with Rachel, but he had been hiding it for so long, he wasn't even sure he'd know how to start.

"It's just that it's pretty hard for a simple person like myself to compete with a woman as perfect as that," Jessica told him. She looked fragile sitting on the ground, a strand of her hair caught in the corner of her pale pink mouth, her eyes large and a little lost.

Ron had to suppress the almost hysterical laugh that bubbled up inside of him. He suddenly felt driven to change the subject, anything to lead Jessica away from this conversation. He carefully redirected the conversation by telling her funny ski stories. He could see that she was hurt at first, but then she seemed to let it go and listened to his stories with interest.

"So, this very overweight lady just stood there, with her ski overalls down around her ankles, yelling at the snowboarder as he tumbled down the slope," he finished. "It was a hot day and she had nothing underneath. It wasn't a pretty sight for anyone to have to look at."

"When the snowboarder collided with her, it snapped her straps?" Jessica had begun to recover and even laughed, a small broken sound echoing off the rock.

"That's right. Damnedest thing I'd ever seen. Every time she'd try to pull 'em up, she'd start slidin' downhill and she'd stand up to stop, and down her bibs would go again." Ron laughed with Jessica. "By the time I got on the scene, and pulled up the bibs, everyone on the chair lift gave me applause."

"I bet they did!" Jessica gave a small smile. "Remind me to never wear bib overalls if I try skiing."

They packed up everything in the cooler, and Ron returned it to the Discovery. They spent the rest of the afternoon taking pictures of the beautifully crafted tower, and Jessica sketching quick roughs. At one point her cell phone rang, and it was Alex checking on her. Ron tried to be discreet, but he didn't go off too far. He wanted to hear how much of an edge his competition still had on him. After all, Alex's other wife had made it clear in every way that marriage to the honored Alex Dawson wasn't all it was cracked up to be.

Chapter 9: Rachel Wasn't Alone

A Summer Trip to the Trading Post

The sky was a brilliant turquoise like only a July Arizona sky can be. The sun had risen early, and the cool of the evening still hung in the courtyard of the Dawson residence. Jessica whistled for Chili, who came lopping around the corner of the house, ready for anything. Her leg had healed, but she'd never rejoined the other cow-dogs, trading her work for a luxurious life of sleeping on Ralph Lauren sheets at the foot of the bed, and hanging around the studio hoping for leftovers. Jessica had been trying to train her for the usual dog stuff like sitting, and shaking hands. But Chili had her own idea of what a smart dog should do, and dog tricks were not among them. To Jessica's amusement and frustration, Chili picked which commands to follow, and the others she would completely ignore.

On occasion, the dog stayed with Will in the barns, but only if Jessica was gone from the ranch. This was a choice Chili made, and Jessica suspected it was because Dorothea refused to spoil the dog as she and Alex did.

It had only been two weeks since Alex had taken Jessica to her first Home Dance on Second Mesa out on the Hopi Reservation. The religious dance of the sacred Kachinas was an experience she wasn't likely to forget for the rest of her life.

Not only was the vision of the ceremonial dance unforgettable, but also the fact that Mac had told her that her life was in danger. And in fact, warned her that her husband's alibi, the night of his first wife's death, was a lie.

Jessica had tried to call Mac so she could ask him why he would make such an accusation, since they hadn't been able to talk at the time. She'd left him a vague message that he had not returned. She even drove by his attractive two-story house in town and found it shut up and looking deserted. That was when she realized it was summer break at the University and she was frustratingly sure he was out of town.

Her level of frustration was heightened by the fact that she had no friends or family in Arizona with which she could discuss this kind of disaster. And she had no experience to draw on; what did one do when someone accuses one's husband of murder? A husband you'd only known about six months?

She didn't feel as if she could confront him. The man wouldn't even talk about Rachel, and Jessica couldn't imagine asking him if his alibi was valid. In the first place, if he were innocent, it would show her mistrust of him. In the second, if he were guilty, why would he just admit it to her?

After a lot of quiet thought, Jessica finally decided that she couldn't be that wrong about a man. Alex was a wonderful person, and she believed in their love, didn't she? In the end, she made the decision to talk to Johnson Longname about it. He was a long-time friend of Alex's, just as Mac was, and she trusted that he'd be honest with her. Over the months, she and the Navajo had grown to be close, and while she hesitated revealing the chink in her new marriage, she needed that friendship.

Before kissing Alex goodbye that morning, she'd stood silently in the doorway to his office and watched him there at his desk. He was handsome and intent, bent over his paperwork. She had tried to quiet her feeling of uncertainty before kissing him on the cheek, saying she'd be back shortly.

As she'd left Alex's office, she'd seen Dorothea lurking in the shadows of the hallway. There was a battle between her and the housekeeper, who was still in a cold war stage. Neither of them had really admitted how they felt, but it was plain that they didn't harbor any real affection for each other.

There had been two social dinners, and one full-blown party at the ranch over the months, and each one had gone well. Jessica had to admit that Dorothea had been invaluable, and that everything had gone off without a hitch. She always did everything Jessica asked, and she was reliable and very efficient. But still, there was something Jessica just did not like about her. She wondered if it was because Rachel had hired her and her husband Ralph, or because she seemed almost obsessively protective of Alex.

Jessica was also beginning to learn the ins and outs of the political scene in the southwest, and she was sure now that Alex had a good shot at State Representative. It was only a matter of time. They both were excited because Alex had plans that would help the environment and the economy of Arizona.

"Come on, girl," Jessica called. "Let's get going." One of her excuses for driving into Cameron that day was to purchase a gift for Gary, her agent. Gary had been extremely patient, working with her on deadlines and trying to get her regional illustration work. Gary's birthday was a week away, and she wanted to buy him a nice piece of handmade pottery for his home.

Jessica closed up and set the alarm in the studio as she always did. She had some strange feeling that Dorothea would snoop through all of her stuff given half the chance, and Jessica was not comfortable with that. She often had the feeling that the housekeeper was either psychic or had a surveillance system set up in the house that no one else knew about. She always seemed to know everything before she was told, and it gave Jessica the creeps. Alex, on the other hand, thought her ability to anticipate his every move was what made her so valuable.

Opening up the back of her new green Discovery, she let Chili jump into the car. Jessica climbed into the driver's seat and waved to Will walking to the house as she drove off. He was probably coming up to go over the books with Alex.

Before going to the Home Dance, life on the ranch had become every day for Jessica. The typical routine consisted of her and Alex getting up early, and doing meditation for thirty minutes. Then, weather permitting, horseback riding for thirty minutes or so after breakfast. Will's lessons had given her confidence she now showed off whenever she and Alex rode. She had to laugh at herself. She had given up high heels for hiking boots, Gucci for North Face, and her new life really seemed to fit her better.

Often after their morning rides they'd each go their separate ways, she to the studio, he into his office or out on calls. Then they would regroup in the evening for dinner and then to bed. She had enjoyed the consistent, lazy pattern and had looked forward to seeing Alex every evening for dinner. Of course, all that changed after the dance.

Alex had loved her idea of changing the upstairs sitting room into a second small living room for them to enjoy their evenings. So Jessica had thrown herself into the project and redecorated the room in a traditional ranch style with built in bookshelves and Navajo rugs. Rachel's old closet had been carefully converted into a media room that had all the equipment she and Alex needed to work on his digital photography, a hobby that he'd picked up with her encouragement.

The couches were recovered with a soft, deep-green chenille and pillows covered in a southwestern tapestry. She and Alex would often take a walk in the evening or just read quietly with Chili lying on the rugs that covered the re-varnished hardwood floors. It was one of the few rooms in the house that did not have Rachel's presence.

One day, Emma had called to ask if she wanted to join her for lunch in Flagstaff. Jessica had enjoyed hearing from the Navajo woman and agreed to meet her the next week.

She and Alex had fallen into the habit of taking breaks from work on the weekends, and going on adventures out into the incredible land of Arizona. Hikes down the throat of monstrous canyons to look at ancient rock art, a drive out to the reservation's vast land to see a seven-tiered waterfall of what looked like chocolate milk, made by the run-off from the desert rains. They took hikes amidst the Ponderosa pine forests, and visited ancient ruins of the missing Anasazi in the vast lands of the Four Corners area. In all these adventures, Alex always brought his camera along to photograph, later taking the images to a new artistic level using his creative skills on the computer.

Driving up to the Trading Post, Jessica parked her truck in a space far away from the tourists. July was a busy time for Cameron because all the buses and vacationing people going to the Grand Canyon would stop at the Trading Post to take a break and, of course, purchase a souvenir.

Jessica took Chili with her, knowing she couldn't leave her in the hot car. The temperatures at the Post could top 100 this time of year because the elevation was around 3,000 feet lower than the ranch, and qualified as desert.

She went to find Johnson, knowing that he worked out on the grounds during the summer, keeping the Inn's courtyard gardens beautiful and blooming. Over the months, she had learned a lot about this quiet man and now knew that tending the garden was a choice in lifestyle for him.

In the many times they visited, she had learned that his wife had left him seven years before, and that he lived with his mother, now in her eighties. His father had been with the Code-Talkers in WWII and was now dead, and that Johnson had three children who were married with their own children. He had a B.A. from Northern Arizona University, and he still lived in the same hogan in which he'd been born.

He seemed to accept her friendship simply as if it just was, never questioning or talking about it. Jessica speculated that he liked her artistic talent, and often turned the conversation toward her work. But most of all, he loved her dog!

"Hello, Johnson," Jessica called when she found him in the courtyard, "Can you watch Chili while I shop a little?"

Johnson looked up from his raking. "That old dog? Why, I'd as soon get tied up with a bag of skunks," he grumbled. As soon as she saw Johnson, Chili's tail wagged with enthusiasm. Without hesitation, she dashed toward her friend and started jumping on him, barking a welcome. Johnson laughed and tried to look dignified. "Here, here. Stop that, young lady. Behave yourself!"

Johnson always tried to pretend he disliked Chili, but it was all just a show. Chili would follow the man around for hours, keeping him company and making sure no one messed with him. It entertained Johnson when someone would approach him, and a protective growl would issue from low in Chili's throat. Jessica was the only other person that Chili protected the same way.

Leaving the dog a bowl of water under a large cottonwood tree, Jessica went into the Trading Post to shop. After some deliberation, she made a purchase of a small Acoma pot from New Mexico. Jessica decided that its simple lines and modern look would go well in Gary's home in San Francisco.

She also bought a couple of sandwiches and chips, with sodas and two huge chocolate chip cookies. A rawhide chewy was something Jessica was forced to get for Chili on every visit to the Trading Post, otherwise the dog would sulk for days. For some reason, their chewies seemed to have some magic about them, at least to the cow-dog.

Walking back to the cool garden, Jessica set up the lunch stuff under a shadowy arbor, overlooking the courtyard's large fountain.

The first time Jessica had done this, Johnson had been reluctant to join her. But when she finally came to realize that he was embarrassed by what he perceived as charity, she helped him know that it was in return for his kindness that she would offer him lunch. Now, it had become a companionable break in their week for both of them.

After sitting down with him under the arbor, they opened their sandwiches, his was always egg salad, hers turkey and cheese. They ate in companionable silence, a summer breeze rustling the large leaves of the cottonwoods overhead and Jessica was reluctant to ruin the mood by bringing up the real reason for her visit. It ruined her appetite. Johnson took noisy swigs out of his bottle of orange soda, his favorite.

Putting her unfinished sandwich back into it's plastic wrap, Jessica reached down to pet Chili, who was hunkered next to the bench gnawing on the rawhide she'd been handed earlier. The dog gave a small growl high in her throat, a playful threat.

"So, our last dinner party was pretty successful," Jessica began, "I tried some new things on the menu, which Dorothea complained about, of course. That woman hates anything that isn't her idea."

"Mm," grunted Johnson, biting into his sandwich.

To hell with being casual, Jessica thought. "Alex took me to my first Hopi dance a while ago," she said, gathering up her trash and stowing it in the paper bag. Her forgotten sandwich was wadded up with it.

"Did you take plenty of water and wear a hat?" was all Johnson said.

Jessica had to snort as she remembered how thirsty Alex had gotten, and how he had ended up loaning her an ugly fishing hat.

"Actually, no," Jessica said. "Alex got thirsty and I got sunburned. Mac was the only one prepared with water and a hat." Getting up from the bench to pick a blossom on a hanging plant, she turned toward Johnson, still sitting in the arbor's shade. "Johnson? How well do you know Mac?"

"Oh, pretty good I guess. Why?" Johnson asked her, his dark eyes squinted in her direction. He never wore sunglasses no matter how bright the sun.

Neither of them said anything for a few moments. Jessica pulled the blossom she'd picked into tiny pieces and fed it to the breeze.

"Oh, I don't know. He said something yesterday about Rachel's death that left me feeling a little uncomfortable." Johnson didn't say anything. He took the last bite of his sandwich and munched thoughtfully, watching Chili gnaw rhythmically on her chewy.

"Johnson," Jessica said, a little nervous about telling him her story, "Why won't Alex talk about Rachel? It's been over a year since she died, but he still seems to really mourn her death. I think I'm going crazy. I really do."

"How do you mean?" he asked quietly, setting aside his orange soda giving her his complete attention.

"I don't know. Alex gets upset every time Rachel's name comes up, and she seemed so damned perfect. Everyone loved the woman. I'm beginning to feel as if I'm trying to fill her shoes, and I'll never succeed. I know that probably sounds stupid, but I don't know," she finished lamely, giving a shrug and turning away from him. She knew she needed to talk about Mac's comment, but had chickened out and diverted to her paranoia about Rachel's ghost instead. She felt ashamed for her cowardly maneuver.

There was quiet in the courtyard, the only sound was Chili's chewing, the dribble of the fountain, and the breeze rustling the tree leaves above them. It was mid-day and the heat had risen. Most of the birds were sleeping somewhere high in the branches and Jessica began to wish she were one of them. Then Johnson surprised her with his next comment.

"She wasn't really the person you think," was all he said.

Jessica turned and looked at Johnson sitting bowl- legged on the bench with Chili laying at his feet. He took a last swig of his orange soda, emptying the bottle and setting it on the bench next to him.

"What do you mean?" Jessica asked stunned.

"You think she was a good person," he answered using his napkin on his thin mustache. "Some people have beauty outside, but they have a dark inside that you have to look through the beauty to see."

His statement astonished Jessica. "But everyone loved her. She was a model of goodness. Alex loved her so much he still grieves for her."

"Is it grief?" he asked.

She was silent in her surprise for only a moment before saying, "Of course it is. What else could it be?"

Johnson didn't answer her right away, and when he did, he'd changed direction. "I didn't really know Rachel that well," he said in his clipped English. "But I know a man who did. If you really want to know the truth about her, you should talk to a man named Jim in Flagstaff."

Jessica just looked at him for a moment. Then she said, "The truth about her?"

"Jim drives a taxicab for Kachina Taxi." Johnson gathered up his trash and stood up, taking it to the black trash bag he'd been using before she arrived. "Jim is a good friend, you can tell him I told you to look him up."

Johnson again began raking under a huge cottonwood, litter that had blown in from the parking lot. Scooping up a small wad of trash, he carefully placed it in the bag, all the time not looking at her.

"There was a restless spirit in Rachel," Johnson went on to say, shaking the bag. "She was not alone on Blue Moon Bench the night she died."

Jessica tried not to show her shock. The fact that he had just echoed Mac's exact words had her frightened. Was it possible that Mac was right about his other accusations? That Alex was being deceptive about his alibi?

Johnson had turned his back to her and made busy work of tying off the bag of trash. She sat down on the bench, her knees too weak to stand. Chili had fallen into a nap in the heat of the afternoon but somehow sensed her distress and woke up, sleepily blinked at her. *Rachel wasn't alone that night on the Blue Moon Bench.*

"Oh, I almost forgot," Johnson said, walking over to his gardening cart, "I have something for you. My cousin makes these, and I thought you might like to have one," he held up a small leather sack suspended on a leather thong. "It's a medicine bag," he said as he brought the bag back to Jessica.

It was about the size of a very small change purse, and made from light soft leather. The leather thong, long enough to wear as a necklace, was the same color as the bag and made up the drawstrings.

"You put in small items that bring you luck. Maybe a penny, or a flower petal," he snipped a white blossom from a flowering plant and opened the strings of the little bag and pretended to put the flower inside and closed up the strings. "You then wear it around your neck, hidden from everyone, and this good magic will always be with you."

Jessica fingered the little bag as she put it around her neck, still shocked by what she had just learned. She felt a small item in the bag and opened it, gazing inside. There, nestled in the leather bottom, was a small, flat bear carved out of turquoise. She carefully closed the bag, got up from the bench and went up to Johnson.

She disliked the fact that most Native Americans thought it inappropriate to hug, and Johnson was definitely one of them. Still, she held out her hand and said thank you to him. When he put his hand in hers, she covered it with her other hand, smiling into his wise eyes. She felt her own begin to tear up.

"The bear is a mighty symbol of strength," was all he said. She wondered if he knew how badly she needed strength right then. Johnson had become a kind of spiritual friend to her, one she valued deeply.

Jessica turned toward her dog. "Well, Chili, I guess we need to get, if we're going riding before dinner," Chili's ears perked up at her name, but otherwise didn't move from her cool shade. "Come on girl." Jessica picked up the chewy, now almost gone and soggy from Chili's attention, and threw it into Johnson's trash can. She then slapped her thigh, giving Chili the command to heal and the dog jumped up, immediately coming to her side.

"Good girl," she said as a reward, petting the dog's head. "Ok, Johnson, it was wonderful to eat lunch with you, as usual. Take care of yourself. Chili will come and visit you next week. And thanks again for the gift," she touched where the bag hung on her chest under her shirt. He simply dipped his head and smiled, waving before he turned back to his work. When she arrived at the truck she fished out the two kernels of corn she'd found on the rez while hiking. She had been keeping them for good luck and placed them into the bag with the bear.

She rode back to the ranch deep in thought. "Jim the cab driver," Jessica said to herself in the silence of the car. Why would Rachel know a cab driver in Flagstaff? Even more important, how would Jessica ever go about finding the cab driver herself?

She also realized that before her conversation with Johnson, she had believed Mac had to be wrong in his accusation. She had believed Alex had loved Rachel, still loved Rachel, and would have no motive to kill her. But now, she began to wonder.

That night when she and Alex had finished a quiet, uncomfortable dinner, Jessica went out to the studio to close up. She'd begun doing what was called preliminary practice in the Tibetan tradition. She had created a meditation and practice space where she could do practices that taught how to open your heart with compassion. Alex's schedule was so busy it was hard for him to join her, but they often practiced together when possible. Today was not one of those days. She was feeling disconnected and knew she needed to reach inside and become centered.

After finishing her practice, she hunted up Ron's phone number that he'd given her the day she'd bought her boots. He had told her that if she ever needed a friend, he would always be there. Well, this was the time when she would call in that promise.

Jessica now dialed his number, hoping that she was doing the right thing. He answered on the second ring, sounding sleepy and disoriented.

"Oh, geez Ron. I didn't mean to wake you," Jessica said, looking at the clock. It was only eight in the evening.

"No, no! I was just reading the paper and fell asleep in the chair. Goes to show what old age will do to you if you aren't careful." There was humor in his voice.

They spoke for a few moments about simple things and then Jessica told him the purpose of her call. "I need to find the cab driver and talk to him," she told him at the end of her carefully abridged story. She'd decided not to tell him everything until she understood better what she was dealing with.

"Okay," Ron said. "Can I ask why?"

"I'd rather not tell you right now, if you don't mind. It's really just a silly personal matter. Believe me, you'd hardly be interested."

"Jessica. If it involves you, I'm always interested," Ron said seriously with more than friendship in his voice. "Why isn't Alex helping you with this?"

"Ron. Come on," Jessica said to him, thinking she shouldn't have called him after all. But, he must have heard the concern in her voice, because he answered right away.

"Okay, okay. So this cabbie's name is Jim? Do you know which company he works for?"

"Kachina I think. Plus, he was a good friend with Rachel. Do you think you can find him with just that much information?"

"Flags a small town. I'm sure one phone call will do the trick. But why do you need me to do this? Why not just find the guy yourself?" he asked her. Jessica had already thought about that and decided not to take the chance of everyone knowing it was Alex Dawson's wife who was interested in talking to a cab driver who had known his dead first wife. Until she better understood what she was up against, she wasn't taking any chances. She simply told Ron that she wanted to remain anonymous and he laughed.

When she didn't join him he grew silent over the phone and then simply said, "Okay. If that's what you want. No more questions asked."

Jessica let out the breath of relief and thanked him. He told her he'd call as soon as he knew where and when she could find Jim, and hung up after they said goodbye. Jessica felt a little guilty making the call behind Alex's back, but the alternative was to confide in him about what she knew, and she wasn't quite ready for that yet.

After closing everything down and setting the alarm, she came out onto the front porch and shut the front door. Turning toward the west, she raised her arms above her head and gave a good stretch, yawning loudly. The sun had already dropped behind the mountains, but there was still a bright orange glow along the horizon.

Suddenly, a lone rider was silhouetted against the brilliant sky. Jessica stood still, staring at the rider and wondering who would be riding so late in the evening on the ranch. The horse reared its head and rose up on its hind legs as the rider pulled the reins in, twisting the horse in a 180-degree turn.

Jessica instantly realized the horse was Salt and Pepper, Rachel's horse. Taking a few steps to the end of the flagstone surface of the porch, she squinted. The rider had a long, blond ponytail and wore a long-sleeved white shirt. It looked just like Rachel, Jessica realized as a chill froze her where she stood.

The rider turned the horse once more and disappeared over the horizon, riding down the hill on the other side. There was nothing but silence, except the sound of Jessica's elevated breathing. She realized that her heart rate was up, and a rush of adrenaline had surged through her body. For one split moment, she believed it was Rachel. But it couldn't be because she was dead, right? Was someone playing a stupid trick? She decided to ask Will about it. Perhaps it was something as simple as he had a friend visiting, or maybe someone from a nearby ranch had ridden onto the Monte Vista without realizing it. There had to be a logical explanation.

She shivered as she turned toward the main house and Alex. While she knew it wasn't Rachel, it gave her an eerie feeling when she thought of how the rider had looked. Perhaps Rachel's specter had come back to haunt her. Jessica grimly smiled to herself. It wouldn't surprise her at all.

Chapter 10: A Master of Disguise

Joe's Bar, Flagstaff

Jessica kept blowing the horn of her truck. She was in no mood to be nice. The two Navajo boys turned their heads and looked at her for a few moments before spurring their horses into action. The small herd of shaggy churro sheep finally made their way into a wash west of the highway, and she eased the Land Rover down the two-lane road in frustration. She hoped it would be easier finding the cab driver in Flagstaff than it seemed to be getting there.

Alex was away in Los Angeles at a conference with other academic men in his field, but Jessica decided to stay home to continue her investigation. He wouldn't be back until the weekend, probably excited and full of new ideas. That would give her plenty of time to visit with the cab driver, who apparently knew a different side of Rachel than the one she'd encountered so far.

Jessica couldn't hide the fact that all this sneaking around actually had to do with what Mac revealed to her at the Hopi dance. She couldn't even begin to believe that Alex had anything to do with Rachel's death; she just couldn't. She loved him damn it, and she knew she couldn't be so wrong about someone. Alex was a man with too much integrity. She trusted him, right?

The second thing that had prevented her from believing Mac's insinuation was Alex's still-apparent love for Rachel, which left him with no motive in Jessica's eyes. However, when Johnson hinted that Rachel might have been something less than perfect, it had planted a seed of fear inside of her. Did Alex really still have an attachment to his dead wife, or was she just imagining that? And if Rachel was less than lovable, well then, that brings another view into the mix. So, she decided that she needed to know who Rachel really was and how she died.

Ron had returned her call with the information she'd needed, telling her the cab company was headquartered in a small, local bar called Joe's Place in Flagstaff. The cabbies often waited for fares there, and that was where Jim could be found when he wasn't driving a customer.

Jessica pestered Ron until he agreed to help her with a disguise of some sort. She was too embarrassed to let this Jim guy know who she really was. And she sure as hell didn't need anyone seeing the new Mrs. Dawson hanging out in a bar at ten in the morning. That was the time Joe's Place opened, and she decided to stalk this mysterious Jim guy as early as possible while the audience was at a minimum.

Jessica didn't want to chance meeting with Ron when she picked up the disguise, afraid that he'd try once again to talk her out of the plan. It was a good thing, because when he called to tell her where he was hiding her stuff, he insisted on knowing exactly what she was up to.

"Jessica, why are you doing this? Who is this guy?"

"Please, Ron. I can't tell you right now," she told him. "But thanks for helping. I owe you." She felt really bad for using Ron's friendship like this, but for the moment he was the only one she felt she could trust for something like this.

He had become so insistent that she finally made up a lame story, but she was pretty sure Ron bought it. At least he stopped asking questions. She wondered at his pushy curiosity and finally told herself he was probably just worried for her safety.

It was Thursday morning and quite a few people were already on their way to work. First, she drove over to the library and parked. It was an elaborate stone building that had a modest amount of visitors, and Jessica went inside to search the archives of the local newspaper. Finding the articles written about Rachel's death made the whole thing more real. When she saw a picture of Alex and his family at the funeral, his head was bent in sorrow, and his hair was stringy and obviously neglected; she felt a stab of sadness for him. There were a few new, unimportant things about Rachel's death that Jessica hadn't known, but nothing that really gave her any new insight. The body was found, the car was deserted, and no foul play was evident. Just an accident, it said.

When she was finished, she headed for the old downtown area, finding a place to park well away from the traffic, and walked the few blocks to the upscale shopping cluster where Ron had hidden the disguise. It was in a plastic garbage bag stuffed at the bottom of the trashcan, under a liner bag already in the can.

Inside the stall of the bathroom, she examined the tight jeans, black top and thick black-soled boots that Ron had put together for her. Putting on the clothes, she carefully removed any identifying jewelry of her own, and when she finally slipped on the boots, she wasn't surprised to find that everything was too small and barely came close to fitting. Damn, how small did Ron think her feet were anyway? She tucked her medicine bag inside the shirt, refusing to give it up, and hung the two strands of colorful beads around her neck that were in the bottom of the bag. She topped the whole thing off with a short, hole-ridden jean jacket with a huge beer label embroidered on the back that had seen better days and was the only thing that fit.

Coming out of the stall, she stood in front of the mirror and quickly stuffed her hair up in the long black synthetic wig, topping it with an odd, flat red cap. With her makeup scrubbed off and the black hair smoothed down around her ears, her angular face looked completely different. Dangling earrings and a pretend nose ring completed the look.

The last thing she did was put on some silver retro sunglasses she'd once impulsively bought but had never worn. They just didn't seem to be her style, but now they gave her a hippy, I-don't-give-a-shit look. She barely recognized herself in the mirror when she was done chewing the stick of gum she had thought to include.

She wrapped her own clothes in her jacket that she'd turned the wrong-side-out, and stuffed them into the bag, returning it to the trash can, ready for her return. Stepping out into the back alley, she changed her walk and headed for the main street. The day was blustery and warm. The wig felt weird, and the shoes were already killing her feet, but she trudged down the alley determined. Playing spy wasn't really her thing, and she worried about pulling it off.

By the time she reached the downtown area, it was ten thirty, and Joe's Place was open for business. She strolled past the front door, looking around her to be sure no one she knew was watching, and then entered from the side door. Ron had told her the place was a popular local hangout that usually catered to the University crowd. A long bar flanked one wall, the other wall sported a long padded bench that had tables intermittently placed along its length. Sitting in the middle of the black and white tiled floor were two pool tables with long lights suspended over them. In the corner was the required jukebox playing a smooth Rolling Stone's tune. Jessica hoisted herself up on a stool and looked up and down the length of the bar. There were already two serious drinkers starting their morning constitution.

"Excuse me," she said to the bartender. "Do you know where I can find Jim?"

"Which Jim?" he asked without looking up from his cleaning.

She thought for a moment. "The cab driver?" she asked with hesitation.

He then looked up at her, apparently gauging whether he wanted to give her such top-secret information. "He's in the back, cleaning his cab," he said while twitching his head in the general direction of the alley.

"Be right back," she said to no one in particular, trying to appear casual when she felt very out of place. A man two stools down glanced her way while flicking his cigarette ashes into a cheap, tin ashtray on the bar. Without a word, he went back to his beer.

Jessica went out the back door and into the alley. A white four-door sedan was parked in a pullout, and a man was washing it from a bucket of water and suds. She slowly walked over to him while popping her gum. "Are you Jim?" she asked, studying her nails, playing the part.

"Who wants to know?" the man asked without pausing at his task.

"Candy," Jessica said, giving the fake name she'd chosen. He barely looked up at her. Dropping the sponge into the bucket, he picked up a hose and turned on the spray, rinsing off the vehicle with an economized amount of water because it was such a premium in Arizona. He then started to dry it off with a chamois. He was a middle-aged man with a surplus of white hair and he looked tough.

"I used to be friends with Rachel and just got back into town and found out she died," Jessica said, giving her best-standing slump. "Johnson Longname told me you were friends with her, so I thought I'd come by and say 'Hey'."

Her speech barely got a raise out of him. He was ringing out the chamois when Jessica then said, "Look, I was just wondering if you knew what happened to her. Johnson didn't know much and he thought you could tell me more. It was a real shock."

Jim stopped drying his cab and gave her a long look. "Sorry. I'm just a cab driver. I don't know anything, I don't see anything," he went back to drying his car. "Have a nice day."

Jessica stood there several more minutes and asked him two more questions to which he simply shrugged. Then defeated, she stepped back around the corner and re-entered Joe's Place. Hoisting herself back up onto a stool, she stared slightly sick at the huge head of a dead animal on the wall above the bar.

"It's an elk. The owner shot the S.O.B. and had it stuffed. Do you want something?" the bartender asked her. Jessica quickly swallowed her nausea and looked at him for a moment. As a Buddhist, she considered all life precious and she felt sorry for the poor animal whose head now hung on the wall in a smoky bar. On the other hand, it fit her mood perfectly. She was so discouraged. She hadn't realized just how important this visit was until now. She wanted to know more about Rachel, and if what Johnson said was right, she was sure this Jim guy could answer some questions.

Suddenly she stopped breathing, staring at her odd image in the mirror behind the bar. The bar, the cab driver's evasiveness, and the odd story from Johnson—had all left her feeling disjointed, and now she knew why. Intuitively she knew that she needed to learn if Rachel was bad enough that a husband might want her dead, especially a husband like Alex who wanted to run for State Representative. Why hadn't she thought of that before? She felt cold fear enter her heart. This did not improve her mood. Without realizing it, she had begun to believe Alex might have murdered Rachel.

She was still staring at her image, and was jolted from her trance when the forgotten bartender snapped his fingers under her nose. "Yes," she told him when he repeated his question, "Give me a beer."

"What kind do you want?"

"I don't care. Something cold and creative," Jessica answered while taking the gum out of her mouth and depositing it into her own tin ashtray. When the bartender served her, she saw that it was a Japanese beer in a huge bottle, cold and open before her. She took one long swig, and let out a huge belch. She looked so stunned that the bartender laughed.

"Real lady-like," he said.

"Very funny," Jessica replied, and took another swig. "The world stinks, and I don't care if I burp or get drunk. Maybe it will do me good. Maybe I'll forget my troubles."

Suddenly, the reflection in the mirror behind the bar showed Jim coming in the back door. To her surprise, he came up behind her, and reached around taking the beer out of her hand.

"This cute lady and me are goin' for lunch, Dave," he said to the bartender. "I'll have my radio on." Then he placed a kind hand on Jessica's shoulder, "Come on, and let's go get a couple of tacos next door." Jessica turned to him puzzled, and then jumped off the stool, pulling down the crunched-up top so her midriff wasn't exposed. Following him out onto the sidewalk, remembering to slump while she walked, he led her to a very small Mexican restaurant one door down.

They sat at a wobbly table in the corner, and Jim ordered her two beef tacos. She felt her stomach surge slightly and was sure it was the beer so early, and the smell of grease coming from the kitchen.

"Make mine bean tacos please," she said with what she hoped was a smile.

When the tacos arrived, however, they looked very tempting, and after a few seconds, Jessica tried a bite. They were the best tacos she'd ever had in her life, and she had eaten many tacos. She ate both of them before remembering her mission, or her host.

Glancing up into his watery blue eyes, she realized they were actually very kind, almost like a puppy. As she watched, he started his second taco, and gave it his full attention.

"Thanks for the tacos," she said, popping the last bite into her mouth. "They're delicious," she mumbled, mouth full.

"So Johnson told you I was friends with Rachel?" he asked Jessica just before taking a large bite of bean and cheese.

"Yeah, and he thought you might know what happened to her, why she died," Jessica said, thinking discouragingly that if she were in his shoes, she wouldn't tell a snoopy black-haired woman anything. But to her surprise, he began to talk.

He looked at her with speculation for a few minutes. "I don't rightly know exactly what happened to her," he finally said, taking another bite of taco and chewing thoughtfully.

"Well," Jessica interjected, "I always thought some bad ending might come to her eventually. She was cut from a different cloth. Johnson agreed with me, she had a bad side for sure." She fiddled with her napkin, hoping he didn't see her nervousness.

"Johnson said that?" he asked, just getting the words around what was in his mouth.

"Actually, I think his exact words were, 'She had a dark side that you had to look through the beauty to see,' or something like that."

Jim wiped his hands on a tiny paper napkin that could barely handle the juices from the taco. "I suppose that was true," he said looking away as if he were remembering.

Then he did a strange thing. He stood up and went to the men's room without saying a word. When he came back out, his eyes seemed red-rimmed and his single sniff gave him away.

"Are you from Flagstaff?" was all he said after sitting down again.

"Yeah. I used to work up at the Snow Bowl on the patrol years ago. I was on my way to Flagstaff and stopped off at the Trading Post, talked to Johnson and he told me the news. All he knew was what he read in the paper." Jessica was starting to feel bad about visiting all these bad memories on this kind man. Not something a good Buddhist would do without remorse.

He looked down at his empty plate and then sniffed once more and leaned back, tucking in the front of his shirt. "I'm sorry I was a little gruff back there in the alley," he told her. "It's just that Rachel was special to me, and it's tough talking about her."

"I'm sorry," Jessica said, meaning it. They sat there for a few moments in silence. Jim finally waved the waitress over to their table.

"Bring us a couple of coffees, honey," he said to the waitress. The dark-haired lady smiled at him and went back to what must have been the kitchen.

Their coffee arrived and Jessica found the restaurant's ability to create wonderful food stopped at caffeine drinks, but then again she really was particular when it came to coffee. Pouring the creamer into her mug, she saw that it barely changed the offensive liquid's color. She didn't bother stirring, just pushed it aside and gave Jim her complete attention.

Jim left his coffee black, stirring while watching his spoon go round and round, clinking on the side of the ceramic mug. His radio suddenly let out a blast of static, making them both jump, and he immediately nabbed it and pressed a button. "1084, available," he said. The dispatcher requested a pickup at the airport to be brought into town. What Jessica assumed to be another driver came across and said he was near the airport and would catch the fair if Jim didn't mind. "Nope," Jim said simply, "1084, clear and on the side."

He took a sip of coffee and carefully set the mug on the table. "Rachel wasn't as happy as most people thought. I don't know how long you knew her, but she had been really depressed the last year," his statement was made with regret, "Sometimes I tried to help her, but she seemed bent on self-destruction."

"Destruction? What do you mean?" Jessica asked, trying not to sound too interested. She was finally going to get some information.

Jim hesitated for a second and then said, "I don't know. I know she loved living, she played hard, and she tried to experience all the color there was in life. But she was going down the road in a fast lane that was headed to nowhere."

The cliché statement surprised Jessica. "Yeah," she said, trying to sound as if she understood. "She always did like to live on the edge."

He sighed and became tight-lipped for a moment. Jessica decided not to push him so he could tell the story at his own pace so he wouldn't become suspicious of her motive. He finally let out a breath and said with resignation, "Rachel got herself into drugs the last couple of years before she died. She'd been kinda going downhill, drinking too much. But that winter she really bottomed out." Jessica nodded her head in understanding, feeling sincerely shocked to hear this. Gone was the pristine beauty; in her place was a different Rachel who had gotten mixed up with the wrong crowd.

"Alex was very nervous about her habit," he told her. "She told me the whole thing. He felt that it would jeopardize his chances of getting elected as State Representative, and understandably." Jessica went suddenly still and tried not to show a reaction while fear coursed through her.

"She was very discreet about her addiction, but still, something like that would be impossible to keep from the press if they ever got a sniff of it," Jim told her. "Alex put her through detox twice. Neither one of them took hold. The second time he cut off her funds, gave her an allowance so she couldn't afford to buy drugs. Don't know where she was getting the money, but it sure didn't stop her."

"Geez," was all Jessica could get out at first. After a few moments she realized he was expecting more, so she added, "I had no idea. We'd lost touch in the last year because I'd gone overseas. Now I'm sorry I didn't call her more often. Maybe I could have helped her." When she looked at Jim's face, he seemed overcome with emotion again. She realized that he'd probably needed someone to talk to about it, and she'd arrived at just the right time to be a friend. She carefully looked away to give him time to gather himself. It was obvious that the man had really cared about Rachel.

"The thing was, her drug use had gotten out of hand." He said the words with great regret and sadness. Jessica looked back at his face, watching the play of emotions. "At first she said it was just the stress of trying to be the perfect Mrs. Dawson." His lips tightened again. "She worked hard to please the Dawsons, but I swear to God, it just wasn't enough."

Jessica thought quickly and said, "I remember her complaining about all the parties and dinners." She could barely get this statement out. Her head was reeling, but she couldn't afford to put it all together right now. Later, she thought, when she could be alone. In the meantime, she allowed herself to be Candy. As if separating herself from reality would help her deal with what she was learning.

She wondered if Jim had ever talked about this with anyone else. Right at that moment he seemed needy, lonely and sad. He went on to say, "Exactly," in reply to her statement, "I used to drive her to her connection. I was the only one she trusted." He looked reflectively down at his coffee. "I hated the guy. Heathcliff. What a jerk." Jessica was barely listening. He went on to say, "She always wore a disguise so no one would recognize her, she was really careful about that." Jessica quickly looked at him, trying to detect if he had seen through her own disguise. But his attention was in the past, remembering Rachel.

Jim rapidly blinked a few times. "It was a real shame, such a beautiful woman with so much to offer the world."

Jessica suddenly wondered what this man would do if she revealed who she really was. Tell him that he was actually talking to the new Mrs. Dawson, and that his story was chilling her to the bone.

So here was the story of Rachel. Probably the real Rachel, the dark-sided Rachel, Jessica thought to herself, just as Johnson had said. Had Johnson known these things? She took a deep breath and realized that Jim was silent.

"I'm so sorry for bringing all this up now," Jessica told him sincerely. She suddenly had a flashback to when Ron had told her about Emma. That she was a known user of drugs and a friend of Rachel's. The pieces were coming together, and probably faster than she cared for.

Jim shrugged and twisted his cup back and forth by the handle. "She was what she was. I just wonder if I shouldn't have done something more to help her."

He pulled out a pack of cigarettes and looked like he was about to light one when Jessica guessed he remembered the ordinance that didn't allow smoking in public places. He stuffed the pack back into his shirt pocket and motioned for a refill on his coffee.

"Ya know," he went on, "it was strange that night she died. She broke a hard fast rule, probably the only one she lived by for years. She had her crowd up to the ranch for a party, something Alex would never let her do."

Jim went on to say, "Alex didn't approve of her crowd of course. They were a rich, spoiled and wrecked group, some of them. Why she broke that taboo is a puzzle."

"So where was her husband that night?" Jessica asked, feeling as if she were insane. She reminded herself that she was Candy, asking questions about her dead friend Rachel.

"He was at a conference up in Page, the north part of the state. Out there for the weekend." He set his empty coffee cup aside and she saw that it still had not gotten refilled. Once again he drew out his cigarettes but didn't light it. "She had to know that Alex would find out, and that he'd be furious with her. I have no idea what she was thinking. By that time we had started losing touch. She had someone else gettin' her stuff for her, I guess."

Jessica looked down at her own coffee. It had gotten cold, and the cream had formed a skin on the top of the liquid, making it look like a cataract in an eye. She stared down at it and felt dismay. Rachel. The woman she had been frantically trying to live up to. The woman everyone loved and thought was perfect. It seemed she was human after all.

Another call came over the radio and this time Jim had to take the fare. Jessica was disappointed because she had more questions to ask, but was resigned when Jim rose ready to leave. "It's been nice meeting you, Candy. I'm sorry you just learned about Rachel's death. It was a sad thing." She stood up, thanking him and giving him a hug to show her sincerity.

He left after telling her that he was always in Joe's Place because the bar owner also owned the Cab Company. They weren't allowed to drink while on duty, but if she came by after midnight, he was off duty, and they could share a beer.

"Thanks for being so kind," Jessica told him. "You're a nice person. Rachel was lucky to have you around."

"Thanks for saying that. But I'm guessing I wasn't a good enough friend. She isn't here to thank me herself." With that comment, he left the restaurant.

Chapter 11: Just Us Girls

Beaver Street Brewery, Flagstaff

Her conversation with the cab driver had left her with a feeling of betrayal. Why hadn't Alex talked to her about this? Why hadn't he told her about Rachel's drug habit, her need for parties and the characters that can come with those kinds of addictions?

When Alex came back from his trip, she thought of confronting him with what she knew, but a deeper instinct told her to wait. Or maybe it just told her she didn't really want to know what he'd say. Jessica convinced herself that if he did indeed have anything to do with Rachel dying, it had to be for a good reason. It had to have been self-defense, or an accident, something that would explain how she could have been so wrong. She just didn't believe Alex could be capable of taking a life.

When he returned they seemed to fall into their old daily routine with one difference. Jessica knew she could never be comfortable again until she discovered the truth about Rachel's death, but she also knew that she couldn't bring herself to talk to Alex about it. Not yet.

So instead, she found excuses that kept her busy in the studio all day, getting up early in the morning, and not coming back into the house until well into the evening. She found herself even avoiding making love with him, claiming to be tired or not in the mood because she was afraid he'd know something was up.

On Friday, Jessica almost forgot the lunch date with Emma in town because of all that had been happening. She almost canceled, but at the last minute, decided to go simply to keep her mind off her troubles.

She arrived at the Beaver Street Brewery promptly at noon, parking in the last space in the busy parking lot. The day was warm and summer was in full bloom with the smell of freshly cut grass and a dog barking in the distance. As Jessica walked across the asphalt, she could almost let the weight of her worries leave her. Almost.

The restaurant was crowded with laughing people, so Jessica picked a table in the back that was out of the noise and traffic, letting her stress drain away. Soon she realized that she was hungry for the first time in days and hoped the food was as good as it smelled.

Five minutes later, Emma breezed in smiling, bringing with her a whirl of perfume and fresh air. Her long black hair was down and moved around her in an elegant curtain around her strong Navajo features. Her clothes were a strange combination of fashion and function. She wore a short, black leather skirt with a bright pink blouse. Her shoes were black sandals with thick, two-inch soles. But the thing that most caught Jessica's eye was the bright pink textured hose that covered the length of her legs, and her nails were now black with pink spots to match her outfit. Her style and panache made Jessica's simple Ralph Lauren shirt, jeans and hiking boots feel almost frumpy.

"I'm so glad we're having lunch," Emma told Jessica. "I was afraid you'd bail on me."

"Why would you think that?" Jessica asked, feeling guilty for a moment.

"Because… I don't know," she shrugged. "I thought that you might think I was weird. A lot of people do."

Jessica just smiled at her and said, "Well, you're wrong. Here I am." They talked about menial things like the weather, and Emma's job with the University. She asked several pointed questions about the ranch and Jessica's studio, as if she was hoping to get an invitation to come out.

"You're welcome anytime, Emma. Alex and I would love to have you visit," Jessica told her sincerely.

Emma smiled hopefully and said, "Really?"

"Of course. I'll give you a tour of my new studio. In fact, it might be fun to have you out for a weekend and you and I can go out painting together."

They ordered their lunch and talked about the ranch and Flagstaff. Emma was full of life and Jessica really found herself enjoying the visit. By the time their food arrived, they were laughing like best friends.

That changed, however, when they were in the middle of their meal and Emma broke off mid-sentence and turned pale under her usual coffee-with-cream colored complexion.

"Well, is that our girl Emma?" a voice said from behind Jessica. She turned her head and saw a man who could only be described as uniquely different. He was tall and skinny, and moved with overdone elegance and grace that Jessica found amusing. She was sure that he had a complete awareness of the audience he was drawing. But, when she turned to look at Emma, she immediately knew this visitor was not welcome. Emma's expression was less than friendly.

"Hello, Heath," Emma said with a forced welcome in her voice. She looked down at the table and made sure her fork and knife were perfectly straight alongside her plate.

"Well, darling, get up and give us a hug," the guy said, opening his long skinny arms, his hips twisted and one knee cocked as if getting ready to dance. Jessica was surprised to see Emma slide reluctantly out of her seat and give him a perfunctory hug, while throwing a mock kiss into the air next to his check.

"It's so good to see you, girl," he said, flapping his hand in the air as Emma sat back down in the booth. Next came the mundane niceties, so Jessica tried to discreetly take in the show.

The guy's black and purple hair was laboriously styled, some shaved, some braided and some curly. The curls hung directly over one eye, bouncing as he talked with enthusiasm. He looked to be somewhere between twenty-three and thirty, and was obviously going for the vintage rock band look. His purple shirt was expensive silk and opened at the neck. It was covered with a short, black leather coat that had chains, studs and numerous buttons attached like the chrome from a vintage Chevy. His embroidered red pants were well tailored and fit his skinny legs snugly, but flared into a wide bell-bottom. His platform shoes sported huge buckles that could be seen because the pants barely came to his ankles, intentionally leaving the Coca-Cola socks exposed. Several earrings studded both earlobes, making it hard to tell if he was gay, straight, or just fashion crazy. Jessica suspected he was all three. He seemed to be a mix between a sexy man, and a flirtatious woman. Another lost soul searching for identity apparently.

"Haven't seen you around the hang-out lately," he was saying to Emma. "Why haven't you come to see ol' Heathcliff? The family misses you, girl," he said, simpering. As he delivered his message, one of his ring-clad hands elegantly laid on his hip, while the other fingered the lower lip of his pouting mouth.

So this was the notorious Heathcliff that Jim had mentioned, Rachel's supplier. And it was obvious that he and Emma had some real history behind them.

"I've really been busy, Heath." Once again Emma played with her silverware. "I promise I'll come to see you next week. My mom sent me some money for my birthday, and…" she quickly glanced toward Jessica, then up at the waiting Heath, "…I thought we'd get together next week."

"Goooood!" Heath said with enthusiasm, "Did you hear that, boys?" He turned to two very young men that had been standing behind him. Jessica hadn't noticed them before because Heathcliff seemed to fill the whole room with his panache. Now she saw that both young men nodded their heads in the positive to answer Heathcliff's question. They looked to be fourteen or fifteen and wore the same clothes and haircut, like bookends.

"OK, dear. We'll see you, say… Monday or Tuesday?" he asked Emma. After she nodded yes, he asked, wiggling his fingers at Jessica's face, "And who is your pretty friend here?"

"Oh, this is Jessica Dawson," Emma said. "Jessica, this is Heathcliff."

Now both of his long, slender hands were on his hips. "Really?" he squeaked, the single word coming out like a girlish squeal. "As in Alex Dawson, your Alex's new wife? Well, well, well. Did you hear that, my boys?" And again he deferred to his twin companions, "Alex's new wife. So Emma, bring her along next week," he said while keeping his speculative eye on Jessica. "We can all become acquainted. That would be such fun. Just us girls," he said while waving in the air again with his expressive hands.

No wonder the conservative, elderly Jim hadn't liked him. Jessica smiled up at him, finding him amusing, but not his lifestyle. Judging from Emma's reaction to him, she knew he wasn't a good guy.

Emma smiled stiffly while Jessica just sat and watched. After their farewells, Heath took his leave, swishing out of the restaurant and spreading greetings here and there. It was then that Jessica realized just how much of an impact on Emma the visit had had. The poor girl seemed deflated and depressed.

Jessica didn't say anything. She didn't care to let Emma know that she knew exactly who and what Heathcliff was. Emma looked down at the napkin in her lap, fiddling with it until it was smooth and to her satisfaction. Then she looked up and smiled at Jessica. It was obvious she was trying to control her tears.

"He's just a friend, actually, an ex-friend. I don't really like him anymore, but he's hard to get rid of. You know, like a bad case of acne," the humor was forced, but Jessica admired her for her show of strength.

She reached across the table and put her hand over Emma's. "It's OK, Emma. You don't have to pretend with me. I really am your friend," Jessica said, and she meant it. She felt sorry for this woman. She seemed to be alone and trying hard to make something of her life.

Emma looked around and saw that the tables next to them had emptied. She looked over at Jessica and quietly said, "He used to be my connection. I used to do drugs. I don't anymore; I've been straight for five months. I just owe him some money." She looked down at her lap.

Jessica sat quietly to let Emma talk, but she looked embarrassed, and as if she could use a lifeline. Jessica decided to tell her she understood how tough addiction could be. They had become close enough in the short time they had talked that Jessica felt compelled to be a real friend to the girl.

Emma went on to talk about how Rachel had been the one to introduce her to substance abuse, and that she kept her in supply. She and Rachel had gone through detox once together, but it hadn't worked for either of them. And then, without any encouragement she told how Alex had cut off Rachel's funds, just as Jim had told her, and that it hadn't stopped them from using.

"Where did you get the money to pay for your supply if Alex cut her off?" Jessica asked.

Emma looked out the small window behind Jessica and then took a deep breath, letting it out as she said, "You probably don't know this, but… Rachel was in love with someone else besides Alex."

A train suddenly went by outside, the whistle and the rumble filling the restaurant, blasting its way into the conversation. Jessica watched as Emma's eyes followed the trains passing, a dart to the right and then back, a dart to the right and then back, and then resting when it was gone. For a moment, all conversation had stopped in the room, but in a few seconds, people began to pick up where they'd left off. The sound of silverware clinking against plates, glasses being tinkled against other glasses. All normal everyday sounds, as if Emma hadn't just told her something awful.

"It was Mac," Emma continued. "You might as well know. Mac and Rachel were having an affair and Mac was giving her the money she needed to stay alive. When Alex cut off her funds, it was with the belief that she had stopped using. Well, she hadn't. She lied to him. She bailed out of the center and didn't tell him. Mac was in love with her and came to her rescue. That was when he divorced his wife, he was hoping Rachel would marry him."

Jessica sat there in shock. "Did Alex know this?" she asked in a soft voice.

"No. No one knew but me. They came to my place to meet when they wanted to be alone. They were very careful and never met in public together." She looked guilty. "I think I was hoping she'd divorce Alex and I'd have a shot at him." She smiled sheepishly. "I've always had a crush on him, but he has never given me a second glance. He thinks of me as a little sister." She smiled at Jessica. "Rachel didn't really deserve him, ya know."

They both waited as the waitress cleared the table, taking an order for coffee from both of them, and dessert for Jessica. After the waitress left, Jessica tentatively asked Emma, "What do you think happened to Rachel out at Blue Moon Bench that night? Do you think she jumped?" She couldn't help it. It seemed the perfect moment to ask the question, and it seemed if anyone would know besides Alex, it would be Emma.

"No!" Emma said emphatically, "Absolutely not. Rachel had finally gotten her life in order. She had every reason to live."

"Why do you think that? It sounds like she was making a pretty good mess of her life, drugs, an affair, and a husband who wouldn't give her any money. It sounds pretty awful to me," Jessica told her.

"No," Emma answered. "There are other things you don't know. Just before she died, she'd stopped using. Mac really helped her, not just by putting her in a center, but by staying with her. They enrolled in a program at a wellness center in southern Arizona, and Mac stayed with her the whole time!"

"You're kidding? So she was off drugs? Why didn't she just divorce Alex, then? She didn't need his money for drugs anymore."

"She was going to," Emma told her, fiddling with her coffee. "If you ask me, she and Mac were going to have a baby. I think she was pregnant when she died." Emma said it as if she were telling Jessica what day of the week it was. She knew that Emma could have no way of knowing that she had just delivered a home-run motive for Alex wanting Rachel's life to end. She was having another man's child! Was it possible that Emma was right?

She just sat there. The bomb had left a crater inside her. Rachel had been pregnant with another man's baby when she died. She felt a great remorse. "Did Alex know any of this?" she asked, terrified of hearing the answer.

"I told you, he knew nothing of their relationship. Rachel was afraid he wouldn't give her a divorce because of his possible nomination for State Representative. He had already told her once that he needed to stay married at least until he got elected, then he'd consider it. She couldn't wait that long. She wanted to marry Mac and then the two of them planned to move to Australia."

Jessica felt sick. She couldn't believe what she was hearing. Now she wondered why Mac had been acting like he had toward Alex. Was it possible he had gotten it into his head that Alex had taken Rachel's life out of revenge? She finally decided that Mac must have been under the delusion that Alex had known about their relationship. That he had known about the baby and their plans. Had he? Had Alex really been at the conference like he said? Surely the FBI had checked out his alibi, collaborated his story with others at the conference, hadn't they? Regardless, she felt great compassion for Alex, what an awful time it must have been for him.

Chapter 12: Could You Have Evidence?

The Museum of Northern Arizona, Flagstaff

The Museum of Northern Arizona was filled with people dressed up and meandering. Children ran from room to room like kids do when their energy was too big to be contained by mere walls. Jessica tried to blend in, wandering from display to display. They were having a Navajo Weaving show, one that was given every summer. The blue ribbon winner was too large to hang, and lay on the floor, roped off for everyone to admire but not walk on. As Jessica studied it, she thought that the intricate and colorful menagerie of tightly woven wool echoed her own feelings. It was difficult for her to imagine how long it must have taken the weaver to create such a piece, and felt lost in its complex pattern.

Ron came up behind her and whispered in her ear, leaving a wisp of garlic and cigarettes. “I can get you a ten percent discount if you want to buy it,” he told her. His comment pulled a smile from her. She knew that the $10,000 price tag was actually within her grasp now that she was a Dawson and that purchasing it would help the artist, and the museum. She entertained buying it but couldn’t imagine walking on such beautiful work, and they didn’t have a wall big enough to hang it on.

“Not likely,” she said to him, moving away from the crowd. “Let’s go outside; I need something to drink." She had asked him to meet her here so they could talk privately without being completely alone.

They moved into the courtyard and Ron got a white wine for her and something in a white paper cup for himself. As they began talking, Ron moved them back into the building and out a side door.

"What was so urgent?" he asked her, puzzled.

"I needed to ask you a couple of questions, and they couldn't wait," Jessica told him as he maneuvered her to a path that traveled through a grove of Ponderosa pines, moving along the ridge of a small canyon behind the Museum. It had trail signs that identified different plant and animal species for the hiker. A few others had found their way to the walk and stood in little groups, laughing and drinking. She made sure no one was close enough to hear the conversation.

"Do you remember when we talked about Rachel up at the Canyon?" she asked him. When he answered her with an affirmative response, she went on. "Well, I'm in desperate need of more information." She turned to face him, keeping her voice down, the trail forgotten. "I know about her drug habit and her affair with Mac. I'm pretty sure that you know more than you told me that day. I'm frightened, Ron. I need to know the truth about how Rachel died."

Ron just stood there, his square hands on his hips, strands of his blond hair escaping from his ponytail. He stood there in silence so long that she was afraid he wasn't going to tell her anything, so she turned and continued down the trail, testing him.

When she heard his footsteps catch up with her, she felt relief. "Wait," he said. By this time they had reached the bottom of a shallow, rocky canyon. There was water trickling through the thick reeds that almost choked it still. Birds darted among the trees and brush, while a rustling in the undergrowth told of small wildlife making their way in this isolated riparian world. Jessica stopped on a rock to the side of the trail and turned to face him, their faces now even. Ron stared at her for a moment. Then he turned away and adjusted his sunglasses.

"I suppose you might as well know. Someone else would tell you anyway." He sounded disgusted. "I was the one who first introduced Rachel to Heathcliff. I used to use it many years ago, recreational, fun, social," he shrugged on the last one. "Rachel begged me to include her, and how could I resist." He walked to a makeshift bridge constructed of a split log and snapped off a dead reed to twist and worry.

"I came to hate her eventually. I saw her as a user of people, and tried to stay away from her. When she started the affair with Mac, I knew she was bent on destroying him. I didn't really care, Mac was a fool for getting involved." He hesitated, and then turned to Jessica. "But I have always hated Alex more, the boy with the golden spoon in his mouth. So I decided to tell him about the affair."

Jessica stared at his back. "So he knew! And you were the one who told him. When did you tell him? How long before she was found dead?" she asked, feeling as if her world was folding in on itself, silently and in slow motion.

"It was the Wednesday just before the weekend she disappeared," he answered, turning back to her. He dropped his hand to his side, letting the reed fall to the ground, forgotten. "I shouldn't have gotten involved. It was none of my business. But Alex had almost caused me to lose my job with River Excursions, the company I was working for then. He gave some constipated story to my boss about drugs. He was just mad that I got Rachel started. I hated him and wanted him to pay, wanted him to know his world wasn't perfect, and that he didn't have mankind by the tail. That, in fact, it had him by the balls instead." There was silence as both of them stood motionless, she was stunned by his admittance and he was stunned by his own candor.

"You have to believe me," he assured Jessica. "I had no idea that he'd kill her. I thought he'd just divorce her and lose his political career. I never dreamed he'd take her life."

"We don't know that, Ron," Jessica told him, forcing her voice to sound confident. "Alex has to be given the opportunity to defend himself. He's my husband, I love him."

Before she could react, Ron was across the distance between them, grabbing her shoulders and shaking her once. "That's just it!" he said almost in a whisper, "No one cares! She's dead and the damn FBI says, 'No Foul.' It's typical Dawson, don't you see? He killed her and no one cares."

"Stop it Ron," Jessica said, knocking his hands away and almost falling as she lunged away from him, dropping off the rock onto the trail. "I'm going to ask Alex, give him the opportunity to tell me his side of the story."

"Oh, and you think he'll just confess? Well of course. He loves you, right? He's an honest kinda guy, right?" Ron's face was red with anger. "Well, he isn't or he would have told you this before now. He would have talked to you about all this before now."

Jessica had turned and was headed out of the canyon. "It doesn't matter, Ron." She turned at the top of the trail. "He's my husband, and no matter what you say, I have to give him the chance to defend himself. He'd do the same for me." She turned and started back to her car. Behind her Ron shouted, "Don't be too sure."

Jessica cornered Alex when she arrived back at the ranch. She suspected that he saw something along the lines of conviction in her eyes, because he gave a large sigh and set aside the paper he was reading when she walked into his study. Jessica wiped her sweaty palms on her jeans as she stood in the doorway. He came around the desk, gently closed the door behind her, and gestured for her to take a seat in one of the overstuffed leather chairs. He sat in the chair next to her, a small table and lamp between them.

"I thought there was something bothering you. I'm glad you finally came to talk to me about it." He took a deep breath and leaned back.

"Please Alex," she started with her eyes closed. "Tell me about the night Rachel died. I need to know the truth. I can't wait any longer to figure it out. I'm losing faith in you. Please tell me your side of the story," she begged with tears in her eyes as she looked up at him.

"I wasn't at the conference in Lake Powell, I was at the motel in Page that night," Alex told her without hesitation.

Jessica suddenly felt detached, as if she were watching a movie, the camera angle rather boring, the colors oddly mismatched in the scene. Her blood hummed in her ears making it difficult to hear what he was saying. He sat calmly, hands on the arms of his chair, oddly unmoving, and he quietly told her his story while staring out the window into the courtyard.

He told her that he had actually gone to the conference on Friday. Saturday night, he'd made a call to the Ranch and found that Rachel was giving a party.

"I was furious with her. She knew the rules. And I learned from Dotty that the whole drug crowd was there, something we'd both agreed wouldn't happen." They'd fought on the phone and Alex told her that he had come to the end of his rope. He told her that he was going to leave the conference, come home and everyone better be gone. But on the way to the ranch he changed his mind. As he passed by the small motel at the Cameron Trading post, he swung in and decided to get a room, cool off and sleep off the alcohol he'd consumed at the conference happy hour. He called Rachel back and told her his change of plans, letting her know that when he got back to the Ranch on Sunday, they would need to talk. He wanted a divorce, and he refused to pay her debts, threats or no threats.

"What do you mean, threats?" Jessica asked.

"I had received a phone call about five months earlier from a person named Heathcliff," Alex told her. "He said Rachel owed him around $100,000. Apparently she'd bought drugs from him for both herself and her friends," he became visibly upset. "I was under the impression that she had stopped using. She'd told me that she was clean," he told Jessica. "Anyway, he said if I didn't pay him the money before the next week, he'd expose Rachel's drug use to the press in order to ruin my chances of running for office."

Jessica's eyes had grown wide. She'd known that his political career meant a lot to him. As State Representative he would be in a powerful position to help push legislation through that would send more of the state funds toward special interest conservation groups that he favored, a political stand that had made him popular with many voters during the campaign. How far was he willing to go to save that political career? Murder? Should she believe him? Was he telling her the truth?

"What did you do?" Jessica asked him.

"What could I do? I refused to pay him. I wasn't going to be controlled by some pusher." Alex shook his head. "I decided I needed to divorce Rachel before everything started landsliding. My only mistake was that I didn't start proceedings right then. Instead, I set it aside, I guess I just didn't want to deal with it."

"So," Jessica intervened, "he never followed through with his threat. I wonder why," As she waited for his answer, she was pretty sure she knew. Mac had probably paid off Heathcliff to bail Rachel out. She hadn't known an Anthropology Professor made that kind of money.

"I don't know why Heathcliff didn't follow through with his threat," Alex said, giving her the answer she suspected he would.

"And so, you slept at the Cameron Trading Post motel that night? Did you tell that to the FBI?"

"No. I didn't have to. I'm not sure what happened. I remember the FBI saying, 'You were at the conference for the weekend, right?' and I said yes. Then they immediately went on to talk about when I got home on Sunday. They never asked if I left the conference. I found out later that a good friend of mine at the conference had told them I was there all weekend." Alex looked frustrated. "That's how he remembered it, and I never got the opportunity to correct it."

Jessica now got up from the chair and walked over to the window, her back to Alex. Looking out at the pastoral scene before her of a brilliant sunny day and grazing horses, she was having trouble believing they were talking about something as gruesome as death.

"Alex, did you kill Rachel?" Jessica asked him outright.

There was no immediate response from him. She heard him get up from his chair and knew he had walked across the room and was standing behind her.

"I can't believe you even asked me that," he said. She heard the hurt in his voice. Still, he didn't immediately deny it.

There came a sudden knock on the study door, and both she and Alex turned. "Come in," Alex said.

It was Ralph, Dorothea's husband. "Sir, its Mr. McInerney and two gentlemen. They say they want to talk to you."

Alex said, "Let them in, Ralph. And where is Dotty? Could you ask her to bring us some coffee, and some kind of sandwiches? I'm about to pass out from hunger." Jessica knew that he hadn't eaten any breakfast, and lunch time was long past.

Ralph left the door open, and soon three people entered the study. Jessica moved behind one of the leather chairs where she could observe, but be discreet. She felt an intuitive flash of unease. Who in the world were these men in suits, and why was Mac with them?

The first man to enter the study was wearing a dark gray suit, well cut and lightweight. He was a big man who walked with authority, but

Jessica thought there were just enough things wrong with him that, for her, the authority was undermined. His red tie was slightly crooked and frayed at the top, and a cowlick feathered in the breeze as he walked. He also tried to keep the girth of his stomach confined inside his jacket, the single button rebelling against its job. He had medium brown hair that was cut short, and a thin dark mustache.

The second man followed at a slower pace, looking around the study as if he were a potential homebuyer and assessing if his desk would fit next to the window. He had on a dark brown suit that looked like it had seen better days, and both hands were buried deep in the pants pockets. The suit hung on his thin frame like an old friend, and he rattled the change in his pocket as he crossed the room to where Alex stood. His light brown hair receded away from a high forehead, which had apparently seen some Arizona sun. It was reddish and shiny, and Jessica could see it was already starting to peel.

Alex and the two men shook hands, but when he turned toward Mac, there was no handshake. Mac looked away with what Jessica feared was an odd expression.

"Gentleman, this is my wife, Jessica Dawson," Alex told them. Both men bobbed their heads in her direction, and the thin man gave her a studied look. "Have a seat," Alex indicated the two leather chairs, while he went around to the other side of his desk. The power position, Jessica thought, Alex must have thought he would need the advantage. Both men sat down in the chairs, exchanging glances, while Mac stood to the side.

"Mr. Dawson, we're with the FBI," the thin man told him, "I apologize for intruding like this, but some new things have come to light in the death of your former wife." The man spoke with respect and familiarity. Jessica wondered if Alex had met him before, but discarded the idea when she heard Alex's voice.

"New things? New things in regards to what?" Alex asked with scorn.

"Well, actually," the bigger agent stood up and took a folded document out of his pocket, handing it to Alex. "We have a warrant for your arrest, sir. You are being charged with the death of one Mrs. Rachel Dawson."

Jessica gripped the back of the leather chair, staring in shock. Arrested? Alex? She then looked over at Mac and saw that he had a grim look on his face. "Mac, why are you here? What do you have to do with this?" Jessica asked.

Mac just looked at her. The skinny agent answered for him. "Actually, Mr. McInerney insisted on accompanying us. It seems that he was able to bring new evidence forward that was previously overlooked in Mrs. Dawson's death."

"This is insane," Alex said, looking stunned. "I didn't kill Rachel. How could you have evidence? I didn't kill her!"

"You know you killed her!" Mac said. "You made her life miserable. And when you couldn't any longer control her, you took her life!" Mac lunged for Alex. The large FBI agent quickly stepped between them, stopping him in mid-step.

"We'll handle this, sir," he said. Then he turned to Alex and read him his rights, while Mac stood watching. Alex was told that he would be given his one call after they booked him in Flagstaff. The larger man again apologized and told Alex that he wouldn't handcuff him, as if that made up for arresting him. Jessica stood there in shock, not moving.

Dorothea arrived suddenly with a tray filled with Alex's favorite sandwiches and set them on the desk. Jessica thought that it was all like a bad play.

"Don't worry, Jessica," Alex told her. "Call our attorney, Mr. Howell, and then let my parents know what's happened." He cupped her face in his big hands and said, "I'm just sorry you had to be here through this. Please trust me, I didn't take

Rachel's life. I love you." His look was so sincere she felt tears well in her eyes.

They took Alex out to their waiting car and put him in the backseat. He sat there with little expression and Jessica assumed he was in shock just as she was. Dorothea arrived with two sandwiches and an apple wrapped up in plastic for Alex to take with him. One of the agents inspected the food and then handed it back to Alex. Jessica felt tears sting her eyes as she watched her husband's familiar profile through the metal grate covering the windows. He looked so alone and empty.

After the car drove away, Jessica made her way back into the house and toward the study, wiping the tears from her hot cheeks. She was so stunned that she needed to think through what she had to do next. Her mind seemed to be off on its own agenda, skittering from place to place and not able to land on one thing.

Mac was hanging up the phone as she walked into the study. Dorothea followed her into the room and stopped by the door. "Why did they take Alex away?" she asked abruptly, standing just inside the room.

"They've arrested Alex for Rachel's death, Dorothea," Jessica told her, all the time staring at Mac in accusation. "Mac apparently has turned against Alex. He gave the FBI new evidence that lead to his arrest."

Dorothea looked at Mac. The two of them stood staring at one another, Dorothea with an angry look, Mac appearing stern and purposeful.

"You stupid old fool," Dorothea told him. She went to the desk and picked up the tray of uneaten sandwiches.

"You are very wrong to think him innocent, ducky!" he shouted at her. "He killed her! He was jealous because she loved me, and you know it!" He was so angry his face was red, and spit sprayed into the air when he screamed the words. "It was Alex that made her miserable. She told me everything that happened in her life. She wanted to leave Alex and marry me! She asked me to devise a plan so she could get out of his clutches."

Dorothea simply looked at him and snorted a disgusted, dismissing laugh and then turned and walked from the room.

"Mac, I would appreciate it if you'd leave now." Jessica pointed the way in punctuation to her words.

"Are you loony?" Mac asked, pointing at her. "Your precious Alex is guilty of murder. His car was seen at the scene of the crime the night of her death! He wasn't at that damn conference and he lied to the police about it. He's guilty. He killed Rachel, and you're too blind to see it!"

"Get out!" Jessica said quietly pointing at the door. She was surprised that she had it in her to be so calm.

He stood staring at her for a moment, and then he spun around and abruptly left the study with a straight back and raised head. At that moment, Jessica had great compassion for the Australian for his conniving mind. She knew he was creating karma for himself and that in the end it would harm him. The Buddha's first teaching is that all beings are suffering… and the only end of suffering was compassion for others, not unkindness like he was practicing.

She stumbled out of the room and into the great room, standing for several minutes and staring out the window into the courtyard. She felt weird, like her body didn't belong to her, but that she was in it, watching as it moved toward their bedroom. Once there, her knees collapsed and she crumpled to the floor in shock. She wrapped her arms around herself, and her sobs were almost inaudible at first, but then she released the control she'd been holding onto and allowed the damn to break. Her husband, the man she loved beyond anything, was arrested for murder. He had killed his first wife! She didn't really know him, she couldn't! She had to fight having the wrong view of him.

She looked up and saw the beautiful things around her, the familiar room where she and Alex had made love, slept in each other's arms, fought over little things and laughed over them later. How could it all be pretend? Did this mean he didn't really love her? That he had lied to her, shut her out, kept from her his biggest secret? He asked that she trust him, but did he trust her?

The grief and shock didn't leave her, but the crying finally left her so exhausted and drained she had to quit. She found herself stumbling to the bathroom almost like she was on autopilot, and washed her face. She started feeling almost absent but found her way to her altar and sat down on her cushion to meditate for ten minutes, to quiet her mind, and to pray for all of them.

After her mind quieted and she felt calmer, stronger, she headed for the kitchen. Her mouth was dry and her stomach growling. She went straight for the refrigerator and looked for a Coke, but could only find apple juice. She drank down a whole glass just as Dorothea walked into the room.

"Have you had anything to eat?" She said with solicitation. Jessica was surprised, "Sit down and I'll heat one of those chicken pot pies I made yesterday so you can eat."

Jessica stared at her a moment, surprised at her kindness, and then sat numbly in the kitchen nook. Dorothea served her the pie and a small salad, and then stood at the sink cleaning up and running water. Jessica thought it was so comforting. As she ate the savory pie, her stomach settled, and she felt satisfied. She knew she looked a mess but didn't care, the kitchen's ambiance soothed her.

"So, what did Alex say?" Dorothea began. "I mean about Rachel? Did he talk to you before they took him?" She continued to wash the few dishes in the sink and Jessica wondered why she didn't use the dishwasher.

"No," Jessica answered. "He didn't have the chance to say anything. They simply read him his rights and took him away."

Dorothea turned, wiping her hands on her apron. "Did the FBI say what evidence they had?"

"Max said something about his car being seen I think, and maybe witnesses," Jessica told her, poking her fork at the discarded crust in the dish before her.

"I'm sorry for what's happened," Dorothea told her with a note in her voice that sounded almost kind. "I'm sure it will sort itself out."

She couldn't believe that she was feeling gratitude toward the housekeeper, but she was. At that moment she thought Dorothea was almost motherly, and decided to give her a hug in thanks before leaving the room. Dorothea seemed a little taken back, but accepted the kiss on the cheek by giving her a pat on the arm before turning back to the sink.

Jessica left the kitchen, and went to the coat closet to grab a sweater and her coat because the evenings were getting cooler. Such a small detail when her world had turned on a single moment, all because of Mac.

As she drove into Flagstaff she called her in-laws and told them Alex had been arrested for the murder of Rachel, and that she'd fill them in with the details as soon as she arrived. They expressed the same shock and disbelief that Jessica felt, but she knew it had to be worse for them because they'd had no idea there were still questions about Rachel's death.

She then called Mr. Howell as Alex had asked her to, telling him what had happened. He advised her to go directly to Alex's parents' house and wait for his call, saying he'd reach out to a few people who he felt could help them, and get right back to her as soon as he could. Jessica pushed the end button on her cell phone feeling even more frightened. Talking about the situation out loud finally made it real, no longer a bad play.

When she pushed the disconnect button on her cell phone, Jessica's thoughts turned to Dorothea. All this time she'd felt dislike for the woman because she could be so overbearing and controlling. But suddenly, Jessica began to wonder if it hadn't always just been that she didn't want to be controlled. Setting that aside, the woman had seemed half-human in the kitchen.

Jessica finally arrived at the subject she wanted most to avoid. In the silence of the truck, as the miles ticked off on her way into Flagg, she found she could no longer stay numb to what had happened. Did she believe Alex was guilty of murder?

Jessica stopped the truck and got out to take in some fresh air and just get some space. She saw the beautiful day around her, summer slipping into fall. Tall ponderosa pines lined the road on both sides, and the wildflowers were at the end of their bloom. The summer monsoons had been enough to make everything green for the summer and added an abundance of color from the Coral Bells and Butter'n Eggs. She looked at the majestic San Francisco Peaks, still carrying a snowy top, and the brilliant blue sky above. This moment seemed auspicious, quiet, and she knew it was a corner she was turning in her life. She felt faith. Things would turn out well. They had to.

She closed her eyes for a few moments and looked into herself for peace and that feeling of comfort she knew from her meditations.

Tibetan Buddhism was very mystical, and miracles had been known to happen, she'd seen many. Years before, just out of curiosity, she had visited a small Buddhist temple in Sedona. While the beauty of the altars, the brocades and the artwork gave her joy as an artist, her experience was much more than that. She was immediately intrigued by the intellectual approach Buddhism had to a spiritual and moral understanding of the universe and how it works. How meditation can change the mind, but more importantly, it is true that it can change your world around you. She found out that Alex had also been intrigued by Tibetan Buddhism, and had visited Tibet, crossing dangerously over the border before China was allowing visitors. When they found out they shared this special spiritual path, it deepened their connection immediately.

Getting back into the car, Jessica pulled out her mala and began to recite "Om Mani Padme Hung" and ticked off one bead for every mantra, 108 in all, dedicating the blessing of the ancient recitation to the end of suffering for all, not just herself; a meaningful Tibetan Buddhist practice.

After three mala's worth of mantra, everything became clearer, and hope rose up around her. They were going to make it right for the woman who died at the bottom of a canyon, alone on a cold night. She promised herself that.

Chapter 13: A Walk in the Park

Flagstaff, the Dawson's House

The day was dry and breezy. Jessica could see the peaks of the mountains through the stately ponderosa pines around her. There were still fields of flowers contrasting with the dark ponderosa patches, and with the fall days approaching, the temperatures were only reading the high sixties. Jessica loved the correlation between her feelings and the weather, but wished the summer monsoons would come back and wash everything clean again.

She had gone to the Tibetan Buddhist group in Sedona and sponsored a food offering ceremony for Rachel's auspicious rebirth, asking that she not be born to suffer another day by being reborn in this realm of what was called samsara. The Tibetan Book of the Dead taught that we could plan for our death, and our rebirth if we had faith and the right prayers are made with the right intention.

She was staying with Alex's parents in Flagstaff while they tried to sort out his bail, and each day was a miserable mixture of optimism and disappointment. Alex's parents were nicer than they had ever been to her and she felt a weight of guilt for suspecting their son of murder. Alex's father, Stan, was a typical suntanned ranch owner, with thinning hair, crinkles around his eyes, and a sparkling smile. When Jessica had first met him, she could easily see where Alex had gotten his height. When Stan had swooped off his large white cowboy hat in a bow that day, he had won her heart. Alex's mother, Patsy, had come as a surprise though. With dark hair clipped stylishly short and contemporary clothing that complimented a slim figure, her appearance hid her years of living on a ranch. She was a kind lady who always seemed to know the right thing to do.

Both of Alex's parents were now considering her part of their circled wagons to save their son, and Jessica sometimes had to hide in the guest room they'd given her, door closed, pillow over her head as she cried.

To add more pain to an already horrible situation, a group of reporters had shown up at the courthouse the day before, having scooped the story of Alex's arrest from somewhere. Jessica had been whisked out of the building by two protective policemen, and into the Dawson's Land Cruiser. Just before she was able to climb into the car, a dark-haired woman shoved a microphone in her face and shouted, "Can you tell us how you feel about your husband killing his first wife? Aren't you worried?" She looked vicious and determined while she tried to shove the police officer who was protecting her aside. Jessica slid into the car's seat, frightened and angry all at the same time. She watched the dark-haired woman out the window as she stood in front of the courthouse and spoke into a news camera. Her mouth was moving silently, and Jessica imagined she was filling in for the public what Jessica hadn't said. "Alex Dawson's current wife fears for her life and intends to leave for Barbados as soon as things cool down."

Alex's father was a real statesman and literally knew everyone who was anyone. Jessica had been relieved when he took over the problem of judicial red tape, since the most she knew about court and bail was what she had seen on TV.

As it turned out, they would not release Alex on bail because of the severity of the charge. He was safely in what they called an "executive cell," which had some comforts like a phone, computer and furniture. That was where he would have to stay until the hearing, over a month away. She took out her phone and entered the date of Alex's hearing in the calendar. Stan and Patsy invited her to stay the month with them, but Jessica still felt as if she were floating in the sea of unreality. She was meditating every day, trying to calm her mind and emotions.

The Dawson's house was an old, historic two-story home that was white clapboard with a wood shingled roof and three stone fireplaces. Large old oaks grew in the yard and a beautiful garden skirted the backyard, which was filled with birds and squirrels. An old, orange tomcat seemed to live in a large, white wicker chair on the back porch, and almost every morning, the deer grazed in the front yard. It was so completely different from the ranch house that she was surprised they were still in the southwest. It sat on the sunset side of the old downtown area, right at the base of a healthy hill.

Jessica had decided to take a walk up to a large observatory that lived at the top of that hill and found that she had to sneak out the back so the reporters didn't spot her. Coming out from behind a hedge in an alley, she began the ascent up the winding paved road that got almost no traffic. She noticed in some places, leaves were beginning to turn color and the air smelled like fall even though it was only September. The sun shone down on her head and warmed her cheeks, chilled from the little breeze that challenged her along the road.

When she reached the top, she was rewarded with a magnificent view of the entire town, the San Francisco Peaks as a backdrop. When you were out in the Arizona desert, driving toward Flagstaff, the peaks rose up out of the horizon, everything around it flatter and lower. From here it was easy to see that the mountain range was really the leftovers from a thirteen thousand-foot volcano, now covered with aspen and pine trees, topped with rock and wind. The town was snuggled amid smaller mounds of lava at an elevation of seven thousand feet, sitting at the base of the majestic mountain range.

Jessica sat for a while to catch her breath and then continued up the road to the observatory. There were a few visitors on this summer weekday, but for the most part, the parking lot was deserted. The visitor's center was built from local lava rock and two older observatories, which now sat in disuse, flanked by wooden shingled buildings that looked like they had been built in the forties or fifties.

Jessica walked among the buildings, and then wandered off onto a trail that meandered into the woods. She picked up a broken branch and began a methodical snapping of the little twigs that protruded from it. Soon, it became a good walking stick.

She had almost stripped all the bark from the stick when her thoughts began to finally address the real reason she'd needed this alone time. How could she have been so wrong about someone? The joke was on her it seemed. When she had finally found the man she wanted to make a commitment to, he ended up being arrested for the murder of his first wife. She was only now really grasping the meaning of what had happened. Her husband was in jail for murder, his alibi was a lie which he admitted, his second alibi was un-collaborated, and she was being asked to wait and trust.

The trail she was on began twisting and winding along a natural rock cliff, with small outcroppings of flowers and grass growing in the crevices. She had stopped to look at some tiny, exquisite white flowers when she distinctly heard stealthy footsteps behind her. She turned and saw that the path twisted, preventing her from seeing if someone had followed her from the parking lot.

Jessica quickly knelt down behind some large boulders just off the trail, keeping her stick handy. Her auburn hair lifted and started floating around her face, so she was forced to reach up and tame it. As she crouched there, motionless, she heard the footsteps stop, and then continue on. She watched as the man came into view, crouched and almost tiptoeing, turning to look up the trail where she should have been.

His back was to her, but it was evident that he was wondering how she had disappeared. He looked back where he had come from, and then up the trail ahead and scratched his head in puzzlement. His hair was long, blond and in a ponytail, and a cast shone whiteley on his injured arm. Jessica couldn't mistake him. It was Ron!

She stayed where she was for a few moments, surprised at seeing him. She quietly scaled the rocks, looking down on him from her perch. She cleared her throat, and Ron immediately dropped into a martial arts stance, spinning to face her.

"I didn't know that you knew karate," Jessica said with her hands on her hips. The look on his suntanned face was priceless.

"Damn, girl! You scared the crap out of me! You should be more careful, I might have hurt you!" He looked serious, but Jessica gave a small bark of laughter.

"Not a chance, I'm too quick for you," she told him. Moving to one of the rocks, she half leaned, half sat and looked down at him. "Why were you following me?" she asked him.

"I wasn't," Ron told her, making his way up the rocks to get closer. "Stan and Patsy told me you'd gone for a walk, and I wasn't sure if it was you I was seeing. I didn't want to approach some stranger and have them think I was weird."

Jessica crossed her arms. "You are weird, Ron," she said smiling. "Why were you looking for me?"

"I just wanted to see how you were holding up. I was worried about you." His blue eyes had become serious. He was standing right in front of her now and he looked down into her upturned face. "Patsy said you'd been depressed and thought you might need some company."

Great, she thought, nothing like sending an ex-boyfriend to do her daughter-in-law a favor. But of course, Patsy couldn't have known her and Ron's history. It was Ron who had helped her secretly investigate Rachel's death by supplying her disguise anyway, and she knew but didn't like to admit that he still really liked her.

She was pissed at herself for noticing he was most definitely attractive in a rugged, outdoorsy sort of way. Tallish, solidly built and funny, when his eyes sparkled in your direction with a flash of white teeth, he was hard to resist.

But Jessica had figured out early that he was the roaming type. He hated to be tied down by anything. He'd been running rivers for twelve years and didn't plan to stop soon. He lived with any friend that would have him, and most often they were women.

But now, that blond hunk stood before her, bemused and smiling at her with a look that sent a warm flush through her cheeks. Before she knew what was happening, he had cupped her face in his hands and slowly melted his lips to hers. They were warm and hungry. Too quickly, he slid his tongue searchingly into her mouth. She felt his passion and knew that she was responding without will. She had been feeling so frightened and alone that she found his attention comforting, even though she knew it was wrong. He tasted like a sweet orange, and his hands smelled like the peel, spicy and pungent. She knew vaguely that he must have eaten one. Her eyes had drifted closed and she floated into the kiss. It was almost too easy to get lost in the thought of giving herself to him. She needed someone to hold her and tell her everything would be all right.

Ron's hands slid up under her blouse and skimmed along her back, snapping her bra free before she knew what he intended. His broad, warm hands spread across her back and began to slide around to her breasts, nipples already hard in anticipation of his touch. His thumbs worked them in lazy circles, creating a shock of sexual electricity through her body as his tongue explored her mouth. He pressed his hips against hers, moving them both against the wall of rocks behind her, his erection against her belly, making clear his intention.

Some kind of autopilot kicked in and Jessica pushed away from him and broke off the kiss. His cast clunked awkwardly on her collarbone and she covered her mouth with the fingers of both hands and turned away from him. "God, Ron. You shouldn't do things like that," she told him in anger. "I'm married." She awkwardly re-attached her bra, spinning away from him when he gestured to help.

"You think I don't know that?" he asked her quietly, standing away from her now. "I think of that every night when I crawl into my lonely bed. I imagine you with him and it makes me crazy. I love you Jessica, and I want you back."

She turned and looked at him in surprise. "Ron, you never had me. We were just friends."

"You can't say that you didn't have any feelings for me," he told her in accusation.

She took a deep breath and let it out to calm herself. He was right. She had harbored some feelings for him, but she had harbored more reservations. He spelled danger for any woman who really fell in love with him, and she knew it. Besides, she'd fallen in love with Alex and that had ended any thought of him. "Ron, listen carefully. I love Alex," Jessica told him, knowing that what she was saying was true. "I don't love you. I'm going through a tough time right now, but it will pass." She straightened her blouse. "The end. No other comments, no other questions. It just is. Get over it." She felt mean, but they had already been down this road twice, and she was getting tired of telling him.

"Alright, alright. So you told me." He continued to look at her with love in his eyes. "But I still love you, Jessica." He walked over to her and stopped just a foot away. She had crossed her arms in front of her and stood her ground. He put both of his broad hands on her shoulders and let them slide down her arms, resting at her elbows. She started to pull away but he tightened his hold. "If you ever need someone, I'm here, OK? I know Alex has been taken in on charges of first-degree murder. I know that they think he killed Rachel. If you need anyone, let me know. I'm serious, OK?" He finished his speech with the most serious note she'd ever heard him use. He tried to bend down and look at her face. She felt obligated to show her appreciation.

She gave him a quick smile and then looked back down at his chest just inches from her own. "Thanks Ron. I really do appreciate it."

"OK," he said, kissing her on the top of her head.

Then he dropped his hands, posed in a runner's stance and said, "Now… the first to make it to the parking lot wins!" It was an old game they used to play and while Jessica chased after him, she knew he just wasn't going to go away. He was a true friend who really did want to help.

They arrived back at the house and Jessica said goodbye to him on the porch. Apparently the reporters had lost interest, because the front yard was now devoid of vans and waiting cars. Jessica was afraid of asking Ron in, because she was sure Patsy would invite him for lunch. On the walk back to the house, she had made a silent decision to move back out to the ranch, and she wanted to get started as soon as possible and a long lunch would get in the way of her plans. The ranch was the closest thing she had to a home, and she missed it. She decided that she wanted to be in her studio with all her books and canvases around her. She missed Chili and Will, and she missed riding in the morning. And she planned on visiting Johnson and telling him about her aching heart. He always seemed to know the right things to say to comfort her without any emotional entanglements. He was a much safer friend than a dangerously handsome ex-boyfriend with an emotional attachment to her.

Chapter 14: The Clever Coyote

The Chinle Formations, Navajo Reservation, Arizona

The land looked as if God had reached down, selectively handpicked mineral-tinted dirt from different parts of the reservation and then carefully mounded it, color upon color, leaving the rain to work it into sensual formations. The water had sculpted each mound with care until it seemed as if you were driving through endless hills of slightly melted ice cream sundaes, different flavors, some crowned with a sprinkling of petrified wood, like roasted nuts, spilling from the top.

Jessica had been told the formations were called the Chinle', a Navajo word that meant something like "where all things come together." As an artist, it was one of her favorite places on the reservations and she knew many famous artists like Georgia O'Keeffe and Ansel Adams had tried to render it, but failed in her mind. It was simply too majestic and resisted capture.

Earlier, as Jessica left the ranch, she again saw the blonde horsewoman high on the ridge overlooking her studio. She quickly gave Will a call on one of the radios they used on the ranch and told him where she'd spotted the mysterious woman. Will immediately dispatched two ranch hands to the spot, and she watched as they disappeared over the ridge, trying to catch the culprit. Later, she was told they had no luck. The rider wasn't anywhere in sight by the time the ranch hands had arrived. It seemed that the horsewoman had disappeared into thin air.

Jessica had then driven to the Cameron Trading Post hoping to talk to Johnson Longname but discovered that he was at home taking care of his ailing mother. Joseph, the shop manager, recognized her as a good friend and gave her directions to his hogan.

Leaving the Trading Post and taking the highway north, Jessica followed the directions of turning opposite the Tuba City turn-off, and headed west instead. The wide, graded dirt road took her right through the Chinle formations and out onto the vast plains of the rez. She bounced along keeping certain geologic formations in their respective places, Pillow Mountain always to the left and so on, and she soon found her way to the newly painted hogan of the Longname family, nestled in a desert ravine.

Hogans were a style of small, round dwellings that Navajos had called home for centuries. The only door always faced to the east so it could be left open to welcome the sunrise every morning with a sprinkle of holy corn pollen.

Johnson's hogan had a small sheep pen built from mesquite sticks just west of it, with a canyon wall as one side of the pen. She noticed the brightly painted generator sitting next to the house and knew it was the new one Johnson had recently bought for his mother. The outhouse was sturdy, but small and unpainted.

The yard was neat and tidy around the buildings, and in the distance she could see the familiar, triangular shape of a ceremonial sweathouse made from sticks and looking like part of the land. And beyond that were two more hogans, probably used by extended family. Johnson's blue pickup truck was parked next to an older white sedan, both cars dusty from the rez roads.

Jessica parked her car at a respectful distance from the hogan, waiting for the required acknowledgement from its inhabitants. On the Navajo reservation, it was considered impolite to walk up to the door and knock. It was so quiet on the reservation Jessica knew that the sound of her car would be heard. If the Longname family were accepting visitors, someone would come to the door, look out briefly and acknowledge her, then duck back inside.

Jessica saw the door open and the outline of a man as he looked out and then went back into the house. She knew that was her signal to knock. Johnson answered, and he smiled shyly when he saw it was Jessica.

"You have come to my house," was all he said.

"Please excuse my intrusion. I need to talk to you," Jessica told him politely, feeling a little uncomfortable about visiting without an invitation.

"This is my mother. Mother, I would like you to meet my friend, Jessica."

They nodded to each other. His mother was an ancient woman sitting in a rocker next to a wood stove. The stove was lit even though it wasn't that cold outside. She wore a shawl that was made of fine red wool and draped with fringe. Her face was etched with lines, and her hair was like fine white cotton thickly braided down her back. A long, full, ruffled skirt showed under the shawl, and peeking out of the bottom were white and purple Nike tennis shoes and new white socks.

Jessica saw that the room was simply furnished. A double bed was against one wall and covered with a handmade quilt. The bed was constructed of pine logs and had a small head and footboard. A little refrigerator sat in one corner of the room and was running off a car battery, which sat next to it. A table that looked like something out of the 1950s was arranged in the middle of the room with four chairs around it. It had a yellow Formica top with chrome trim and the chairs were upholstered in yellow and white plastic, decorated with several rips patched with duct tape.

Jessica wondered why the generator was needed when she noticed there was a small electric light on a table next to the bed. There was also a bookshelf at the end of the bed with a very tiny television sprouting rabbit ears. She wondered if they could even get channels so far out. She also noticed the Monopoly game on one of the shelves and remembered Johnson had told them his Mother had finally accepted electricity so she could see to play Monopoly in the winter evenings. There was a lantern hanging over the dining room table and she wondered if this was more from habit than necessity because there was also an electric light hanging next to it.

It was obvious to Jessica that the Longname family lived the simple life of the Dine' by believing material things should be in modest quantities.

"Please," Johnson said. "Have a seat. Would you like some coffee?"

"Oh, yes," Jessica said. "Actually, I brought you something. It's in the car. Just a second." She quickly went out to the truck and brought back a liter bottle of Orange Soda, Johnson's favorite. Alex had taught her to always bring something when visiting someone on the rez, so she had purchased the bottle before leaving the Trading Post.

Johnson was pleased with the gift, as Jessica hoped he would be. But she was surprised when his mother clapped her hands together and smiled a toothless grin. "Oh, orange soda. My favorite," she told Jessica. Johnson smiled at her.

"Mother doesn't usually get soda, but I guess we can let this be a treat, huh?" He poured her orange drink into a small jelly glass that had the Flintstones running around it, painted in bright colors. Her eyes sparkled and she sipped her soda like it was a fine wine. Jessica was charmed and delighted all at once.

"So, why have you come all this way on our dirt roads to see me? Is everything OK?" Johnson asked her, as usual coming to the point. While Navajos were known in their area for their subtle, polite talk, allowing the visitor to bring up the purpose of their visit, Johnson was unique. He rarely wasted words or made small talk.

Jessica cleared her throat and glanced at his mother. She wanted to talk about Alex, but not with an audience, so instead, she made some mundane comment about her dog Chili. She guessed that he'd understood her hesitation, because a few minutes later he said, "Mother, I'm going to show Jessica the new sheep pen we built this weekend. Is that OK?"

His mother tipped up her orange drink for another sip, and then she said something to him in Navajo. Johnson smiled and waved his mother's comment away as they headed out the door.

"What did she say?" Jessica asked him when they were far enough from the hogan.

"To take my time," Johnson told her. "She is dressed to go to the doctor and hopes she will miss her appointment." Johnson laughed. "She would rather see a medicine man, but I made her an appointment at the Tuba City clinic."

Jessica knew that family was very important to Johnson and she was touched to see this side of him. He'd been too private to say much, but one of the waitresses in the restaurant who had become friends with her once divulged the sad story of his adult life. His wife had been working in Flagstaff during the week, making the two-hour drive back to the hogan each Friday. She had gotten a degree from NAU and was making good money, helping to support the family while Johnson kept the homestead. It wasn't until he'd been married 5 years that he found she also had an in-town husband. Because of this, his marriage to her had never been legal. It had broken his spirit, and he claimed that he would always be married to her in his heart. So he stayed on the rez with his three children, now in their teens, and seemed to enjoy his life working at the Trading Post, and living on the reservation. He said a simple life was the best, and at this moment Jessica could see how well it suited him.

The two of them walked out to the sheep pen, and Johnson

explained how it was put together. Two of his younger sons were tending a herd of sheep on a hill, and waved casually as they walked out. Johnson lifted the rope loop that kept the gate closed and three well-trained dogs herded a second tight pack of sheep out. Although rez's dogs were usually mutts, they seemed to be some of the happiest animals Jessica had ever come across.

She had read somewhere that once the dogs were trained, they knew to take the sheep out to graze in the morning, keep them together during the day, and then bring them back to the pen when it started getting dark. A young dog often learned by example from older ones and about the only thing that could distract a dog from his duty was a jackrabbit. Once Jessica had clocked a rez dog at forty-five miles an hour in her Discovery. He was running parallel to the road, dead set on catching the jackrabbit, but soon gave up to return to his herd.

As Jessica and Johnson circled the pen, he told her a story about his dogs. He said one was almost blind, but followed the herd by sound and kept the two younger dogs in line. Last spring a lone coyote had tried to cull out a lamb to kill, and the older dog fought with the animal. Johnson, hearing the fight, went out to find the coyote dead, and the old blind dog circling the lamb. The rest of the herd had been lead back to the pen and were safe, but the blind dog wasn't able to find his way back without the sound from his companions. He'd continued circling the young sheep keeping it safe until his master had arrived. Johnson said he'd brought him home that day and let him retire from herding, to keep company with Grandma until one day he'd peacefully passed in his sleep.

After the tour of the new pen, she and Johnson walked up to the top of the hill and sat on a flat rock that overlooked his little family settlement.

"They arrested Alex yesterday for the death of Rachel," Jessica told Johnson.

"I know," was all he replied.

"How did you know?" Jessica asked surprised.

"The people who gossip on the Reservation are faster than the phone," he answered. "It's already being discussed among the people at the Post. Alex is a well-liked man from our area, his arrest is news to us."

Jessica told him how Mac had brought new evidence forward after a year and how they had to wait for the hearing and couldn't get Alex released on bond. When the whole story had spilled out of her, Johnson and she sat in silence, looking out across the land.

Two black ravens made a slow, wide circle above them. They were drifting on an updraft that was rising out of the canyon next to them. One bird circled clockwise, while the other drifted counter-clockwise.

"I just don't know if I can believe Alex when he says he didn't kill Rachel," Jessica sadly told Johnson watching the birds circle above them. She would never admit this to anyone else but Johnson.

"Do you believe Alex is capable of taking another's life?" Johnson asked her.

She thought about his question for a few seconds. "Not the Alex I know," was all she could say.

Johnson looked at her for a moment and then said, "If there is another who took Rachel's life, you must find him." When he finished, he went deep into thought before adding, "There is a sheepherder, Billy Manygoats. He lives over by the Little Colorado River. He is the man who found Alex's wife in the Canyon. You should go visit with him," Johnson said.

"Why?" Jessica asked, "Does he know something?"

"Most of us know things we do not understand, and until the right person hears it from us, it is undiscovered," he said, standing up and walking a few feet away, looking down on his mother's house. Jessica knew he was probably getting worried about her being alone for so long, but he went on to say, "You know, you outsiders are not very smart. When you are in another country, you should learn to live by their beliefs, even if it is just for a few hours." Jessica puzzled over what he'd said, but made no comment.

"Did you know," Johnson asked, "that the Navajo are nothing like Christians? We don't believe in an afterlife. When someone dies, they just stop existing for all those left behind." This was the most Johnson had ever said in one visit. He started back down the hill, and Jessica had to get up and follow him to hear the rest of his story.

Before turning away from the canyon, she noticed the two ravens were now only one. The other had flown off, leaving the one lone bird to fly high, now a black speck against the brilliant blue sky. She turned and quickly followed Johnson. "We don't have a heaven or a hell," Johnson went on to say, "but we do believe that after someone dies, the spirit is confused and does not understand what has happened, so we do not speak their name for seven days in fear they might hear it and come."

By this time, they were standing in front of Jessica's Discovery. Johnson finished with, "Do you know when the FBI might have questioned Billy?" he asked.

"I don't know," Jessica said, not understanding his change in subject.

"I hear there were dead coyotes hanging from sticks around the Manygoats home right after the body was found. The clever coyote knows how to scare the spirits away, and Billy seemed to think he needed their help," was how Johnson answered her, walking to the door of the hogan.

"I need to get Mother to the doc. You drive safely going back. And bring that bad dog of yours by next week. I gotta new toy for her." He walked toward the hogan and waved goodbye before closing the door. Jessica stood for a moment, mulling over what he had said. Then she climbed into the Discovery and started her drive back to the ranch.

Chapter 15: A History of Being Unstable

Flagstaff Medical Center, Flagstaff, Arizona

Emma's small face looked pinched and pale, lying on the white hospital pillow. Jessica stood beside her, worried and feeling helpless, while gazing at the sleeping woman. Just when she was about to rope and drag a nurse into the room, the doctor arrived.

"Hello. Are you family?" he asked Jessica abruptly as he checked the monitors around the bed. She just stared at him for a moment.

It was the day after she'd visited Johnson, and she'd received a frantic phone call from Emma early that morning. She said she was in the hospital and she needed Jessica to come get her. Jessica immediately asked for details, but Emma would only tell her that she needed her to come quickly. So Jessica had gotten in her truck and driven into town at breakneck speed, responding to the sound of desperation in the young woman's voice.

Since she hadn't answered the doctor's question, he now said, "Please leave if you aren't family. No one but a family member are admitted until visiting hours, which is," he paused as he checked his watch, "two hours away."

"Thanks," she said. "I'm not a relative; I'm a friend and Emma called this morning asking me to come get her. Is she alright?"

The sound of their talking must have woken Emma, because a weak voice said, "Oh, Jessica! Thank you for coming." Jessica looked at the now-awake patient and moved to the bed, happy to see her conscious. Emma reached out her hand with desperation and when Jessica took it gently, Emma's eyes immediately filled with tears.

She leaned over her and asked, "Emma, what's wrong? Are you OK?"

The doctor moved to the other side of the bed, holding the clipboard in front of him while making notes. "Emma, I'm glad you're awake. How are you doing this morning?"

Emma looked sheepish as she answered the doctor's question. "I'm better this morning, doc. This is my friend, Jessica. She's come to take me home. Jessica, this is Dr. Dean, my jailer."

The doctor looked at Jessica, this time giving her more attention. Then he turned to Emma and said, "I thought you were going home with your Uncle. He's been called."

"Doc, would it be OK if I talk to Jessica alone for just a sec?" He gave Jessica another look and then consented.

"I'll go check the others on this floor and be back before I leave. But don't get out of bed!" he said while pointing at her. "You'll find that you're still a little weak and I don't want you walking by yourself." He moved to the door and closed it quietly behind him as he left, rattling the clipboard into a holder on the outside. When he was gone, Jessica turned back to Emma.

"What's going on?" Jessica asked with concern.

"Oh, God, Jessica," was all Emma said at first, turning her head away, looking toward the window with tears welling up in her eyes. The other two beds in the room were empty, although one bed had a Hershey bar wrapper and a well-thumbed Glamour magazine strewn across it. Jessica pulled up a chair so she could sit next to the bed, holding Emma's hand. It was obvious this was going to take some time. She patiently waited until Emma was ready to talk. When she did, Jessica was stunned at what she revealed.

"I tried to hurt myself last night," she said in a small voice after a few moments. In response to Jessica's intake of breath she added, "I didn't mean to. I mean… I meant to but I didn't mean for it to be a big deal." Jessica stared at her in shock while Emma closed her eyes in shame. "I'm pregnant and I just can't deal with it." Emma finally admitted in a strangled breath. "Oh, God, Jessica, what am I going to do?" She began to sob.

Jessica stood up and gathered her into her arms, sitting on the bed. "Come here," Jessica told her, and then let her cry it out. When she was done, Jessica found a box of tissues and brought them for Emma to blow her nose and wipe her face clean. She didn't have a stitch of make-up to run, but her eyes were still red-rimmed and puffy.

"Emma," Jessica said gently. "How could you possibly think of taking your life, and that of your baby's?" She reached up and tucked a long strand of black hair behind her ear. Emma's small face looked pale against her black hair, eyes enormous. "Don't you realize how lucky you are? You're going to bring a new life into the world. A child that will be unique and yours alone to love."

Emma's eyes again started to shimmer. "But I can't do it alone. I'm not strong enough. The baby might…" And that was where she lost it again. "Please," she said between sobs, "can't you just take me to my house? I want to call my mom in California and see if I can stay with her."

"What about your Uncle?" Jessica asked her. "They've called him and I guess he's on his way."

Emma started shredding the damp tissues in her lap. "I won't go with my uncle," she said tightly. "That's why I called you. I thought you'd help me get to my apartment so I can find my mother's number. I could'na call anyone at work, I don't want them to know. And Alex usually helps me... but now."

Jessica sat there for a moment. "Why won't you go with your Uncle?" she asked gently, ignoring her comment about Alex.

Emma didn't hesitate. The hate was evident in her voice as she said, "The doc should have called my mom instead, and that's all."

"OK," Jessica said, realizing the young girl had made her choice. "I'll go to your apartment and get your mom's number. You can call her from here." She stood up and collected her coat and purse. "Where's your key?"

"It's in my purse," she said while pointing to the floor. The large black handbag she'd carried since Jessica had first met her, sat next to the bed on the floor. Jessica handed it to her, and while she fished the key from its depths, she asked,

"Can your mom come out here and get you?"

"No. She's gotta work. But I'm sure she'll let me come and stay for a week or something." Emma handed her the key and then gave her directions to her apartment, and told her where she could find her address book. Jessica gave her a brief hug and left the room with a wave and assurance that she'd be right back.

The first thing she did after leaving the room was find the doctor. He was still doing his rounds on that floor and she waited to catch him between patients. She intercepted him in the hall and said, "Dr. Dean, please. My name is Jessica Dawson, and it's important that you tell me how Emma is really doing." She put a note of pleading in her voice and tried to communicate her sincere concern.

He looked at her with more interest and said, "Alex Dawson's new wife? Well, I'm very pleased to meet you." He shook her hand with enthusiasm and a surprising grin. "Your father-in-law made this new wing possible. Any Dawson is welcome here."

Jessica was a little taken back, but grateful for his willing confidence. He took her arm and led her to a small, private waiting room and handed her into a chair while asking one of the orderlies to get them coffee. Once they were seated, he began to tell her what had happened to Emma.

It seemed that she had turned on the gas heater in her small apartment after blowing out the pilot light, attempting to end her life by breathing the unburned natural gas. She'd blocked under the doors with rugs and towels and taped up the doors and windows so no fresh air could get in. What she hadn't counted on was the pet door. She had fainted in front of it, and just enough fresh air seeped in to keep her alive until a neighbor smelled gas and called 911. The doctor said that she would suffer no consequences, but the baby was another matter. It would be some time before they could tell if the lack of oxygen had done any damage to the child.

The doctor went on to say that, while Emma was an adult, he was hesitant at releasing her without counseling. He was concerned that she might try to take her life again if left alone.

"She has a history of being unstable," he went on to say. "When she was seventeen she slashed her wrists. It wasn't a threat or a way to get attention. She was serious. That was when the Dawson's helped out. They helped find her a foster family in town while she received counseling until she graduated. Then your husband, Alex, helped her secure a job at the University, giving her the independence she'd always wanted."

Jessica was surprised to hear this. Alex had never mentioned it to her, even though they had talked about Emma a couple of times. Still, perhaps he hadn't said anything in difference to Emma's privacy.

"Doctor? What if Alex and I had her stay with us at the ranch? Alex could use some help with the business, and it would give Emma the chance to see things from another perspective." Jessica hadn't had time to give it much thought, but somehow it felt right.

Neither she nor the doctor had mentioned Alex, and so Jessica was surprised when he said, “It would probably be good company for you too, until Alex is released.” He hesitated fiddling with his hands. “By the way,” he began again, “I absolutely can’t believe Alex had anything to do with Rachel’s death. He’s too good a man.” Jessica felt her face flush slightly, but smiled at the doctor and thanked him for his kind statement.

They both agreed that her plan would work if Emma agreed. There was some concern about her job, but Dr. Dean said he’d call the head of her department, an old college chum, and see if he couldn’t get her a medical leave of absence. He suggested Emma stay where she was for a couple more days anyway, until he was sure that she and the baby were stabilized. When he mentioned that Emma was only three months along, he also told her that she’d already had two abortions and had completely discouraged her from a third. He had some concerns about her even being able to carry this one to term.

Further saddened by what she had just heard, Jessica went back to Emma’s room and told her the plan that she and Dr. Dean had devised. Emma agreed immediately and seemed excited and relieved. So Jessica went to her apartment and got her address book so she could call Emma’s Mom, and also brought her some pj’s and a book she found on a nightstand that Emma had been reading. Out of compassion, she hurriedly cleaned the apartment, stripping the doors and windows of the tape that was still there, a grim reminder of how much Emma needed help. She was just happy that Emma hadn’t died and was still here for her baby. She wanted the apartment to be welcoming when Emma came home.

Now that she knew she’d be going to the ranch, Emma seemed more willing to stay in the hospital for a couple more days for observation.

“You know,” Emma told her, “I never thought I’d be in this kind of trouble. I thought I was smarter.” Jessica smoothed her hair, and gave her a reassuring hug. With a promise to visit the next day, Jessica left the hospital feeling happy that she could play a positive role in Emma's recovery.

She made the decision to stay in Flagstaff with Stan and Patsy again, and after giving them a call, headed downtown to visit with Alex. They told her he was being moved to another cell and couldn't see any visitors, so she left the building frustrated and headed for the Edge a few blocks away.

She hadn't stopped thinking about what Johnson Longname had asked her, how soon after Rachel's death did the FBI question Billy. She understood that Billy probably had more to tell now that Rachel's death was over a year ago, but what could he reveal? That crafty dog, Johnson, would never have said anything if he hadn't thought it was significant. Jessica reluctantly hoped Ron could help her.

He was shaking out sleeping bags that were on display when she arrived. The store was completely empty except for one other employee busy with key chains in the front.

When Ron turned and saw her, his face actually lit up with happiness. She hesitatingly gave him a brief smile in return. Ron moved forward and hugged her as a friend would, but Jessica pulled away quickly and stepped a safe distance from his strong body. After the incident up on the observatory hill, she wanted to be careful not to give him the wrong impression. It was hard enough for her to be there as it was, but he was the only one who could help her with what she needed.

"Can we talk for a sec?" Jessica asked him. He nodded, hollering up to the other employee in the front of the store, telling him he'd be in the back. He then led her into the relative privacy of the back stockroom, its large open door giving Jessica some sense of security from her own runaway feelings.

Ron took a large backpack off a chair, tossing it onto an empty table, and motioning for her to have a seat. She shook her head and leaned against the table instead, crossing her feet.

"Look," Ron started before Jessica could say anything. "If this is about what happened on the hill, I just want to say it won't happen again." He crossed his arms and leaned his shoulder against a post in the middle of the floor. "That is, unless you want it to." He added a small, warm smile.

Jessica couldn't help but return it, and rolled her eyes to the ceiling. They had been friends for a long time, and she didn't want to lose that. The humor in his smile helped to break the tension and she was glad he'd brought it up. "I'm not here about that, Ron," Jessica told him while studying her boots. "But thanks for saying something. I think I was just tired and needed someone to say everything was going to be OK." She looked up at him and smiled again, "And you just happened to come along the trail at the right moment."

Ron snorted and gave a quirky grin to his sensual mouth. He dropped his arms and hooked his thumbs in his pockets. "So, why are you here then? Want to visit a bookie at the race tracks and need a disguise?"

"You think you're so funny," Jessica said, moving away from him. She started fiddling with some climbing rope untangled from its spool on the table. "Actually, I do need your help."

He gestured with his hand, palm up, urging her to continue, blue eyes intense as they reflected the light from the window. His tan had faded a little from being indoors more and Jessica thought he looked a little distracted. "OK," he answered her. "What is it?"

Jessica dropped the rope and turned to give him her full attention. "You once told me you knew someone with the FBI, and if I needed to get information, you could help me. Do you think you could do that for me now?" Jessica asked him.

"Sure," he shrugged. "What's up?"

"I just need to know how long after Rachel's death the FBI

questioned Billy Manygoats, the sheepherder who found her body," she said.

"I'm sure I can find that out for you. Why? Or should I ask?" he looked at her with humor.

She was sure he was referring to the fact that she hadn't been willing to tell him why she'd wanted to talk to Jim, the cabbie. Now she felt a little guilty for using him, but pushed it aside. She needed to know this.

She took a deep breath and blew it out. "Look Ron, I'm married to a man who first wife has died under mysterious circumstances. He won't talk about it with me except to tell me he doesn't want to talk about it. What am I supposed to do? I want to know what happened." She shrugged her shoulders.

"Believe it or not, I understand. I'd want to know the same thing," he said as he moved to a wall of lockers. He used the combination lock to open it and then removed a daypack from its depths. Out of one of the pockets, he pulled a small black address book, one like every male used to carry before cell phones and computers. He quickly made the call, but the man he knew wasn't in his office, so he left a message for him to call later. Jessica was disappointed, but Ron promised to call her at Stan and Patsy's with the information.

They said their goodbyes and the quick hug of thanks she gave him was more sincere than her greeting. She arrived at her in-laws' house tired and hungry. She spoke to Alex on the phone for almost an hour about ranch and university business.

Then they talked about Emma staying with them at the ranch, Jessica talking like he was getting out tomorrow, when in reality the hearing date wasn't for another week. Still, Alex said the same thing as Dr. Dean, Emma's company would be good for her until they straightened his situation out.

When she asked about Dr. Dean's comment regarding Dawson's

helping Emma when she was younger, he filled her in.

"I found Emma in an old deserted gas station out on the rez, beat up and terrified," Alex told her. "I knew her and her family and knew she had moved out to the reservation from L.A. to live with her Uncle. Apparently her Uncle was sexually abusing one of her young male cousins and she'd kept quiet for the two years she'd been living there because her Uncle had threatened to kill her if she said anything. When I found her, she had threatened to report him, and he'd beaten her until she almost died. She barely escaped with her life."

"Oh, God! So that's why she ran away!"

"Exactly. They pressed charges when they discovered the truth after she escaped the beating, and two other family members admitted suspicions they'd had about the Uncle. It was all kept extremely quiet, and her Uncle was immediately no longer her guardian. He served time for his offenses and we helped her find a foster home in town until she graduated that year. After that, I helped Emma get a good job at the University, hoping that she would be able to start over. She worked her way through college and now she has her degree."

As they were getting ready to hang up, she found herself asking him how much he loved her. She cringed at hearing herself, but she needed to hear him say the words even though she told herself she didn't. His warm, sultry voice comforted her fears as he lulled her into the security she so badly needed. They said their final goodbyes with the promise to talk the next day and Jessica hung up with a sigh. She had lied to herself and pretended everything was OK just to get a fix.

She closed her eyes and tried to imagine Alex as she first saw him. Tall, dark-haired and so handsome it almost made her cry. She thought back on their first kiss in the hallway of the El Tovar Hotel during a New Year's Eve party. He had trapped her against the wall and cupped her face with both hands, studying her for moments before diving into the kiss like it was oxygen to a dying man. It had taken her own breath away and even though they had known each other only a month, she knew he was the man she wanted to spend her life with.

She didn't find out until later that he was wealthy, or that he had a dead wife. She hadn't cared. She'd just wanted this tall man who turned a key inside her to always be where she could be a part of his world. Well, she got her wish. "And now what?" she wondered.

Later in the evening Ron called with her information, as promised. His friend had told him that Billy Manygoats was questioned the very next day after the body was recovered from the Grand Canyon. He had been quiet and reluctant to talk much, but they found that was usually the case with Native Americans. He'd simply confirmed that he'd been collecting stray sheep in the canyon and seen the body among some rocks. And only questions being asked, with him answering yes and no, had pulled that information from him. That was it.

After they hung up, she made her plans, deciding to wait until Emma was ready to go home with her. Then, once she got Emma settled at the ranch, she'd take an afternoon and head out to Blue Moon Bench, leaving Emma in Dorothea's capable hands.

She wanted to meet Billy Manygoats and find out why he would nail up coyote carcasses on posts after he'd found Rachel's dead body.

Chapter 16: Spirits Can Walk Walls

Blue Moon Bench, Navajo Reservation, Arizona

The wind blew with indifferent determination across Blue Moon Bench. The land of the Navajo Reservation undulated far into the distance, spotted with small scrub bushes and snaking dry washes that would gush with water in the rain. There was silence except for the brisk wind that blew through, making a dancer of each bush and creating a thousand whispers around her. The occasional, solitary call of a raven echoed across the canyon. The cry was suddenly met with the call of Jessica's Navajo flute. A friend of Johnson's had taught her to play and she found that it gave her solace when she was alone.

As Jessica played, sitting on the edge of the Grand Canyon, she watched two ravens drift higher as she made high notes, and lower as she made low notes. Somehow, she knew they had become a part of her own mind, so she played for a while, watching them rise up and drift down, catching the wind currents as they rose out of the canyon. The Buddha taught that all beings are not separate, that they are all one. She finally stopped playing, feeling deeply connected to the land around her, and when her flute notes stopped, both birds glided off in different directions.

The graded dirt road she had followed out here had moved west along the Little Colorado River Gorge for about ten miles, and just before the Gorge met with the Grand Canyon, it took a sweeping bend north. A small two-track dirt road shot off her main one, just where it curved, and continued west to the Grand Canyon rim, looking down on a point where the two rivers came together at the bottom of the canyons, called 'the confluence.' This was where Jessica was now parked. She had gotten out and carefully looked over the edge to see the two snaking rivers below her, one a bright turquoise and the other a muddy brown. Jessica immediately leashed Chili because she was afraid the dog would go over the edge because of her insatiable curiosity. They sat several safe feet away from the edge while she imagined this to be the very place where Rachel had fallen to her death.

To the west, the north rim of the Grand Canyon rose before her. It was about a thousand feet higher than where she sat, and with the difference in elevation, it was easy to see the distant geologic layers looming up before her. It was a magnificent part of the reservation, isolated and very quiet.

Jessica looked to the east, and saw that the land sloped away from her. She could barely see the few hogans that were situated between the Canyon and the road a few miles away. They were tiny specks, here and there, with little signs of life. Those hogans were the home of Billy Manygoats and his family.

She was on a mission. Johnson had given her detailed directions to the man's hogan, and she had arrived ready to ask questions. But Billy Manygoats had not been at home. The suspicious family had said he was out, but hesitantly invited Jessica to stay until he returned. Reluctant to stay with a family that was so uncomfortable and formal, Jessica excused herself and told them she had another errand to run, but would be back around three o'clock. They smiled and nodded as she drove off. The family's odd behavior made her wary. She wondered if they were just misleading her and Billy was actually out back, hiding in the outhouse.

To pass the time, she'd driven back out to this point drawn like a magnet. Why did Rachel come out here that night? It was forty-five miles on a dirt road in the dark, to a place that was isolated and remote. She couldn't think of anyone less likely to do that drive than social, fun-loving Rachel. That night she had been hosting a party at the ranch for her friends. Why would she venture out here alone and eventually end up at the bottom of the Grand Canyon?

Jessica first made sure that Emma was settled at the ranch before she drove off, leaving Will in charge of keeping her supervised. The doctor warned Jessica that Emma might attempt to take her life again if they weren't careful, and an appointment was made for her with a psychologist. Someone from the ranch would drive her the twenty minutes it would take to reach the clinic on the east side of town three times a week for her sessions.

Jessica had been pleased when she'd taken Emma out to visit the horses on the ranch and found that she'd had a real interest in animals. So she'd left her with Will, learning how to groom a young pony. It was obvious that Emma and Will had a history by Emma's body language, and it took Jessica one minute to realize that Emma had an attraction for the foreman. She wasn't sure Emma was ready for a relationship, and there was still the question of who the father of her child was. Emma refused to reveal her secret to anyone. But at least she had friends around her that would keep her and the baby safe.

Just before leaving the ranch that morning, Jessica had seen the spooky horsewoman apparition for the fourth time, but this time, she stood with her horse just inside a wash, watching as Jessica drove her Discovery up to the gate to leave the ranch. Jessica felt a surge of fear and wondered why she was being haunted this way. Jessica just sat in the truck with the engine idling, watching as the apparition sat on the black and white horse, watching her back. She wondered if it was indeed Rachel's ghost or a reflection of her own mind like the Buddha taught. "All things in your life are a reflection of your own mind." The horsewoman's blond hair shimmered in the sunlight, and her white shirt was brilliant and shining like a mantle. She suddenly turned the horse and broke into a gallop up the wash and behind a hill. Maybe Rachel's ghost wanted her to solve the mystery of her death. Jessica didn't even bother calling Will this time. How was he going to find a ghost?

With an uneventful drive to Blue Moon Bench, she was here on the canyon edge waiting until three o'clock so she could finally ask Billy Manygoats the questions she needed to ask him.

Jessica looked up from her thoughts and noticed that Chili was getting restless at the end of her tether, and so was she. She got up from her perch on a rock and stowed her flute back in her daypack. She began to walk north with no destination, just wanting to move around while she waited until it was time to head back to the hogan, taking Chili with her.

They were a ways from the rim now, so Jessica released the dog from her leash and let her run, keeping an eye on her zigzag progression. Her mind wandered to Alex and she wondered what he was doing right then. Probably working on paperwork for the ranch. Each time she spoke to him, he'd tell her about the business he and Will were working on or the report that he'd started on the cave he'd discovered just before they'd met. He continued to maintain his innocence and after each conversation, she felt a lonely ache and anger at the same time. She very much needed to know Alex had not killed his first wife. Somewhere inside she believed that but needed to find proof, both to free him and to vindicate her belief in him.

She looked up to find Chili and saw that the dog had found an odd outcrop of rocks she was exploring a little too close to the rim.

"Chili! Come!" she commanded. The dog responded and ran to her side. Jessica reattached the leash and explored the rocks herself, finding a trail that dropped down off the rim hidden among them. They walked its length, Jessica keeping a tight grasp on Chili's collar because of the steep drop-off, and found a shallow cave at the end just a few yards along the cliff wall. It was low and a tumble of rocks but otherwise uninteresting.

They made it back up to the cliff top and continued to walk along the rim, Jessica glancing at her watch with impatience. Looking up, she saw a mesa directly ahead, rising like a prow of a ship, over the canyon wall. On top, it looked like there were ruins of some kind mixed with juniper scrub trees. Jessica and Chili scrambled up the narrow, natural steps that were flanked by tall boulders on each side, the only way onto the mesa. Once on the top, the ruins lined the side and created a charming village with a small central plaza. Even with the crumbled walls it was obvious that the village had been a magical place for the inhabitants. Just the view alone was enough to take the breath from anyone.

Chili kept pulling on her lease, excited to explore and insistent. Keeping her close with a short leash, they wandered the ruins.

She followed Chili in and out of the rooms, trying to imagine how it must have looked when the inhabitants lived there. One room still had a small opening in the wall, a window that must have let in light and fresh air. The view from it was magnificent and the little shelf under it gave a real human quality the others didn't have. Chili suddenly pulled hard, and Jessica let the leash go its longest length since they were in a walled room, while she continued examining the shelf.

When she turned to leave the room, she didn't see Chili, but noticed the leash snaked into a hole in the floor of the room. She called Chili's name and suddenly, Jessica could hear scrambling. Unexpectedly, the dog popped up from a natural hole in the floor that Jessica hadn't noticed earlier.

"You clever girl," Jessica told her, ruffling her ears. "How did you find that?" Chili wagged her tail with enthusiasm and pleasure at the attention. Jessica walked over at a different angle and looked down the hole curious. Inside was a tumble of rocks and debris. A stash hole, she thought and wandered back out onto the square with Chili next to her. They explored the other rooms and found more windows and one small grinding stone where the owner had ground corn. It was smooth and worn to the touch and probably still sitting where the original inhabitants had left it centuries before.

Back outside at the end of what would have been the village center was a six-foot wide natural indentation in the stone floor of the mesa that still had a clear pool of water from the last rain that Chili drank from. Birds twittered and darted among the juniper pines and a light breeze danced around the ruins. It was a delightful place and Jessica wished Alex were there to share the story of just who these people had been.

It was now almost three, so she headed back to the Manygoats' after returning to the truck with Chili. This time Billy was there, and waiting outside for her arrival. He was a man in his forties who had obviously lived much of his life outdoors. His blue jeans were worn and rolled up at the bottom to make them short enough for his work boots, which laced up his ankles for protection from snakes. His blue flannel shirt was open only enough to reveal a sliver of clean white tee shirt underneath. His white cowboy hat sat low over his eyes, and he respectfully removed the hat as soon as he saw her coming, holding it against his chest as if he were taking a pledge.

They shook hands lightly as most Native Americans do, and Billy shifted from one foot to the other, looking a little uncomfortable. Jessica tried to put him at ease by asking him questions about his sheep and the pen that looked much like Johnson's. Encouraged by Jessica's interest, he talked about his mother, who was a weaver, and how all the wool came from their own sheep. Jessica explained that she was also an artist and told him how she appreciated the work his mother put into her rugs.

He seemed interested in her work, so she talked briefly about her latest project, all the while keeping to the Navajo protocol of not talking directly about what she came to ask until all the formalities of polite conversation had been completed. Earlier in the hogan, she'd seen beautifully colored wool, and diverted the conversation by asking how his mother went about achieving the colors. He went into a long explanation of how she gathered different plants from the land around them and boiled large pots over an open fire, cooking the plants for the pigment. He took her around the back so she could see where she worked and by the time they found a rock to sit on, he was more at ease and seemed willing to talk about the night he'd found Rachel's body. Granted, his story was told in pieces and with hesitation, but he finally got it all out.

The story began the night before he found Rachel's body. He said that he'd gone out to his truck for some horse tack, and while standing next to the truck, he'd seen what he called 'spirit lights' along the canyon wall. He gestured to the west, and Jessica looked to where he was pointing. It was the mesa with the ruin on it where she had just been, from here looking even more like a great ship, sticking out into the Grand Canyon. But the prow itself was a sheer mass of stone that continued beyond the lip of the canyon, too steep for anyone to have lights.

"Do you mean lights in the ruins?" she asked Billy, puzzled, knowing that this was information the FBI had probably not learned.

"No, no," he answered in his clipped Navajo accent. "On the walls of the canyon. Spirits can walk the walls."

Jessica just smiled like she understood and this was an everyday occurrence, while she wondered at his description.

Billy went on to tell her the story of how the next day he found Rachel's body, a gruesome and sad tale that enforced his naiveté. A sheepherder gathering stray sheep in the canyon and seeing circling vultures, just like in the movies. He'd thought that it might have been one of his stray sheep, but found Rachel instead.

"Billy," Jessica asked as they sat there. "Why did you hang

coyote pelts on posts the day after you found her?" She asked this because Billy hadn't explained it in his story. But now he only seemed uneasy and looked away, speaking about something completely different. "When the spring comes, the mesa is surrounded by flowers. They are the spirits of the animals who gave their lives so the families might eat."

Jessica had to shift her thinking. She felt confused and asked him to repeat what he'd said. Then she realized that he had completely changed the subject from coyote to wildflowers. She tried once more, but he just looked off into the canyon and shook his head no, while making a small grin that never reached his eyes.

She knew then that she had stepped over some boundary, and stood up, thanking him for his help. She decided she would think about what he had said when she was alone. He also stood and accepted her hand in another gentle handshake. They both walked back to the hogan, and she waved as she pulled the Discovery's key from her pocket, and watched as Billy entered the hogan. She turned and used the remote to unlock the doors to the truck.

Before she could open the door, however, Billy's cousin, Kenneth, came out of the hogan and trotted toward her truck. "Mrs. Dawson?" he called.

"Yes?" Jessica asked, turning with her hand on the door handle. Kenneth was an attorney and distantly related to Billy. She remembered him from one of their dinners at the ranch and Alex telling her that he had gone to law school on an academic scholarship to Harvard and practiced business law for five years before returning to the reservation to help his people. Jessica guessed that he had arrived at the hogan after she went for a walk with Billy because he hadn't been there earlier.

"Mrs. Dawson, was Billy able to tell you everything you needed to know?" he asked, slowing his walk while putting both hands in his Khaki pants pockets.

Jessica looked at him for a moment, a little unsure. "Well, we talked. He told me some things I didn't completely understand. But I guess that's to be expected." She smiled to soften her comment.

"Do you have just a second?" he asked her. When she nodded yes, glancing at her watch, he gestured that they should walk away from the hogan. With Kenneth leading, they headed for a small hill in the opposite direction of the canyon, Chili still in the truck waiting for her.

Kenneth squinted against the sun and shaded his eyes as they reached the top of the hill. "I heard that Alex was arrested for Rachel's death, and I was sorry to hear that. He is a nice man. If we can do anything to help, please let me know."

"That's kind of you, Kenneth. That's why I'm here, to see if I can find out anything that might help him." He nodded his head as he walked to an outcropping of large rocks and sat down on a wide, flat boulder that looked well-worn. Jessica guessed this was a place family members came to think. As she joined him, she saw why. The view of the Grand Canyon was spectacular. The sun was still high in the fall sky, big, brilliant blue and crystal clear. The scene took Jessica's breath away, and she sank next to Kenneth in wonder.

"It's beautiful, isn't it?" he asked her, smiling.

"Amazing, I think."

"Of all the places I've traveled and lived, I always know that I have come home when I sit here on this rock. My ancestors for centuries have sat here, and probably the ancient Anasazi." After his comment, they both sat still for several minutes in silence.

"Kenneth," Jessica said, hating to break the spell, but knowing this was an opportunity she might not have later. "I asked Billy a question that he was careful not to answer. And... Well, I'm wondering if it would be inappropriate to ask you." She felt her cheeks flush and it made her mad. This was all so new to her, she didn't want to step into a place of taboo, but she also needed to know.

"What was the question?"

"I asked him why he hung dead coyotes on fences around the hogans after he found Rachel's body. He didn't answer."

Kenneth smiled at her, and leaned forward, dropping his hands between his knees, playing with a piece of tall, tan grass he'd snagged. "You have to understand this world we live in, we Navajo. When we are here, we see nothing unusual in our way of life. It is our way. Our world is immersed in superstition and romance, but we don't know that. We only know it as the way of the *Dine'*. The way we have been taught to live." He used the Navajo word for his people with reverence. "We teach our children with stories that have been passed down for hundreds of years, and believe even when we do not anymore. I come back with a college education, but when I am here, I am still Navajo, and I still believe."

Jessica heard him with her heart. When she sat there on that rock, looking at what his ancestors had seen for so long, she believed and understood. She felt humbled and wondered if his answer meant he would not tell her about the coyotes either. But he suddenly began to speak.

"What I am about to tell you is taboo to talk about among the *Dine'*. I would be careful talking about this with anyone else. Alive, the coyote is mischievous and cunning, performing feats impossible for other animals that live on his land. Stories and fables of the coyote have come down through generations of our family, helping to teach us as children some of the most important lessons in life. As a traditionalist, Billy still believes these stories." He hesitated and looked up to see if Jessica was still listening. She was enthralled.

"He believes that dead, the coyote can protect humans against the *chindi*. The *chindi* are the spirits of the dead that have not yet found their way. It is believed that they wander, lost and confused, and those alive have to be careful not to allow them to stay on this plane of the living. That was why he nailed coyotes to posts, to protect his family from the *chindi*. For him, it is taboo to talk about this, especially with a stranger."

"And it's not taboo for you?" Jessica asked him.

He smiled. "Well, I am not traditional. Still, like I said, I still believe. It is hard when you are taught from the very beginning to be careful of the witches, or they will get you in the dark."

Jessica smiled back at him. "Thanks for telling me this, Kenneth. You're very kind. I'm not sure how it will help, but it was good of you to tell me. I'll be sure to tell Alex of your concern for him. He'll be grateful too." Kenneth seemed serious when he acknowledged her statement. She stood up and they shook hands. She noticed his handshake was close to non-natives in how firm it was.

They walked back to the truck in silence, and just as she opened the door of her truck, she turned back around. "Kenneth, he also said something about spirit lights. Do you know what he meant by that?"

"He told you?" he asked. "I'm surprised, he must have liked you. About four months ago he thought he saw some lights bobbing along the walls of the canyon. The next day, one of our sheep dogs was found dead by the rim. Billy got it into his head that the lights he saw were skinwalkers or ghosts, coming for one of their own."

A skinwalker, or in Navajo "yee naaldlooshii" is believed to be a human who has assumed animal form and has supernatural powers that can be considered negative, or black magic. Many Navajos who follow old traditions often have fear that this kind of spirit is around doing negative things like taking the lives of chosen victims.

"Why would a skinwalker want a dog?" she asked, puzzled.

"Skinwalkers are witches that take on the skin of an animal and become that animal to cast hexes. We Navajos believe they are very powerful and can perform supernatural feats. Billy thought his spirit lights were skinwalkers looking for something. The first time he thought they were with the dog that was deceptively a skinwalker, amusing himself for a time. When they left, it left the dog, dead without the spirit of the skinwalker. The second time he saw the lights, he believed they were skinwalkers looking for Rachel to cast spells on her so she would walk off the cliff and die. That is what he believes."

Jessica stood there and stared at him. Wow, she thought, that's amazing that in an age such as theirs, there were still people who lived by superstition like this. She thought it was impressive and had great respect for Billy's deep religious beliefs. Who was she to question it? Buddhism teaches that all religions and beliefs are valid. Each spiritual path, no matter what you call it, is exactly where each human should be at that time, in this life. So each path is perfect, and should be respected and upheld in that way. It also teaches a step further, we are not separate from each other, and karma is exacting. Being mindful every day was a challenge. Oh yes, she knew she had her superstitions. She wasn't different from Billie.

"Do you believe that he really saw spirit lights?" Jessica asked him.

"If Billy says he saw lights, he saw lights. If they were spirit lights or not, I don't know, but Billy isn't crazy; he's just superstitious." Kenneth looked very serious as he told her this.

"Thanks Kenneth. You've really been a help," Jessica said with sincerity. "Before I go, can you tell me if he told the FBI about the lights he saw?" She was remembering what Ron had said about how hard it had been for the FBI to get the story from Billy, that he had been quiet and reluctant to talk much.

Kenneth looked at her, thinking, and then said, "I'm sure he didn't. They were here the next day, and I'm sure he refused to say much from fear that Rachel's *chindi* would haunt him. It's taboo to talk about the dead for at least a week after they die."

"Yeah," Jessica answered with thought. "I've heard that. Kenneth, would you mind talking to the FBI about the lights if I call and tell them? They'd probably want to talk to Billy again."

"Don't worry about it, I'll talk with Billy and I'm sure he'll want to help Alex. It would be nice if you could ask them to send the authorities from Tuba City. At least they are *Dine'* and would understand the delicacies involved. That may help Billy feel more comfortable talking about it."

"I will definitely do that," Jessica told him. "Thanks, Kenneth." She climbed back into her truck, pushing Chili out of the driver's seat. Starting the engine, she waved to Kenneth as she drove away.

As she bounced the miles back to the main road, she contemplated what she had just learned. She wondered if the lights were important, but she wasn't sure just how they would be.

Jessica wanted nothing more than to have Alex home, safe and not guilty. She wanted things back to the usual routine, she in her studio, painting, him in his office, working. She wanted to go back to their morning rides and quiet dinners in their family room, Chili sleeping at their feet. She wondered if they would ever get back to that, and decided right then that if they ever did, she'd learned to really appreciate what she had.

Chapter 17: Scream if You Need Me

Whopper Strip Club, Flagstaff, Arizona

She and Jim, the cabdriver, had agreed on a time to meet up at Joe's Bar. She hid her truck down an alley and walked to the bar dressed in the Candy disguise ready to get this part over with. It was night time and Jessica noticed there were no street lights as they drove across the railroad track and into a darker part of town. After several twists and turns, they arrived at a large tin building that said "Whopper Construction" on the side. Jim, the cab driver, drove into the side alley and there was a door with a tin awning and one single light bulb over it. Several cars were already in the parking lot, and Jim parked in a space that was close to the building and probably his usual.

Jessica sat in the backseat, feeling a little uneasy with her surroundings, feeling a little uneasy with her surroundings. Jim was taking her, as Candy, to see Heathcliff, Emma's drug guy, and she had no idea what was in store. Jim still just knew her as Candy, and was trying to help a friend.

Emma had been at the ranch for over a week, and while her physical health had improved, her mental health was still shaky. Will had come to Jessica two days before and told her that Emma was more worried about the money she owed Heathcliff than her pregnancy. So the next time she talked to Alex, she told him of the problem and he said, "Well, we'll just have to pay her debt off with him then. If she isn't comfortable with what she might see as charity, she can work for us in the evenings and weekends doing paperwork for Will and the ranch to pay it off." This was the Alex she knew in her heart, compassionate. How could he have murdered Rachel?

Alex had left the details to her, advising her to tell Emma, find out the size of the debt, and then contact Dawson's lawyer and let him pay Heathcliff anonymously. But Jessica had already learned from Will that Emma owed Heathcliff around five thousand, and she didn't feel comfortable asking Emma just how they would go about getting the payoff to Heathcliff. In truth, she wanted to just say "Surprise! Heathcliff is paid off!"

So after some thought, she decided to turn to Jim using the Candy disguise just one more time. Her plan was to talk to Heathcliff about the payoff, give him the money on a second visit after confirming the amount, and get the whole thing over with.

It took some talking, but Jim finally agreed to drive her to Heathcliff's office under one circumstance: that he stays with her. She hadn't told him why she wanted to see Heathcliff, but Jessica thought that he was probably guessing drugs. She decided to let him assume, since the truth was probably better left unsaid. How could she tell him without telling him who she really was?

After Jim parked the car, they got out and Jessica followed him to the scratched and painted metal door. Somewhere she heard the distinctive bass of loud music, and wondered where it was coming from. When he opened the door, there was a short hall, and Jessica was surprised to see a guy sitting behind what looked like a ticket window. He greeted Jim and stamped the back of his hand, so Jessica held hers out to get her stamp too. The guy hesitated.

"Do I know you?" he asked.

"No, but Jim does," she smarted back.

"She's OK, Terry. She's a friend of Emma's. Is Heathcliff here?"

Terry, a bruiser type, looked her over and decided she was OK. Her black wig felt hot, and she was sure that the jerk tried to see through her black crocheted top. He stamped her hand and indicated with his head that they could go in. "Talk to Dave, Heathcliff's upstairs."

They entered through the door at the end of the hall, and as soon as they walked into the room, Jessica almost choked on the cigarette smoke. Somewhere, a jukebox was playing a top-forty tune, and it took a moment before she realized she was in a topless bar!

Jim led them to a table in the back and Jessica tried to look casual as a cocktail waitress came over sans-top and took their order. It was obvious the waitress knew Jim, because she gave him a kiss on the cheek.

Jessica had been completely unprepared for the topless thing, and now she was trying to look anywhere but where bare flesh showed. She turned to Jim and started to ask him a question when she noticed the bartender. He looked familiar, but she couldn't quite place him at first. Then she realized that he looked strikingly like the man who chased her in Hotevilla on Hopi Mesa the day of the dances, except he wasn't wearing the red ball cap. Could that be possible? She suddenly wanted to get this over with very quickly.

She turned back and saw a lone man at the next table talking to the waitress while handing her some money. She took the drink off the tray and then she did a little trick where the tray opened like it had a hinge. She took out a tiny zip lock bag with white powder in it and passed it to him, closing the tray back up. Jessica was pretty clear on what it probably was, probably not a sweetener.

Jim lit a cigarette and blew the smoke away from her, as if it made any difference. "Let's get our drinks, and then I'll talk to Dave," he told her. She watched with fascination while their neighbor made a rail of cocaine on the table and proceeded to snort it.

Suddenly, bump and grind music started blasting from some huge invisible speakers. Lights came up on a stage that was situated in the center of the room. It wasn't like all the ones you see in the movies; it was simply a round raised platform with tables all around it. There was a pole down the center and on all four corners, and suddenly a dancer slid down the center pole and went to work. She didn't have to strip, because she was only wearing a G-string and tassels. The men in the audience started whistling and giving catcall encouragement to the dancer, reaching forward and hoping to cop a feel while stuffing a dollar bill in her string. The louder they clapped and whistled, the harder the dancer would gyrate, making love to the pole in a way that made her blush and giggle at the same time. It looked stupid, really.

On the right side of the stage from where Jessica and Jim sat, she saw a handsome Native American who wasn't joining in with the rest of the audience. He sat at a table away from the stage and nursed his drink, keeping his eye on the dancer. Through the smoke, Jessica noticed that he was wearing a red bandana around his head, and two black braids hung down each side of his handsome face and she wondered why he wore dark glasses in the already dark bar. His jeans were tight, and his shirt was nondescript blue, but Jessica thought his broad shoulders and long legs made him stick out in a crowd.

"...He'll probably insist you go up there without me," Jim was saying.

"Huh?" Jessica aka Candy said.

"I said, Heathcliff won't come downstairs, he always meets in his upstairs office. If we let him know you want to talk to him, he'll probably insist you go up there without me." He had to shout almost into her ear so she could hear over the music. Jessica nodded her head and shrugged letting him know that was no big deal. Jim went back to his drink.

Jessica took the moment to look at the rest of her surroundings. The bar was directly in front of her and the stage was to her right. On the other side of the stage and tables was a door, the one Mr. Braids kept glancing at, which Jessica assumed lead upstairs.

She took a long swig from the beer bottle that had suddenly appeared on the table and a loud burp loomed up from deep in her chest. She covered her mouth and set the bottle down. She looked back at Mr. Braids and found him looking directly at her. She blinked and almost smiled when she remembered she was now a married lady. She looked back toward Jim and saw that he had left the table and gone up to the bar. She watched as he talked to who she assumed was Dave, the guy who looked like her assailant from Hotevilla.

She suddenly felt weird sitting by herself in a topless place and shifted in her seat so she looked more casual. She picked up her beer and took a quick slug.

She was doing OK until she noticed the guy at the next table had bought what she assumed was a lap dance. Of course she'd heard of these, but when the dancer straddled his legs and started jiggling her bare breasts around so close to his face he was cross-eyed, she snorted so hard with laughter that she blew beer up her nose.

Grabbing a napkin to catch the foam that was dribbling out of her nose, she quickly leaned over to let most of it drip on the floor. She looked around to see if anyone saw her, and that was when she noticed Mr. Braids heading in her direction and things were getting noisy in her head. She panicked and quickly looked around for Jim while discarding the napkin.

She was surprised to find Jim standing next to her, and he began shouting in her ear, "Heathcliff is ready to see you. Come on!" With that, he grabbed her elbow and led her to another door she hadn't noticed next to the bar. She looked back and saw that Mr. Braids was left standing in the middle of the floor. Once she and Jim were in the hallway, the music was less loud and Jessica could hear better what Jim was saying.

"Go up these stairs and someone will lead you to Heathcliff," Jim told her. "I'll be right here waiting for you. Scream if you need me, I'll hear."

Jessica stood there and stared at him for a minute. "You think I might need you?" she asked stupidly.

"Let's hope not, doll." He winked at her and smiled, taking a draw on his cigarette.

Jessica went up the stairs slowly, thinking that maybe she was making a mistake. She felt that perhaps she was way in over her head. When she gained the top of the stairs, she turned and looked down to see that Jim was casually leaning against the wall, smoking and waiting for her to return. She felt better. A very large man saluted her. "Candy?" he asked, leering at her.

"Yeah," was all she could manage in a croaky voice. Now that she was here, she started having misgivings. What if Heathcliff recognized her from their first encounter at the Beaver Street Brewery? She told herself that the visit had been too short, and Heathcliff too self-involved, but you never know. On the other hand, her disguise was really good, she thought.

"Right this way," he said, smiling at her breasts. What was it with these guys? She wondered if he thought the flesh-colored silky stuff under her crocheted top were her breasts and was looking for her nipples. Dream on, dude, Jessica thought with a smirk. But at least it helped to distract her.

She followed him down a long, dark hall that had several doors. Their destination was the last one at the end. He opened it and motioned for her to enter.

It pissed her off, those movies had prepared her for something completely different from what she now saw. She expected to see a seedy old wooden desk with a bare bulb hanging over it and two bimbos draped across it. Instead, she found an executive office done completely in black, white and …pink. Heathcliff's touch, no doubt. He sat behind the larger part of the L-shaped desk, and he was having a pedicure, evidenced by the woman bent over his feet. To her right Jessica saw another, smaller desk which sported a black, flat-screened computer and an efficient-looking assistant typing away at something.

To her left was a tasteful living room with a large screen TV going full blast with some game show on. Two expensive black leather couches flanked the TV and the two young men who had been with Heathcliff at the Beaver Street Brewery were completely engrossed and eating popcorn. They looked up when she entered and then dismissed her immediately.

"Yessss dear," Heathcliff said to her, "Jimmy says you need to see me. You're a friend of Emma's?" He waved one of his ringed hands in her direction. His hair was still a tangle of braids, curls and half-shaved styling. He had eye makeup that was quite stunning, and his white silk shirt was open to reveal a chest completely shaved of any hair. He was still a weird dude, Jessica thought. She was relieved to see that there was no inkling of recognition in his eyes.

"Yeah, thanks for seein' me," Jessica said. She hadn't pictured this big of an audience when she'd been playing the scene in her head. She tried to think fast. "Can we, uuuh, be alone, do you think?" she asked him. You never knew unless you asked, she figured.

"And why would we need to be alone?" Heathcliff asked. He seemed to be way less 'on' than he'd been in the restaurant. Jessica suspected it was because he had a much smaller audience.

"Well, I kinda need to tell you somethin' private," she said almost in a whisper, leaning toward him over the desk.

"Can't you see that I'm getting my pedicure? I need it so badly this week, I can't possibly skip it." Heathcliff looked back down to his toes and the woman laboring over them while he wiggled his fingers at Jessica, indicating for her to keep talking.

"Well…" Jessica cleared her throat. "It's about some money that Emma owes you and the manner it's being paid back."

That caught his attention. He swung his chair around completely forgetting his pedicure. She heard a scuffle behind his desk and assumed it was the manicurist trying to save her lotions. "What do you know about that?" he asked, his greed overcoming his vanity.

"Well, I might be able to help you get your money. But…" She looked around her, "It just feels a little crowded, if you know what I mean."

Heathcliff snapped his fingers and the secretary and manicurist got up immediately. The two boys, however, didn't respond as quickly. Heathcliff snapped his fingers one more time and they both came to their feet. Only one started to move toward the door, still watching the screen. "Turn that damn thing off!" Heathcliff said in a whining voice.

"Ahh, Heath. The guy is about to win a house in Aruba! He only has one more question to get right, and we're gonna miss it!" one of his twins said.

Heathcliff quickly stood up with an intimidating look on his face and that seemed to be all the incentive they needed. They both scurried toward the door. Jessica shivered a little when she saw how quickly they responded to a physical threat. Jessica's eyes turned warily back to Heathcliff.

He walked out from behind the desk and slipped into a pair of puffy pink slippers. They were so beautifully fluffy that Jessica wondered if someone had the job of grooming them every day.

He picked up the remote control and silenced the TV with a click. Then he turned to her and motioned toward the couch opposite him. They both sat down, and she waited for Heathcliff to say something first.

"And so Candy, what is this little thing about what Emma owes me?" he asked her with a toothy grin. He laid one arm over the back of the couch and lightly stroked it like it was a pet, all the time sitting with crossed legs, bouncing the pink slippered foot.

"Well actually," Jessica told him, "I'm here on behalf of an anonymous party who wants to settle Emma's debt. You tell me exactly how much and how we can pay it, and the money is yours."

Heathcliff looked at her with new interest. "Twenty thousand," he told her, completely serious.

Jessica looked at him for a few seconds and then said, "Somewhere nearer five thousand, I think."

Heathcliff dropped the smile and said, "Are you calling me a liar? Because if you're calling me a liar, we can just get my friends back in here and they can convince you otherwise." He looked at her with the same steely glint she'd seen earlier when he was dismissing his twins.

He suddenly licked his little finger and then swiped both eyebrows and gave an unexpected giggle. He got up and walked to his desk to pick up a business card and waved it in Jessica's direction. "Here's who you make the check out to and you can drop it off or mail it if you'd like." He walked up behind her and delicately handed his business card to her over her shoulder. As she reached for the card, he gracefully caught her thumb and forced her arm into a twisted position that created excruciating pain. A whimper came out of her before she thought, and her eyes began to tear of their own volition. Heathcliff licked his pink lips while watching her pain.

"And it's twenty thousand," he almost whispered in a silky sweet voice. "It used to be five, but the extra fifteen is accumulated interest. And tell your girl that she better not ever come to me for her stuff anymore. She has worn her welcome out in the house of Heathcliff." He abruptly released her hand and did a sexy shuffle in his puffy, pink slippers toward the TV, snapping up the remote and clicking it with anger.

Jessica massaged her arm getting up from the couch to leave. Just as she stood, a voice said, "Boss?" Heathcliff swayed the short distance to his desk and pushed a button on his phone.

"Yes?" he said, obviously not happy about being disturbed.

"I just gotta call. We're about to be busted," a voice said over the speaker.

"Well, make sure there isn't any merchandise on the floor. Get Donald on the phone, I told that damn man we're tired of being raided. He has no class whatsoever." Heathcliff clicked off. "For some reason they keep trying to bust us, but they never get any real evidence. My men are too good. They always figure it out beforehand." He waved his hand in circles over his head.

"OK, well thanks," Jessica told him as she headed toward the door with the card in her hand. "I'll just go now. Jim is waiting downstairs for me and probably wonders where I've disappeared to."

"Yeah, yeah," Heathcliff said, dismissing her and turning up the volume of the TV. Suddenly there were sounds of doors slamming and screaming voices.

She'd just made it to the door when it flew open, and two men busted in with sawed-off shotguns. She screamed and jumped back against the wall, almost stumbling in her haste. The men ran into the room, and one of them shouted, "Everyone, down on the floor." She immediately hit the floor on all fours and looked toward Heathcliff. He had magically disappeared! He was no longer in the room, and Jessica had no idea where he'd gone, or how he'd left that fast.

Jessica was terrified and wanted nothing more than to escape. This was all she needed. She could see it now: Mrs. Alex Dawson was arrested in a bust of a local topless bar while doing a business deal with the drug dealer/owner, Heathcliff!

She scrambled like a dog on all fours out through the now broken door and then leaped up to run down the hall when she saw the heads of more men running up the stairs towards her. She quickly slipped into the first door to her left, and before she could close it she heard Heathcliff's voice. He was talking to another man with him in the next room and she could hear him through an adjoining door which was open enough to hear, but not enough to see them.

"Take this and put it in a safe place," he was saying.

"Damn! This is like the stuff we used to get over a year ago. Is it from the same guy?" a second voice answered him. Jessica peeked through the crack where the door hinged into the room and saw he was holding a gold statue that looked ancient and beautifully made.

"No," Heathcliff answered back. "Mac stopped bringing us stuff after Rachel died. This came from some old couple who learned about me from Rachel. They knew I'd be willing to handle it for them."

Jessica was shocked. Mac? Their Mac? He must have been bringing Heathcliff artifacts to sell for money. Of course, she thought, to pay for Rachel's habit! She just knew a professor's salary wasn't enough to support someone as high-maintenance as Rachel. So that was how he'd tried to keep her happy.

The second voice said, "It must be solid. We should just melt it down and keep the gold."

The nasty sound of a hand against flesh and a grunt told Jessica that Heathcliff hadn't thought too much of the guy's idea. "Idiot," he growled. "That's a ceremonial piece from the Chime in Peru. It's worth more than this whole building, and certainly your sorry ass. Hurry and put it in the hot box. I was worried those fools were going to bumble into its hiding place in my office."

"Yes, sir," the second voice said with respectful fear. Things suddenly got quiet and she guessed they had moved out of that room to a safer place.

She could tell by the light coming from under the door that she was in some sort of storage room and made her way to the back. Another door led into a smaller room with a workbench and some shelves, which she could just barely make out in the dark. She dove under the workbench and pulled a large box of toilet paper in front of her, shrinking down as small as she could.

"Where'd the woman go?" she heard a muffled voice ask. She

closed her eyes and said a small prayer. A light suddenly came on in the other room, and a quick scuffle of feet told her it was being searched.

"Look in there. She has to be here somewhere." Jessica tried to get as small as possible when she saw feet and legs that looked familiar. It was Mr. Braids! He had the same black leather boots with the spurs and that nice tight ass she'd noticed. Now she prayed that the tight ass wasn't attached to someone who was too smart or thorough.

To her relief he left after a cursory glance. "Not in here. She must have gone downstairs when we weren't looking. The guys down there probably have her. Come on." And with that they turned out the light and left.

Jessica stayed there a long time and listened to the sounds of doors opening and closing and feet stomping around the rooms down the hallway. She found a comfortable position and leaned her back against the wall almost napping. When she tried to get up, her butt was asleep and one foot hurt when she walked on it. She started to limp to the door when she heard voices just outside and pulled back against the wall, ready to dart back into her hiding place again.

She stood there for several minutes, and when she didn't hear anyone else coming down the hall, she slowly opened the door and then passed across the hall to enter a room that was a small hotel room look-alike. She made her way to the fire escape she'd seen earlier from Heathcliff's office.

There was no one around to watch her descend the stairs down to the alley, and when she reached the ground, she quickly made her way into the light of the street and walked nonchalantly like she belonged. It was several blocks back to her truck, but when she finally made it, she found herself shaking from the tension. She sat behind the wheel, pulling off the hot wig from her sweaty head before starting the engine. She thought about Jim, wondering if he had escaped or got arrested.

Then her mind turned to Mac and she wondered if he'd felt any guilt at selling the very thing his career as an anthropologist was bent on saving. She couldn't imagine Alex doing such a thing and knew that Rachel had driven Mac to do things that went against his very ethics. She wondered if it could have driven him to murder, and then duplicity against his best friend just to save his own ass.

Chapter 18: Let the Woman Rest in Peace

Monte Vista Ranch, Northern Arizona

Jessica sat resting in the saddle of her grazing horse, elbow on the horn. She had decided to ride out alone on this quiet Tuesday morning to get her mind off of all the things she was dealing with, even though she had plenty to keep her busy in her studio. It was a cool October day. If you were in the sun, the cold, blustery wind was negotiable. She tucked her nose down into her knitted scarf wound around her neck to keep it warm.

She'd been working on a project for a publisher that covered the history of the Casa Grande civilization in the far south of the state. New ruins had been uncovered, and from them, they were discovering more complex details about these early Natives. The book she was illustrating in watercolor was going to focus on what this newly discovered village looked like when it was young, and how the people lived. Her preliminary sketches sat on her drawing board even now, but she'd found it hard to sit in one place, and so decided to take a ride instead.

The day before a call had come from Alex's parents telling her that Alex's hearing had been delayed yet again. The court refused to set bail because of the severity of the crime and because of the discovered evidence, and until the hearing they would not be changing that decision. Jessica was so frustrated that she'd started yelling at Alex's father over the phone and had to make a major effort to get her temper back under control. Stan was compassionate and told her to continue to be patient. Mr. Howell, the attorney, and he were doing everything possible to get Alex released. He felt sure by this time next week, they would all know something more. With Dorothea's help, Jessica found her iPhone, which she had lost the day before, and entered the new hearing date, swearing under her breath.

Other than that, things had been fairly quiet at the ranch now that Emma had fallen into a routine of her own. With the burden of her debt to Heathcliff removed she had actually begun to get her health back, both mental and physical. She'd insisted on paying back the money by working for Alex and Jessica, and began from the moment she'd heard the news. With Alex's agreement, Jessica didn't mention that Heathcliff had insisted on twenty thousand dollars, intentionally leaving her to think that five thousand was all she owed. And Emma was determined to work most of that off before returning to the University at the end of the month.

Jessica dismounted her horse and tied him to a close-by juniper, leaving him to scour the rugged lava rocks for grass. Chili, who had joined her on the trip, came trotting over with a stick for Jessica to throw, a game she never seemed too tired of. Sitting in the sun under a juniper with a thick carpet of needles under it, Jessica tossed the stick for Chili.

When she'd walked down to the barns that morning, she'd noticed Will and Emma working on one of the new cow ponies Will had recently purchased. It was true that they made an unlikely couple, but Jessica had her hopes.

Emma still hadn't confided who the father of her child was, and while Jessica was curious, she also felt that was Emma's choice to make. Emma was also working side by side with Dorothea, and she had turned out to be quite the creative cook. Jessica had taken to eating in the kitchen with Will, Ralph, Dorothea and Emma, and on the nights Emma cooked, the meals were a delicious mixture of Californian, Mexican and Arizona Navajo.

Jessica reached out to pet Chili, who had come to lie under the tree with her. She found her mind wandering to Alex and realized that the inevitable always surfaced: what if Alex really did murder Rachel? The thought absolutely made her blood run cold. She wondered if she could have been so wrong about a person. Could she have been so blinded by his looks and wealthy situation that she completely missed seeing who he really was?

What if she only knew one side of Alex? What if he had a part of his personality that didn't always show its face? She'd read stories about women who had been duped by men in just that way. Women married to serial murderers like Bundy. She shivered in the cold and closed her eyes to collect her thoughts. She had to admit she'd only known Alex for seven months, but was he capable of hiding such a terrible secret? There was no doubt that she'd have to get to the bottom of just what happened that night at Blue Moon Bench.

To escape her thoughts, she stood up while slipping out of her jacket. The sun was warm and her jacket was heavy. She hooked the jacket on the horn of her saddle and wandered down the hill to a creek wash that was dry and filled with tumbled river rock. One of her favorite things was to find stones with interesting colors and patterns to take back to the cactus garden. She picked up a sturdy branch to use as a walking stick, which she used to help her navigate the rocky wash. Chili came with her, sniffing the ground for anything interesting. After about fifteen minutes, as she decided to head back, she suddenly heard her horse whinny in alarm behind her.

Turning to see what the trouble was, she saw a lone horseman grab her horse's reins from the juniper tree and ride off in a scramble. The rider was the Rachel look alike appearing again as if from nowhere, but this time Jessica was close enough to get a good look. The person was thick and muscular - not thin like she knew Rachel had been.

"Hey! Stop!" Jessica screamed, "Come back here!" Chili started barking and ran in the direction of the horse thief, skidding to a stop and then holding a stance of aggression with her hackles raised in anger. The dog knew a threat when she saw one.

The rider disappeared over the hill and a cloud of dust left behind drifted in the cold autumn air. Jessica stopped running and stood in shock on the top of the hill. This time she realized she had to consider that Rachel might still be alive. The idea of seeing a ghost in the distance was one thing, but a solid woman on a horse stealing her own horse was another matter completely. But if she was alive why would she be stalking Jessica, and why wasn't she coming forward and letting everyone know she was alive?

She realized in the next second that she would have to put that aside for now. The ranch was a good twelve miles to the west, and the walk was through rough terrain. They had to get started before it got too late or the weather shifted. Lunchtime was ahead and both of them would be getting hungry. She had no water, phone, or jacket since they were all on her saddle, which was left with her horse.

The Arizona air was so dry and cold that she knew she was likely to dehydrate in an hour simply from the exertion. It was the middle of fall and the clouds were building on the horizon. Today there was a chance for rain, possibly snow. She started to whistle for Chili but realized the dog had not left her side. Knowing instinctively that something wasn't right, Chili was sticking close.

They started their walk, but sinking into the sand of the first wash made her quickly change their course for firmer ground. After a few miles, the two of them came up over another rise and were high enough to see the ranch house in the distance. It was further than she had estimated and the buildings were still a tiny dot on the horizon, although she'd been walking for over an hour.

Jessica stopped and unwound her heavy scarf from around her neck and turned it into a makeshift head scarf/shawl to help warm her. She ran her hands up and down her arms and then started walking again. Chili stayed close and watched Jessica's face, her eyebrows twitching in concern.

"It's okay, puppy. We'll make it." She reached down and gave the dog a reassuring pat, knowing she could use a little reassurance herself. As she started walking again, she began reciting mantra, calming her mind and raising her spirits. Suddenly she wasn't worried. She felt better knowing the horsewoman was human and it would be easier to solve the puzzle because somewhere, there was evidence that could be found.

They walked steadily on, weaving their way among the pinion and juniper trees. It was getting later, and the sun was lower, so they walked fast to keep warm, and to get back to the ranch as quickly as possible before the sunset completely. She avoided the washes when she could because it was just too hard to negotiate in her high-heeled boots. At the top of a hill, she stopped to catch her breath and stood with her hands on her hips.

"Well, Chili, I can guarantee we'll be two cold, thirsty girls when we arrive at the ranch." She adjusted her scarf, her mouth dry and tacky, and the fall air dry and cold against her face. The burn of two blisters inside her boots began screaming as she started down the hill, refusing to give up.

To her surprise, her prayers were answered when she heard the whinny of a horse in the distance. She swung around to see where the sound had come from, and about one hundred feet to the right, her horse was grazing in the brush! Had she not stopped to catch her breath, she might have simply passed by, never seeing the horse in the shadow of the trees. Jessica wondered if the horse whinnied because it heard her voice.

She quickly looked around to see if her thief was still there and saw nothing but rolling hills and small trees.

She slapped her thigh giving Chili the command to heal and walked slowly and quietly toward her horse, not wanting to spook her. She knew the horse would be jittery after being nabbed by a strange rider, and she hoped her canteen would still be riding the horn. When she got to the horse, it shied a little but then stood quietly enough while Jessica spoke to her, checking for the canteen. She was filled with gratitude when she found it was still full. Whoever played this cruel trick had failed to think of emptying it out, probably because they thought she wouldn't find the horse.

She gave Chili a drink from her cupped hands first, and then rinsed her own mouth before drinking. The water was sweet and cold. She then poured a small amount into her hat for the horse. Chili was sitting watching her every move, not looking the least bit tired. She, unlike Jessica, was after all a ranch dog and used to being on these kinds of outings with Will.

She pulled out a jacket she always kept in her saddlebag and put it on before grabbing the rope off the saddle. She tied one end of the rope to Chili's collar, giving her plenty of lead, the other end to the saddle, deciding to keep her close until they got home just in case the kidnapper reappeared. She didn't want Chili to share in the same experience as her horse. Once Jessica began walking the horse, Chili trotted alongside with little concern. Both the horse and dog had worked together rounding up cattle and seemed comfortable with the arrangement.

She turned the horse back toward the ranch, her eyebrows furrowed in anger. She had no idea who had done this, but she fully planned on telling Will it was time they brought in the County Sheriff. She'd resisted telling anyone the last time she'd seen her "ghost," but this time she wouldn't make the same mistake. This time the hoax had gone too far, and it really pissed her off!

They arrived back at the ranch. Jessica was happy to get there before dark, and Chili was happy to be released from the rope. When Will saw them riding onto the ranch, Jessica was relieved to see him come trotting out to meet them. He intuitively knew something was wrong. He grabbed the horse's reins while she dismounted, then handed the horse off to another ranch hand to unsaddle and rub down. At his encouragement, she and Will, with Chili following, went into his office to talk about the incident with more privacy. Will didn't want the rest of the ranch to get nervous until he better understood what was going on. He handed her a hot cup of coffee and Jessica curled her fingers around it while bringing it up to her nose, breathing in the warm, damp aroma and closing her eyes. Chili curled up in front of the woodstove, letting out a great sigh of relief once settled.

While Jessica gave him a quick rundown as to what had happened, he took notes and then agreed that calling the Sheriff was the right move.

"You look whopped," Will said to her. "I'll drive you up to the house."

"Thanks, Will," she agreed. It wasn't so much the walk, as the encounter with the horse kidnapper that had left her feeling very unsettled. Once back at the house, she drifted off into a nap and slept for almost an hour with Chili close by.

They were both awakened by the sound of the doorbell, and a few minutes later, Dorothea quietly tapped on the bedroom door. "Excuse me, but Mr. Ron is here to see you. Should I send him away?" She looked questioningly at Jessica sitting up from her nap, blurry and rumpled.

Now that she'd slept a little, she was feeling better. She thanked Dorothea and asked her to tell Ron she'd be right out. She quickly cleaned up before going out to the great room to meet him. He stood in front of the fireplace, looking up at the beautiful painting of the Grand Canyon by Howard Turpening that hung there. As he turned at hearing her steps on the tiled hall, she was struck by how handsome he looked. Neat, with a blond ponytail, tanned, and fit, he wore a white linen shirt open at the collar with faded blue jeans. His blue eyes were striking in the fading evening light and Jessica had to hold herself away from the attachment she had read there.

"Ron," she said, letting her surprise show. "What in the world are you doing here?"

He walked toward her and stopped politely a few feet away. She was happy to see that he was keeping his promise about not pushing their friendship to something it shouldn't be.

"I brought you these," he said, bringing out a box she hadn't seen him carrying. 'These' were a pair of hiking boots she had lusted after the last time she was in the adventure shop where Ron worked. "They went on sale and with my employee discount, I had to buy them for you before someone else bought the last pair your size."

"Oh Ron, that's amazing!" She took the box, moved to the couch and immediately began to remove the shoes she had on. Ron dropped to his knees to help her. "That's okay, I can do it," she said. "Go ask Dorothea to bring whatever you want to drink and the checkbook. I can't believe you thought to pick them up for me. Thank you so much."

"If you're getting the checkbook for me, don't bother. I bought them as a belated wedding gift. I believe I missed the wedding and wanted to make up for it."

Jessica stopped what she was doing and stared at him for a few seconds. He had been wounded when she'd announced she and Alex were getting married, and refused to come to the small ceremony. She guessed this was his way of apologizing for his behavior.

"I appreciate your gift, Ron. And you have nothing to apologize for. In fact," she said with sudden inspiration, "I think I should take you to dinner at the Trading Post in thanks. I haven't had a real Navajo Taco in ages, and I'm sure Alex would approve if he were here. We'll ask

Emma and Will to go with us. It'll be fun." She bent back down and happily pulled on her new boots and began lacing them up.

Ron agreed to the dinner and Emma and Will joined them with enthusiasm. Jessica quickly ran out to the studio, closed everything down, and set the alarm. The four of them drove down to Cameron in her Discovery, laughing and talking about anything and everything. It felt good to be out with friends, forgetting her problems at least for one evening.

In the middle of the meal, Ron suddenly decided to make a toast to Jessica as the best damn artist in Arizona. She suspected he was a few sheets to the wind but in good humor accepted the compliment. Just as Ron reached over and gave her a quick hug and a kiss on the cheek, a flash went off in their face.

Standing by their table was the same dark-haired newswoman who had been hounding Jessica ever since Alex's arrest. With her was a scruffy photographer still holding the camera with its garish flash as if he were about to take another picture. Jessica sat there open-mouthed with shock.

"So, Mrs. Dawson, would you like to comment on who this handsome gentleman might be? Have you already given up on your husband and decided you need to pave the way for your next marriage?" Jessica could feel her face flame with embarrassment. Will was the only one thinking. He stood up and ordered the woman to leave the table. A Native American waitress hovered close by, but she didn't look as if she knew exactly what to do. Will got directly in the reporter's face and started walking toward her, forcing the woman to back up to the door of the restaurant while throwing rude questions at Jessica. The photographer followed in their wake, all the time snapping pictures of Will herding the woman out of the room.

Suddenly, a man came out of nowhere and forcefully grabbed both the woman and the photographer's arm, escorting them from the room and speaking to them in a quiet voice that none of them at the table could hear. The man was the Native American bartender from the topless club, the guy in the red ball cap from the Hotevilla Kachina dance that had followed her, scaring her half out of her wits! Now he was here saving her from a rude and insulting newsperson. She sat there almost as stunned by that as she had been about the reporter. Who the hell was this guy? Did he have a job at the Trading Post during the day as a bouncer or something?

Will had come back to the table, quiet and angry. Everyone was silent in the wake of the incident and Jessica bent back over her cup of coffee too embarrassed to say anything.

"Geez, Jessica, I'm sorry," Ron said to her. "What a jerk! Everyone will know it's a lie if she prints any of that crap. Besides, you can sue her for defamation of character. She can't hurt you."

But everyone there knew better. If the picture of her and Ron kissing were to be printed, it would certainly hurt them. While Alex's political career was on the skids with the arrest, Jessica still didn't want to compromise the family any further with her simple friendship with Ron.

They decided to cut the meal short and head back to the ranch. Will asked for the check and they all left the dining room, with him paying while Ron and Emma made a pit stop. Jessica went out into the large gift shop to wait, carefully looking around to make sure there were no more reporters.

"Hold on," Will told her, "I'll check the parking lot before you go out there." Emma came out of the women's room and went with Will to make sure there were no more surprises awaiting them outside.

Ron came out of the men's room looking a little tight-lipped and angry. "What is it?" Jessica asked him.

"Nothing," he said as he grabbed her elbow and escorted her through the gift shop to the door.

"Ron," Jessica said, pulling her arm from his grasp. "What is it? I'm not going anywhere until you tell me." She stopped dead in the middle of the floor and looked stubborn, waiting for his reply.

"That damn man who hauled off the reporter was lurking in the hall and followed me into the men's room," he told her with resignation. "He just told me to stay away from you."

Jessica just looked at him before saying, "You're kidding, right?"

"I'm dead serious," he said. The conversation was interrupted when Will returned to say the parking lot was clear and she could come out to the car. He took her arm and walked her across the pavement to the Discovery with Ron following. "And he wasn't kidding," Ron went on to say. 'Do you know him?"

Jessica thought for a moment, trying to put together the connection, but she finally gave up and said, "I've seen him around," she said vaguely. She decided to keep to herself the chase at Hotevilla, and the fact that she had seen him in the topless place in Flagstaff, at least until she could speak to the sheriff. Maybe he was connected to Alex, or maybe he was a part of the horse kidnappers' crew or something. Odd things were happening around her, and she needed to get clarity before involving Ron in the mess, plus it wasn't a good time to talk with others there to listen.

They drove back to the ranch with Will at the helm, and the mood was much more subdued than when they'd left earlier for dinner. Jessica resented the fact that the reporter could have such an impact on everyone's disposition. After they arrived back at the house, Ron gave his goodbyes, and Jessica thanked him again for the boots before he drove off down the dirt road toward the highway. She smiled as the small taillights of his Jeep disappeared into the night. He really was a nice man.

Will left for his house down the hill, and Emma said goodnight before going off to her own room. Jessica stopped in the kitchen to make a cup of hot tea and then headed back out to her studio. She was a little keyed up from the incident in the restaurant and she wanted to do a little sitting meditation to quiet her mind about the crazy evening before going to bed.

When she got to the old adobe building, she was shocked to see that the door was open, so the alarm was shut off and there were lights on in the dark of the evening. She hesitated thinking she should call Will on her cell, but decided to quietly investigate first. She cautiously stepped in the room and stopped on the threshold, her foot making a small crunching noise from the sand still sticking to her boots.

Dorothea turned and jumped back with a startled look on her face, mixed with what Jessica thought was guilt. She had been standing in front of the beehive fireplace with her hand resting on a small mural of a man and his donkey done on tile that had been grouted into the adobe wall. A trim of a darker turquoise-colored tile framed the piece, which looked as if it had been done in the 1950s. When Jessica entered the room, Dorothea had jerked her hand away from the tile.

"What are you doing here?" Jessica asked. From the very beginning, she had made it clear that no one was allowed into her studio unless given permission. She was very protective of her work, and was worried someone might damage artwork that had a deadline. Usually the staff was allowed in to clean only when she was there.

"Oh, excuse me, Mrs. Dawson," replied Dorothea. "I thought I saw lights through the window and knew you were gone. I just came to investigate and it turned out to be Juan, out chasing a dog. I guess the light from his flashlight reflected through the windows, and from the other side it looked as if someone was in here." She smiled and walked across the room to the door. "It appears that everything is in order, so I'll just go."

"How did you get in?" Jessica asked her. "I locked and set the alarm before we left for dinner."

Dorothea looked at her in surprise and shrugged. "It wasn't locked when I arrived. Are you sure you locked it?"

Jessica searched her face for any trace of duplicity, but Dorothea looked back at her with a clear brow. Jessica roamed the room but found nothing out of place. She stopped at her drawing board, looked at the work that awaited her there, and then turned away. She shrugged and replied, "I guess I didn't. Thanks for checking on it." She turned and saw that the woman was already half out the door.

"No problem. I was on my way home anyway. Goodnight, I'll see you in the morning." She gave that odd little suffering smile just before turning and walking with purpose across the flagstone patio in the direction of the small house she and her husband occupied on the ranch.

Jessica turned back to the Casa Grande drawing on her board and realized that she needed to finish the project very soon. The deadline was looming in front of her, and she had been so distracted she'd been neglecting it. She promised herself that she'd sit down first thing the next morning and complete it.

Now, however, she sat down to begin her meditation. Suddenly she saw her situation clearly for the first time. Here she was, rich, living at a beautiful ranch with a handsome husband who appeared to love her. Friends around her who cared for her, her every whim was provided for, and she still was unhappy. She remembered reading that the Buddha said that all beings were suffering and that enlightenment was a way out of suffering. She got comfortable on her cushion and began her breathing exercises before relaxing into meditation. She wanted enlightenment!

An hour later, when she was finished, she decided that she'd have to talk to her agent Gary, about her schedule. She had been lax in her work lately because of all the things that had been going on in her life. As her mind crawled over what had taken place the last few weeks, she came to a decision. Until she and Alex got through all this mess, she needed to tell Gary that she would have to lighten her workload. She was sure he'd understand. With determination, she sat down and picked up her brush. She had about another hour of work, and the piece would be finished, so she decided not to wait until morning. Then, tomorrow she'd book a flight to San Francisco and visit Gary face to face to let him know her decision, delivering the artwork in person.

An hour and a half later, Jessica had completed the painting, and was shutting up the studio, planning to head to the main house and bed. Chili stood up from her basket by the fireplace and stretched with a large yawn. Blinking up at Jessica, she stood waiting for some attention.

Jessica turned and walked across the room, turning off lights as she went, and paused at the door. She thought again about how the housekeeper had gotten into the studio when she was sure she had locked and set the alarm. The image of the woman's jerk of surprise and guilt played itself once more in Jessica's mind, and she knew there had been something odd about her reaction. To Jessica it just didn't read right.

She walked over to the fireplace and studied the little mural that Dorothea had been touching when she'd first arrived. In the dim light, she was just able to see the painting. A man wore a sombrero and baggy clothes and struggled with a stubborn mule loaded high with supplies. Jessica studied the piece and then ran her hand over the painting. It was smooth and cold, the tiles around the outside shiny and slick to the touch.

Suddenly, her finger met something on the left edge of the tile. She tilted her head and saw a tiny wire that had been bent like a loop, its other end disappearing into the grout that held the tile in place. She took her fingernail and flicked the wire, thinking it was left in error, a piece of chicken wire used to reinforce the mortar perhaps.

Smoothly and quietly, the picture swung away from the wall, and behind it was a hidden cubbyhole. Jessica stood there stunned with surprise. She thought about how it had probably been built to hide money and jewelry when the house was first constructed. Now, to Jessica's further surprise, it held a book.

She carefully removed the book from its hidden shelf and tilted it toward the light. The title read, 'The Journal of Rachel Dawson'. Jessica stood frozen.

She walked backward until her legs met the coffee table and ended up sitting down with a thump. The journal was a rich blue with a warm cream label in the shape of a rectangle, perfectly centered on the cover. The title was embossed into the label, so Jessica knew Rachel had either gone somewhere to have it made for her, or it had been a gift. The book was held closed by two long, pale ribbons that looked worn from heavy use.

Of course she'd have to read it. Any woman in her place would do the same. Still, she wondered if she really wanted to know more than she already knew about Rachel. She wondered if the book held the secret to exactly what happened the night she'd died and more importantly, if Alex had played a role.

With determination, Jessica got up and latched the door of the hiding place. She motioned Chili outside and closed the studio door behind her, this time making sure she set the alarm. The two of them then headed for the house, tired from the long day, and anxious to find some rest. Tomorrow, she'd find the time to read Rachel's journal, perhaps taking it with her to San Francisco. And the question she'd ask herself just before she fell asleep was: had Dorothea known the journal was hidden behind that little mural?

Chapter 19: Shadowy People

Monte Vista Ranch, Northern Arizona

The sound of her cell phone woke Jessica from a deep sleep. She was so groggy she'd barely raised the phone to her ear when the rings stopped and there was blissful silence. Looking at the number, she saw it was her agent. He left a message asking if she was up for a badly needed trip to California for a book signing on a project she had illustrated two years before. It fit in with her plans.

She lay still under the covers, thinking about the day ahead. She knew a trip to San Francisco would be good for her, and Alex had agreed over the phone last night that she needed the break from work until they were able to at least get him home on bail.

The frustration and worry about Alex's situation had become enormous, and her thoughts often tried to run in circles, leaving her angry and confused. While he expressed the fact that he was just as frustrated, in truth he seemed rather calm considering his fate. Sometimes she felt trapped by her situation. Should she have married Alex after knowing him for only three months? She even sometimes resented how that impulsive decision had put her in this unreal role of a wronged woman. She knew Alex should have talked to her about his first wife, but also understood how difficult it had been for him. She wanted more than anything to believe in him, and in their love for each other. But it was getting harder.

The trip to California was uneventful, and Gary was almost too understanding. The book signing had a marginal turnout and Jessica had a nagging sensation that he was feeling sorry for her. Pity, that was all she needed, she thought the next morning as she sat in the airport waiting for her flight back to Arizona. With Alex in jail, her uncertainty about his guilt, and all the things that were happening in her life, Jessica couldn't help but feel completely ragged around the edges.

Standing up with a sudden decision, she jumped up and trotted toward the airport door, her rolling suitcase pulled behind her. She hadn't done anything impulsive for ages. Now, she'd decided to take a day for herself and instead of flying back to Arizona, visit a retreat a few miles up the coast just north of the city. She had a brief moment of guilt but squashed it with a call to Dorothea so anyone looking for her would know she was delayed in California. How would they know it wasn't business?

She found the number for *Eslan*, a place she used to frequent when single, and she had to beg them to work her in. Here, the name Dawson meant nothing, and they barely remembered her since she hadn't visited in more than a year.

She had a massage and then went to the hot spring bath setting on the edge of a cliff overlooking the ocean. Her luck held and there was no one else there, so she felt safe and relaxed while soaking in the hot water and coastal silence. After rinsing off, she returned to her room, wrapped herself in full-length white cotton robe and sat outside on her private deck high above the ocean. The day was an unusually mild October day with a hazy sun and a light breeze. She sat there so long, letting her mind drift from thought to thought until she finally relaxed for the first time in months.

Later she joined a meditation group for an hour in the streamside meditation roundhouse, then returned to her room to fall asleep to the sound of a gentle autumn breeze blowing in the French doors, honey-colored sheers billowing into the room. When she awoke, the sun was setting on the ocean, and the evening had cooled. She slipped into white slacks and sweaters, realizing that it was as if she were wearing someone else's clothes. She was years away from that woman who lived on a ranch in Arizona with a new husband who might have killed his first wife. She was an unknown woman, someone who had no name and lived only in this moment, in this place. Time had stopped for her.

She went out on the small deck outside her room, and sat down on her prayer cushion, doing a practice meant to remove obstacles, using her mala to accumulate the mantra. It was peaceful and helped to fill her with inner strength. After she finished, she sat still, quieting her mind, centering her focus on her breathing, stretching the meditation to an hour. A peace descended and stayed with her throughout the rest of the evening.

After, she poured a small glass of wine and sipped it slowly, not rushing the moment. She thought long about what she should do, watching the waves down on the beach below her in the dusk. It was hard not to think about just bailing out of the situation and moving back to California. She could pick up her life here again; her circle of friends still wanted her to return anyway. There was even an old boyfriend or two waiting in the wings. The Tibetan Buddhist temple in Oakland was a beautiful temple, and the members were really kind there. She had once been a part of that circle before moving to Arizona.

Now, sitting quietly, looking out on the ocean and contemplating, she realized she needed to see it through and stay in Arizona. Because of Alex she had become another person with a different life that she had learned to love. She wanted it back with Alex there. He was dear to her in a way no one else had ever been. She wanted to fight for the relationship.

She tried several times to reach Alex but couldn't get through. So she drifted to a small restaurant that overlooked the ocean and ate seafood gumbo rich with tomato cream sauce. She slept so well that night that morning seemed to come almost before she closed her eyes, and refreshed and rejuvenated, she caught the next flight into Phoenix, looking forward to returning to her life on the mountain, her resolve to stay in Arizona and work it out with her husband firmly in her mind.

The ranch was quiet when she arrived. No cars parked outside, the sun was shining and a light breeze was ruffling the large yellow leaves of the cottonwoods in front of the house. The air was dry, unlike the California coastal breezes. It felt good to be back.

She brought her small bag in and left it on the floor of the bedroom, heading for her studio and its sanctuary. Chili met her in the courtyard, her tail wagging so hard even her butt swayed, and after Jessica gave her a long hug, the two of them walked down the flagstone path to her studio.

Coming to the old adobe's door, Jessica punched in the security code as she had done so many times before, and this time found that, once again, the alarm was not set. However, the door was closed, and when Jessica opened it, she froze where she stood.

The studio had been turned upside down. Every book on her shelves now lay strewn on the floor. Her files and drawers joined the debris, the contents half in, half out. Her brushes and paints, inks and charcoals were scattered everywhere atop drawing tablets and canvas. The cushions on the couch had been flung aside and she could see through the doorway that the little kitchenette had not been spared. Her meditation corner was pulled apart, her cushion ripped open and on its side against the wall. The altar was spared, but everything else had been tossed upside down.

The first thing she did was pull out her phone and call Will. The peace she had attained during her stay in California helped her to stay calm and focused. She told Will what she had found and he instructed her not to touch anything. He'd call the sheriff and be there in a few minutes with some help.

Jessica and Chili slowly entered the room, the dog cautiously sniffed around the debris, intuitive to Jessica's concern. She carefully stepped her way through the things on the floor, looking around her in shock. She stopped and turned full circle in the middle of the room, speechless. That was when she saw the other person.

Rachel, Alex's first wife, was sprawled on the floor with her back against the wall! Her head had dropped onto her chest, limp and still. There was no blood, and Jessica could see that this ghost was not a ghost at all. Just as she had suspected during the horse kidnapping, this Rachel was odd, large and sloppy.

Standing there in shock, she stared with disbelief. What was she doing there? Was she the one who had done this damage to the studio? She again looked around the room, and that was when she noticed the tile mural on the fireplace had been left open, the shelf empty. She remembered that she had taken the journal with her to San Francisco; so far she had only gotten around to reading the first few weeks' worth of entries. It was now safe in her suitcase, lying on the floor of their bedroom where she had dropped it when arriving back from the airport. Rachel had probably opened the hidden cubby, looking for her journal.

Turning back to look down at the blond woman on the floor dressed in jeans and a white shirt, ponytail now in disarray, Jessica felt a small surge of determination. As she moved toward her carefully, she suddenly realized that the notorious Rachel was actually alive and laying on her studio floor! So she didn't really die that night out on Blue Moon Bench, and her husband didn't murder her!

As she got closer, she now saw that there was an empty bottle of whiskey, and from the smell she could tell just who had consumed the whole thing. Bending down, she tilted to look into the face of the beloved Rachel. This was a moment she knew would never leave her.

Jessica went utterly still, a small sound escaping with a breath of further disbelief. Standing up straight, she grabbed the ponytail and pulled. The hair came off to reveal an unconscious... Dorothea, her housekeeper! It wasn't Rachel at all. It was Dorothea dressed like Rachel! The horse, the clothes, and the wig had made the deception believable!

Standing there with the blond wig dangling from her hand and a drunk Dorothea at her feet, Jessica slumped. How could this be? Just then she heard a noise, and when she turned, Will and Ralph appeared in the doorway.

"Oh God," Ralph said as soon as he saw Dorothea, recognizing his wife immediately. "I'm so sorry Mrs. Dawson. We've been under some stress lately and she's taken to drinking again." The discarded bottle still lay next to Dorothea. "I can promise you that she'll be very remorseful in the morning."

The sound of voices had probably gotten through the drunken haze. Dorothea raised her head with a bobble and peered up at her husband, her short gray hair smashed and sweaty from the wig. She stood up carefully with Ralph's help, leaning heavily against the wall, and stared at the three of them. The wig in Jessica's hand caught her attention. She stared at it for a few minutes as if puzzled by it, and then reached up to discover it was missing from her head. Jessica then saw blurry comprehension dawn in her eyes, and she lunged for the wig awkwardly, accidentally swatting it from Jessica's hand, sending it into a spin across the tiled floor until it hit a pile of rubble.

"Shiiit!" she said under her breath, trying to stay upright. Suddenly she turned toward Jessica pointing her finger. "You were sup… supposed to be… back yesterday," she told Jessica with a drunken slur.

"Excuse me?" Jessica said, stepping away from the smell of her breath.

"E'cuze you? E'cuze you?" she yelled. "There'z no 'cuse for you!

You stupid bitch. You were supposed… to... to… be afraid… and… and… you were supposed to leave the ranch. Stupid…," the rest of the sentence was said with such a garble it was impossible to make any sense of it.

Jessica suddenly got it. Dorothea had been stalking Jessica disguised as Rachel apparently hoping to scare her away. She glanced over at Will and Ralph and saw that they were just as stunned as she was.

"Dorothea," Jessica said, "I don't understand. What did I ever do to you? Why would you want me to leave?"

"Tell her Ralph," Dorothea answered, not even looking at her skinny husband. "Tell her… howsee... shhe asks too many ques… too many ques…" Before she could finish her sentence, she slumped to the floor, Ralph catching her just in time before she hit her head.

"Okay, okay," Ralph said to her gently. "Let's go ahead and go home. You can tell Jessica later. Right now we both need a cup of coffee." Ralph glanced over his thin shoulder with an apology. Will followed them out the door and Jessica could hear a brief discussion before she saw Dorothea and Ralph pass by the studio's window. Dorothea's larger frame made Ralph seem even smaller than usual, she had come to and was weaving and leaning on his helping arm.

Will came back into the room with a look of puzzlement on his suntanned face. He scratched his head and looked at Jessica. "Damnedest thing I ever saw," he said to her. "Well, I guess the mystery of yer Rachel ghost has been solved. Would'a never guessed, that's fer damn sure."

Jessica shook her head and hooked her hands into the back pockets of her jeans. "I don't quite understand why she was stalking me, but I believe it's a reason to dismiss her. I'm not sure I feel safe having her on the ranch." She looked back at Will.

He stood there a moment and then jammed his hat back on his head.

"S'pose yer right. Hate ta lose Ralph, but what she did wasn't right." He turned and headed for the door, pausing on the threshold. "I'll send some hands over to help with this mess," he gestured toward the things littering the floor. "You wanna tell Alex about Dorothea and Ralph?"

"Why don't you tell him?" Jessica asked. "It would be better coming from you since it has to do with ranch business. I don't want to get into the middle of it now." Jessica had always puzzled about why she preferred to call her Dorothea instead of the friendly nickname Dotty like the others. She decided that somewhere inside she never trusted Dorothea in some way.

"I noticed now and again she'd talk bad about you," Will looked at her kindly. "Seems you had reason enough to let her go even without this." He turned and began to leave, talking to her over his shoulder. "I'll call Alex and let him know. Think I'll wait to talk to Dorothea and Ralph. Best to leave some time fer her ta sober up. Figure she'll be purtty trashed, so I'll talk to 'em come mornin'." He gave her a wave as he turned down the flagstone path.

Jessica walked out onto the porch to wait for help to arrive from the barn. What a helluva week, she thought. It had all started with her horse being taken by who she now knew was Dorothea. She thought about the events of the past few months, trying to piece some things together.

Three ranch hands arrived before she came to any conclusions, and helped her put everything back in its place. There seemed to be nothing missing, and only a few things were broken. The damage could have been much worse, but the inconvenience was enough. Plus she wasn't going to forget soon that Dorothea had been stalking her for months, disguised as her husband's dead first wife. How bizarre.

When the studio was put back together a couple of hours later, Jessica thanked her help and headed back to the house. Emma was in the kitchen cooking something that smelled delicious. She had heard what had happened with Dorothea from Will, and she stepped in to cook dinner. Jessica was glad to have her company, and the two of them ate in peace at the kitchen nook, talking about Dorothea's weird behavior.

"When I first came out to the ranch," Emma told Jessica, "She told me that she hated how you always wanted to run things, that you were always asking her how to do everything when she wanted to run the show herself. I never imagined she disliked you this much though." She set down her wine glass and looked at Jessica. "Are you going to let her go?"

"I have to, Emma," Jessica answered. "She just doesn't need to be here. I'm sure they'll find a job somewhere else. Ralph will get a good recommendation from Will."

Jessica helped with the dishes and then said goodnight to Emma even though it was still early. She was anxious to get to her room so she could read the rest of Rachel's journal.

Closing the door to their room, Jessica removed the journal from her suitcase. She ran her palm over the smooth cover, admiring once again its beauty. She found a seat in the overstuffed chair, propping her feet on the ottoman and pulling a throw over her legs. Chili moved in a circle several times before settling with a sigh in her dog bed next to the chair, muzzle resting on her paws. Jessica settled in, ready to read the entire book, cover to cover.

She wondered how Dorothea had known about the cubby and why had she been looking for it? Did she know there was a journal? And why would Dorothea care about Rachel's journal anyway? She shook her head and pushed that aside for later. She needed to have time to think it through.

Jessica untied the ribbons that held the journal closed, and carefully opened the cover. She ran her fingers over the inside paper: marbled with swirls of green and blue paint, artistic and expensive. The journal pages themselves were made of paper with deckled edges, smooth and rich. She carefully untied them and opened the cover, running her fingers over the inside page. It was marbleized paper with swirls of blue and green that reminded Jessica of the ocean.

The first page of the journal was dated the year Rachel had died. Her handwriting had been beautiful and graceful, just like Jessica imagined the woman had been. It looked almost spidery. The entire book had been written in the same blue ink with a fine fountain pen, both items Jessica recognized from having seen them on Rachel's desk upstairs. The words flowed over page upon page of rich cream paper.

Jessica decided that she deserved to read this journal from cover to cover. This woman and her dead memory had made her life hell for the last several months. Jessica had every right to know just who Rachel was and how she had lived her life. Perhaps it would help her purge the mystery of Rachel from her life once and for all.

She dove into the world, as Rachel saw it, once again and set aside her feelings of discomfort for invading something so private. Like Jessica's own journal, it contained very personal thoughts and musings, never meant for a stranger's eye. Rachel seemed childish and immature in some of her thinking, romantic and greedy in others, all couched in intelligence. Emotionally immature, mentally skilled, in all of it, it was obvious that she'd been ready for a change in her life.

She wrote candidly about her relationship with Alex, obviously on the wane by the end, the affair with Mac and its meaning to her obviously important. The journal revealed how Mac had been paying for her drugs after Alex had refused, and covered how Mac stuck with her through her last visit to rehab. The baby had been a surprise, but one that Rachel and Mac guarded until they could obtain a divorce from Alex. It filled in some of the holes that Emma's story hadn't given. It was sad reading it from Rachel's view, especially the fact that she miscarried the baby a month before she died.

But the most shocking thing it revealed was about Mac paying for her drugs with the proceeds from the sale of artifacts, artifacts that he was selling through Heathcliff to pay off Rachel's drug debt. Artifacts that Mac had been taking from a cave, a cave full of gold and silver, a cave out on Blue Moon Bench. It seemed Rachel didn't really know its exact location, only that Mac depended on the riches in it to pay for her drug habit.

The journal slipped from Jessica's fingers as she sat in the chair, darkness settling on the room as the sun set outside. She could hear the gentle snore of her dog at her feet. She made no move to turn on the light. She sat, putting the pieces together, making the puzzle finally fit.

She tried to remember back when she'd been in the topless club overhearing a conversation Heathcliff was having with someone about artifacts. He said that Mac had stopped bringing him things when Rachel died, but now an older couple was bringing him something of the same quality, the same type. Gold, he said, and he may have even mentioned Asian. Could the older couple have been Dorothea and Ralph?

Jessica got up from the chair and walked to the window. Chili was still sleeping in her bed; a quiet night in the middle of chaos. The courtyard outside was lit by the moonlight, the trees ghostly and pale, colorless in the night.

Finally, a connection with Blue Moon Bench and Rachel, Jessica thought. There was no question that something about the cave and Mac had drawn her out there that night. It must have been important because Rachel had been giving a party. She'd had a lot of guests at the ranch the night she died, yet she'd left around midnight to drive out to Blue Moon Bench. Was she by herself? Had she gone there to meet Mac?

She tried to figure out how Dorothea and Ralph came into the whole thing. She knew they'd only given Heathcliff one gold artifact to sell because Heathcliff had said as much. Maybe they didn't know where the cave was then, or more pieces would have been sold. Maybe they had stolen the one piece from Mac. She wondered if they had even known there was a cave. She didn't even know for sure that Dorothea had known the journal was in the cubby. But what if she had found it while cleaning when the building had been a gardening shed? Maybe the artifact had been in the cubby, and it was the only piece they had.

Jessica shed her clothes, not even bothering to wash her face or brush her teeth. She crawled under the cold sheets of the empty bed, knowing what she had to do the next day. She felt the familiar warmth of Chili as the dog joined her, lying on the end of the bed. They both drifted off to sleep, Jessica dreaming of gold artifacts and shadowy people and a woman riding a black horse in the night.

Chapter 20: Free Falling

Blue Moon Bench, Navajo Reservation, Arizona

The day had a funny haze in the afternoon sky, almost as if a storm were brewing somewhere in the distance and hadn't quite gotten to Blue Moon Bench yet. The light was a weird yellow and the air was still and cold.

Jessica squatted under a mesquite tree, holding onto Chili's collar. In the distance, a jackrabbit was escaping from the two of them. He made no noise as he zigzagged across the desert, his speed his only protection from his predators.

Chili had stopped barking, but now she was whining and trying to pull away to go after the running animal. Jessica struggled to get the lease out of her daypack while hanging onto the dog's collar. She knew if she let go, Chili would be gone in a flash, and she didn't want to lose her to the Navajo reservation.

"Alright, girl," Jessica said to Chili. "Back on your leash. That jackrabbit doesn't need a spoiled cow-dog chasing him."

Before leaving the ranch that morning, Mac had shown up on the front porch looking terrible. After several attempts to make amends for having Alex arrested, he finally revealed the real reason for his visit. He wanted Rachel's journal!

Jessica had to smile to herself now. Nothing surprised her anymore. Of course he'd want the journal. It was evidence that showed he'd committed the crime of selling priceless artifacts, pieces that were on government land, making the offense a major federal crime with up to twenty years in prison.

Jessica had no idea how he had found out about the journal, and later she tried to guess who might have told him. There were several people on the ranch who knew and might have told him including Emma, Will and Dorothea.

She remembered that Will had gotten a call from a ranch in California just a few days after Dorothea and Ralph had been let go. The call was about employment confirmation for Ralph. So it appeared the two had already taken their profit from pawned gold and was working on a new life on the coast. Still, Dorothea may have told Mac about the journal before she left, wanting it back for them all.

Jessica had simply refused Mac's request for the journal, having already called Will the moment she'd seen his truck pull up in the driveway. She'd told Mac the journal, which was now safely with her in her daypack, was not his property. When Will arrived, she'd walked to her truck, thrown her pack in the back, and watched while Will escorted Mac's Toyota off the ranch, both trucks speeding down the road in a cloud of dust. She then drove off, headed for Blue Moon Bench and much-needed answers.

Jessica could understand how concerned Mac was. She had every intention of turning the journal over to the FBI, after she found the cave herself. From the sound of Rachel's journal, it wasn't just any cave. It was a cave filled with gold and silver artifacts that looked Asian in nature, a real anthropological find. Gold that had been left centuries ago by some wandering civilization, or perhaps a Spanish treasure trove stashed for later removal that never happened.

Jessica learned from the journal that the cave had not only yielded enough gold for Mac to pay Rachel's drug debt off, but could also promise a comfortable future for Rachel and Mac when they pulled off the planned disappearance that was apparently thwarted by Rachel's death.

Jessica was sure that the cave was the center of everything: the cause of Rachel's death, Alex's possible guilt, Dorothea's role and probably more. She was certain she would finally get some answers.

Once Jessica got Chili on the leash, and the jackrabbit had long disappeared in the brush, she and the dog continued toward an outcropping of rocks that had caught her attention on their last visit. As they walked, Jessica watched for any worn paths or openings around the monoliths that made up the outcropping.

The countryside around her was silent and smelled of damp earth and juniper. She felt the spring of tension inside of her start to relax. The only sounds were of the two of them, her hiking boots creating a muffled thump with each step, and Chili's claws sometimes scratching on rocks as she strained at the leash to the next rock, sniffing the ground for scents of rabbits gone by.

Coming out of the rocks a few minutes later, there were no new discoveries. They started down the small trail that was perhaps six feet wide in most places, narrowing to a couple of feet in others. It sloped down about two hundred feet, and dead-ended in front of the shallow cave she and Chili had explored on their last visit. As they made their way down the trail, a scatter of small stones showered down on them. They both looked up, but Jessica was sure it was just a small, scrambling animal of some sort and pulled Chili along the path.

They arrived at the cave entrance and the dog became over-excited about exploring. Jessica calmed her down, and then pulled out her flashlight so they could both see well in the gloom. The cave was shallow, as she remembered it, and after some scrambling and with the use of the light, she found a cubby hole to one side that she'd missed the first time.

It was about four feet deep and low enough that she had to crawl on all fours to enter. Inside she was surprised to find a clean metal trunk hidden under a heavy canvas tarp, and a sturdy-looking lock protecting the contents. Carefully searching the area, she found a hidden key and was able to unlock the trunk.

Inside the trunk, Jessica found an expensive collection of rock climbing gear. The equipment looked like the same kind Alex used to climb, and it was in good condition. She carefully closed the trunk, snapping the lock closed and re-draped the canvas tarp. Carefully returning the key to its hiding place, she decided it probably belonged to a Navajo who liked to climb as recreation here on the reservation, and left it here for convenience.

Jessica slipped on her rain jacket against the light rain that had started outside and then securely wrapped Chili's leash around her wrist. Discouraged that her investigation had been fruitless, they began the walk back up the trail. Once again a trickle of sand and small pebbles showered down on them, and this time she had a strange feeling that someone was above them. Both she and Chili stood perfectly still, listening for any other sounds, but soon moved on after hearing only the wind and a hawk far down the canyon.

Just before they reached the top of the trail, Jessica heard the angry buzz of a bee off to her right. She made a rapid swat at it and then tried to pick up their pace, wanting to reach the rim before it began to rain in earnest. Chili stopped on the trail, however, and lifted her head, her ears perked and listening. Jessica gave her leash a tug, and another buzz went by her ear, but this time closer, with a strange crack immediately after it.

Just as she realized it was a rifle shot, Chili let out a loud screaming yelp. Jessica whipped around in time to see the dog catapult into the air, jerking at the end of the leash hard enough to tumble over the edge of the cliff!

Jessica hit the ground to duck away from any more bullets and then looked around her. She could see no one above them. Chili was now hanging suspended over the canyon with nothing but Jessica's stranglehold on the leash standing between her and a plunge to death. She crawled over to the edge while trying to keep the leash secure. Poor Chili was crying horribly and twisting in the air, her harness firm and strong. Jessica was relieved to see that the dog was suspended above a small ledge right below them.

"Hold on girl," she said, trying to reassure the struggling dog. She began an earnest prayer quietly under her breath, tears of compassion spontaneously welling up in her eyes.

The leash painfully cut into her wrist as she tried to lower Chili onto the ledge. Lying on her stomach, she extended her arm as far as possible and still came up short, dust and dirt invading her eyes and mouth. Her arm was beginning to give out from holding all the weight of the wildly squirming dog, but she knew Chili might be hurt worse if she let go. Even if she landed safely, there was no guarantee the wounded dog wouldn't run off the edge of the canyon in confusion without Jessica there to stop her.

She forgot the shooter and edged further over the lip of the canyon, sweat popped out on her forehead and she extended the reach of the leash now growing slippery with perspiration. The sound of the dog in pain was almost too much for Jessica as she strained to stretch over the rim further wanting Chili's landing to be soft. She suddenly felt herself start to slide headfirst into the canyon, tears blurring her sight.

Right before she went over the lip of the ledge, she tried to grab at a small tree that had rooted next to her, wanting to save the dog from a hard landing at any cost. The tree couldn't hold her weight and she went over sideways, landing hard right next to Chili, her legs dangling over the edge. Her shoulder took all the impact and the pain was so intense she almost blacked out.

Lying for several seconds, stunned, Chili's pitiful whine made its way into the fog of her own pain. She looked over and grabbed the collar to prevent the wounded dog from moving, the ledge only about four feet wide, about twelve feet below the rim with very little room to maneuver. The vast space of the canyon was simply an inch away, and it gave her intense vertigo. She immediately sat up and pulled herself away from the edge as much as possible. Leaning her back against the canyon wall while still holding Chili's collar, she closed her eyes, continually repeating an auspicious mantra that always calmed her, perfect faith rooted in ancient practice. A miracle was needed.

Once she gained a little space in her mind, she was able to give Chili a closer look and saw that the dog was lying on her side, her breathing rapid and shallow. Inspecting Chili's wound, she was rewarded with a piercing yowl as the dog tried to jerk away. The bullet had gone through the fleshy part of the right hind leg and exited cleanly. She soothed the dog into laying still, her compassion for her pet enormous, and she was calm with the conviction that it would not end here. She just wouldn't let it.

"Shhh. It's okay, Chili. Don't worry," she said, petting her ears back, planting a kiss on her forehead, her own tears mingling with dust and blood. She suddenly grew still wondering who had shot them, and if they would shoot again.

She knew her shoulder was bad, but the car wasn't far, and if she had to, she could probably tie the small dog into her jacket and pull the whole bundle up to the trail with a rope she always carried. She saw the cliff up to the trail was negotiable with a challenging climb, but doable. If the gunshot was an accident, she could do that, but if it was intentional, the shooter would probably still be up there, waiting. That was something she didn't want to imagine.

She carefully eased her daypack off her sore shoulder, all the time keeping an eye above her, her knees pulled up to her chest. She couldn't think of anyone who'd want to kill her and so hoped it was just an accident, a hunter gone rogue. Unzipping the pack, she looked for the small medical kit she always carried with her, awkwardly making a bandage to help stop Chili's bleeding. She was afraid the dog would die when she saw the extent of the wound and tears continued to roll down her cheeks as she finished adjusting the cotton gauze under a pink bandana.

It began to do more than mist, and Jessica knew that the dog would probably go into shock. She looked above them and saw there was a small overhang that would serve as some cover from the storm, so she painfully shifted Chili so she was up against the canyon wall affording her some protection under the rock outcrop. The overhang was so low she had to stay on her knees to remove her jacket carefully, avoiding her shoulder. She wanted to cover Chili for warmth until she'd made a plan for escape. As she moved to pull the coat off, she looked up and saw a face above her, looking down at them from the rim. To her astonishment, it was Mac! She felt sick to her stomach.

He had moved back away from the ledge, saying nothing to her even though they had seen each other! And with him disappeared the muzzle of a rifle!

Without warning, the sound of the angry bee whizzed by her ear, and this time she heard the gun's report almost immediately. The sound of the bullet making a ricochet off the rock next to her knee was enough to tell her to pull back into the overhang.

She ducked and quickly laid her coat on what little ground there was. She lifted Chili's shoulders with her good arm, and carefully slid the dog onto half the coat, bringing the other half over her for warmth. She felt a tiny rumble in the earth beneath her, and she went pale with fear.

Noise above her caused her eyes to travel along the rim and finally a movement in the shrubbery gave Mac's hiding place away. She quickly curled herself up against the cliff wall leaning over the prone dog, keeping out of Mac's range, trying to buy herself some time to think. After a few seconds, she carefully leaned forward to look below her, wondering if there might be an escape route there. Again the rifle rang out, but this time the bullet hit the rock immediately next to her head.

She quickly leaned back, but not before she'd gotten a good enough look to see there was no escape below. In fact, it was a straight drop into the frighteningly deep canyon. She had to fight the sudden dizziness that overwhelmed her. She imagined falling over the edge, and felt nausea rising in her throat. She closed her eyes fighting vertigo, and swallowed.

Sitting still under the cover of the cliff, she tried to gather her scattered thoughts. They were miles from anywhere, and no one would consider her missing for hours. She usually spent at least a couple of hours when she went hiking, and the only people who knew she was here were Will and Emma.

The raindrops that had fallen on her earlier ran down her forehead and dripped down into her eyes, and she closed them against the sting of dirt and tears. Wiping them with her sleeve, she suddenly noticed her daypack lying on the ledge next to her. Her cell phone! It was in her pack. She had no idea if she had reception, but it was worth a try.

She dug in the pack and found the phone. Pulling it out, she discovered she had service, but it was weak. She hit Will's number as her situation came to her. Sitting on a tiny ledge of the Grand Canyon, a killer above her, and she below trying to call someone on one little cell phone, the only connection to survival. That and her faith that help would come. What would she say? Hello Will. How are you? Oh, by the way, Mac has shot Chili and is now trying to kill me. Can you come and get me? I'm on the third ledge to the left. She knew she was in real danger. How would he find her?

She realized she was close to hysteria. There was no answer on the other end, and so continuing to do mantra, she dialed the office and was relieved when he answered almost immediately.

"Will, I need help," Jessica said to him in a whisper. The reception was spotty, and she wasn't sure he could hear everything she was saying. She quickly relayed the information, knowing her life depended on the phone's reliability. She started to cry at the end of her dissertation, and his response was broken up.

Suddenly, the reception shifted and Will's strong, confident voice came to her, loud and clear, "I'll call the Tuba City Sheriff on my own cell. Don't hang up, okay?" he said, and then he waited until he received an affirmative answer from her. "They can locate you by your phone's signal through GPS." She was so relieved to hear that she let out a loud gasp. She could hear him talking on the other phone, giving them time to locate her as Mac fired one more time. She almost fainted with fear and scooted further into the cliff wall behind her.

"Okay, Jessica," she barely heard him say. "They've got you located. You can't hang up, or they will lose the signal. I'm going to head your way too. It would be good if you… stay low and try to… sight. You… talking to him. It could buy us some time."

"Okay," Jessica whispered back, "I'll try. Please hurry. Please." Jessica realized that Will was no longer listening, had gotten in his truck, and was driving. She gave a curse under her breath and once again wiped her tears with a sleeve, taking a deep breath. She knew she had to be strong and keep a clear mind. She grasped the phone close to her breast.

"Mac?" she yelled, "Mac? I know it's you up there. Can we talk?"

There was no immediate response and again, Jessica raised her voice. "Mac. Chili has been hit with one of your bullets. She's bleeding and I'm frightened for her. Can you help us? Please?" She hoped it would buy them some time to engage him in conversation.

"Help you!" a voice of indignation shouted back to her, "Why would I help you, you bloody fool!"

"Why? What have I done? I don't understand. I'm your friend."

Mac's voice came back to her from above. "You're no friend of mine, ducky. You have Rachel's journal, and I don't want it to go to the authorities. It's that simple. You give me the journal, and you don't go over the edge. It's your choice."

Of course, now she knew why he was here. It was the journal he wanted. Maybe his shooting at them was simply to scare her! But did he know she had the journal in her pack? And she couldn't be sure that after giving him the journal, he wouldn't still want her dead. After all, she had already read its contents.

There was a sudden rustling noise and she realized that he was standing directly above her when a shower of dirt came down in front of her from the overhang. Then there was silence.

Jessica began to wonder about Mac. Now that she was seeing him in a different way, she wondered if he'd be capable of murder, specifically Rachel. Did he have a motive? Maybe he got tired of supporting her drug habit and all that goes with something like that.

"Mac, what happened the night she died? Did you come out here to meet her and something went wrong?"

He had moved to the side and was actually standing at an angle to the overhang now. From there, Jessica was sure he was able to see Chili's tail and her own curled-up leg, both unprotected.

"Mac," Jessica tried again, "I promise I'll never tell a soul. I understand if there was an accident. I know that you didn't really mean to kill her. It's okay." His sudden, explosive response caught her unprepared.

"NO!" he screamed at her, his cry echoing over the entire Grand Canyon, bouncing off the steep walls of rock. There came a blast of gunfire from him. Four bullets showered down onto the ledge, two of them ricocheting into the area where she and Chili lay. One hit her backpack right next to her hand. She let out a scream and dropped the cell phone, watching as it skittered across the ledge and over the edge, spinning into space before falling away.

When the gunshots were fired, Chili had raised her head and her eyes rolled in their sockets from fear. She whimpered and tried to struggle up, but Jessica laid her body protectively over the dog, and put a comforting hand on her head and stroked her ears. She was stunned and terrified, afraid to move, holding her breath, pulling her legs in to remove them from his line of sight, continuing to pray with her eyes closed.

"I have found witnesses, ducky. Blokes that saw Alex out here the night and time she died, and he flippin' lied, telling the FBI he was at that conference. The bloody man is guilty!" He was so close that Jessica could hear his frustrated breathing and knew he was getting more agitated by the moment.

"He was jealous of me, angry that Rachel loved me and not him! What more do you need to know?" His last words were almost a scream. It was obvious that he truly believed in Alex's guilt and therefore confirmed his own innocence in Jessica's mind.

Again he fired onto the ledge in anger. Again the bullets ricocheted around under the overhang. This time one of them ripped into her cheek as it passed. She screamed and reached up to find the sting was like fire when her fingers found the wound. It seemed to be just a graze, but her hand came away with a good amount of blood. She realized she was about to hyperventilate from fear as white spots danced before her eyes. She disciplined herself to breathe evenly and regularly, the spots beginning to disappear, her faith and meditation coming into use beyond anything she had imagined.

"Jessica?" he screamed at her. She lay very still, afraid that he might begin firing his rifle once more, knowing that he had gone mentally over the edge. She heard some clicking noises and realized he was reloading the gun. Sweating in her heavy clothes and covered in goosebumps from a chill, she was afraid her own body was going into shock.

Mac began scrambling around on the rim, and from the sound she thought that he was maneuvering himself into a position to drop onto the small outcrop. "You can't die damn you!" She heard him say, "I need that journal."

The dizziness once again assailed her when she realized that he could easily dispose of both their bodies since there was a several thousand-foot drop directly over the edge. If he found the journal in her pack, that would be the end. She imagined a sheepherder walking the canyon months from now, finding her and Chili's white-boned skeletons. She convulsed at the thought. She had to clear her mind if she was to save them both. She could not allow the negative thoughts to assail her. Instead she imagined them safe at home and well.

Jessica positioned her head so that she could pretend to be unconscious. She thought she could use the element of surprise in her favor if Mac did drop onto the ledge. It wasn't much of a plan, but it was all she had.

Her heart was pounding with fear when he suddenly landed on the ledge with a shower of rocks and dirt, just as she had feared, his feet hitting only about two feet from them. They both lay very still, Jessica holding her breath and leaving her face slack. She closed her eyes completely; sure he would look her over closely at first.

The only noise on the ledge was the crunch of his boots, and his labored breathing. She watched through her lashes and realized that he had used a rope to repel down, but in his hurry he failed to notice the rope now dropped behind him and he was no longer tied off, the end now dangling after his descent.

Jessica, tense and ready to strike in defense if necessary, imagined what he was seeing as he studied them. Chili under the blood-soaked coat, her slumped against the rocks, and a huge pool of Chili's blood on the ground. She also realized the wound on her face was now bleeding from the warm course of blood that ran down her neck.

With no warning, Mac bent over, and reaching for Chili's tail he started pulling the dog to the edge. Chili was screeching out her pain while her eyes were rolling back so far into her head, the whites showed. With ears down and teeth barred with fear, she tried to bite him to protect herself.

It was that small animal's pain that suddenly snapped Jessica awake. Fear for them all overcame any other emotions. She had no consideration for her own safety, just for the defenseless dog that depended on her, and the man standing in front of her, who had once been her friend, now trying to kill them both.

Mac was still bent over when she got up on her knees and pushed him away, while she slid the coat with Chili on it back under the overhang, using her bad arm. The pain shot across her back and neck, causing her to gasp. In his surprise, Mac let go of the dog instinctively and jerked out of her grasp and stood up. She fell back on her butt away from the edge, Chili whining, but once again safe next to her. She scrambled back under the overhang to get as far away from Mac as possible, pulling Chili with her.

Then, before she could realize what was happening, she felt a rumble beneath them. The impact of the dog, woman and finally a large man, had been too much for the unstable ledge. She watched in horror while the cliff where Mac was standing suddenly broke away.

Jessica saw him go over as if it were in slow motion. One moment he was crouched down looking at her, the next, he went down as if on a slow-moving elevator, the look of comprehension terrible on his face. Just before he disappeared over the edge, he made a valiant grab for the rope, but it was too late. She was too terrified to move or scream, frozen with fear.

After, there was perfect silence except for the whistle of a breeze that blew over the lip of the canyon. It had all happened so fast, he hadn't even had the time to cry out. Jessica carefully gathered the dog in her arms, tears mixing with blood and the rain. Bringing the damp jacket up around them, head bent over the small body, she sobbed and prayed. That was how the Sheriff and a team of rescuers found her, when her prayers were finally answered minutes later.

Chapter 21: That's a Cute Angle

Flagstaff Medical Center, Arizona

"It was just pretense," Agent Johnson said. "He was never really arrested, Mrs. Dawson. The night Rachel died, he was with one of our agents out by Blue Moon Bench, but nowhere near where her car was found deserted."

Alex looked down at her hand and gently brought it to his lips. "Please forgive me for not telling you sooner. I know you've suffered, but believe me, it was necessary." He turned to the agent and thanked him for coming. They shook hands and Agent Johnson saluted her before exiting the cafeteria with a slight bow, leaving them to talk it out.

Jessica felt numbed and knew she was having a hard time getting her mind to shift perspective. She shook her head as if to clear it and squinted her eyes. Staring at Alex, she tried to imagine that what she was hearing was the truth. "Wait, you mean, you were with an FBI agent at the time of Rachel's death?" She had to be very clear on that.

"Yes," was all he said?

Jessica looked at him in silence and then spoke. "And so… why did they have to arrest you or pretend to?" she asked.

"Because Mac kept insisting that he had witnesses who saw me that night out there. Well, he did. But I was out there trying to investigate something that involved HIM. We couldn't very well tell him that. So when he kept insisting and then found another witness to testify that I wasn't at the conference I was supposed to be attending that weekend, they had no choice. Mac had started to get suspicious of the agency for NOT arresting me when the evidence was so compelling. So… they arrested me. Or pretended to."

Jessica absorbed the whole story, trying to understand the entire implications. "And so…" she said, "the entire time I was trying to find out what really happened to Rachel just to free you was for nothing?" Her voice began to rise in volume as she spoke. "You were never arrested. I didn't need to ask all the questions I did, or take all the chances I did. You were never arrested?" She had risked her life for nothing. She had almost fallen into the Grand Canyon and died herself, for nothing! "Where have you been all this time, Alex?" she asked him with accusation. "And how many other people knew about this? Did your parents know?" She was pissed.

His not answering gave her an answer enough. "They knew?!" she almost screamed, standing up.

Alex stood with her, "Please, Jessica. Not so loud. It couldn't be helped. My father had to know. He knew too many people. He knew the first time he tried to get me out on bail. He knew I had the right to bail, considering my circumstances. All the evidence was circumstantial. They couldn't possibly hold me."

That didn't make Jessica feel any smarter. She should have known that herself. But it was obvious they thought she was just a stupid artist; a stupid woman who they all believed couldn't keep her mouth shut. She felt so furious that she could barely think straight. Her shoulder hurt like hell, and she wanted to be alone and think. "What car are you driving?" she asked him. "Give me the keys." She held out her hand, palm up.

"No," Alex answered her. "I'm not going to let you drive with your injured shoulder. Let me drive you."

"Give... me...The... keys!" Jessica said to him in a voice that left absolutely no room for argument.

"At least let me drive you to where you want to go."

"Now!" Jessica said to him quietly. "Or I'll walk all the way to the ranch."

"Please," Alex begged her. "Let me call Will then. Have him come to pick you up. You're on medication. You shouldn't be driving." Jessica turned and started for the door of the cafeteria.

"Jessica, come on." Alex pleaded. "Please don't leave mad. Let me finish."

She turned on him in the hallway. "Oh, now you're worried about me!" she screamed at him. "NOW! When I was out there risking my life to prove your innocence!" she said, pointing vaguely out the door. "Do you know what I did for you? Do you know that I went to the topless place and talked to a dangerous drug dealer for you? That I had to wear a disguise and hang out in a biker's bar to get information for Christ's sake? And did you care? NO! You were somewhere, probably staying in some resort here in town and soaking in the hot tub!"

"God! Don't say that!" Now Alex's voice had risen to the same pitch as hers. A few people diverted their paths to avoid them, and others peeked around corners to see who was making all the noise.

"You have no idea what I was doing!" He took a deep breath and quieted his voice in an effort to help calm them both down. "Okay, look. I deserve to be yelled at. But I won't have you thinking I wasn't concerned for your safety." He placed both hands on his hips and loomed over her. "Do you remember seeing a guy in a red ball cap? Long hair, skinny?"

When it was evident by her expression that Jessica did remember seeing the mysterious character, Alex went on. "He's Agent Rand. I sent him to tail you, to protect you. Do you remember the day at the dance at Hotevilla? When you went off to find me? Well, you almost walked into a trade deal with Mac and his friends. My guy diverted you. And then again, when you visited Heathcliff at the topless bar? Do you remember the drug bust? Well Agent Rand set that off when you managed to get yourself upstairs into Heathcliff's office."

Jessica suddenly remembered seeing the man then, and again when they'd been eating in the Cameron Trading Post restaurant, and a reporter had almost attacked her at dinner. The red-ball cap guy had physically removed the reporter from the restaurant!

Alex went on, "Agent Rand couldn't follow you upstairs and make sure you were okay, so I told him to call in a bust to get you out of there."

Jessica blinked at him. "You did that?" she asked.

"Yes," he put his arms down and moved closer. "And more. I was there in the room at the topless bar—two braids, a red bandana—ring any bells? You're very important to me, Jessica. I wouldn't let anything happen to you." He ran his hand down her good arm and took her hand in his. "You scared the shit out of me a couple of times. I thought you were just a quiet artist. How would I know you'd become some crazy undercover spy?"

Jessica was forced to smile, and then tears filled her eyes. All the fear and confusion rushed away so fast it left her dizzy. "You really worried about me?" she asked in a small voice.

"Of course I did," he told her as he tucked a strand of errant hair behind her ear. "Please say you forgive me. I'm so, so sorry. And I'm so glad you're safe, and here with me." He stayed quiet, looking at her with calm eyes.

She kissed him for real this time, Jessica's good arm around his neck. With relief, he dropped his head onto her shoulder and let out a huge sigh, all tension leaving his stance, showing even HE had been worried. After their kiss, they slowly walked toward the door, Alex on her good side, his arm around her waist. She couldn't believe how quickly things had turned around. She was still a little in shock as the reality of what she just learned sunk in.

"I'm taking you back to the ranch and tucking you into bed. The doc says you need rest and time to recoup. We are following the doctor's orders, right?" he asked her playfully as he ran his hand sensuously down her hip. She frowned with disappointment. As much as she would enjoy making love to her husband, every muscle and bone in her body still ached, even with medication.

As they walked out the automatic doors, half a dozen reporters assailed them. Alex didn't avoid them this time, but simply said that they would be receiving a statement in about an hour that would give them their story. Two gave over their business cards to make sure the release went to the right email address, and after a few pictures, they were left alone. Alex helped her into his red Range Rover, and she felt safe for the first time in months. He got into the driver's seat and looked over at her. "Let's go home," he said, grabbing her hand and dropping a small kiss on her fingers.

Chapter 22: Gold Images on the Walls

Navajo Reservation, Northern Arizona

Jessica gave a second glance in the rearview mirror. She was praying to see the telltale dust cloud from another car on the rez road, but there was none. She'd been hoping Agent Rand, her 'tail', was following her in case she needed help.

It had been three days since Alex had rescued her from the hospital. Her shoulder was still hurting, but now it was a dull throb instead of a full-blown scream and she could actually move it without a painkiller. She'd stopped taking the painkillers the day before and found she was better off without them. They had been making her nauseous and now that the pain could be controlled with ibuprofen, she'd tossed the painkillers in the trash with satisfying finality. That chapter was closed.

Earlier that day, Alex had been called into town to help close the McInerney case. Now that Mac had died, the trail to the ancient gold had gone cold. While Alex had told her they'd known that Mac had been bringing artifacts to Heathcliff to pay for Rachel's drugs, they hadn't been able to find out where he'd been getting them. When Rachel had died out on Blue Moon Bench, they'd suspected that the artifacts may have come from that location, but they'd had no luck confirming their suspicions. Unlike Jessica, the department felt that

Rachel's death had been accidental. And for all Jessica knew, they might be right. After all, if the cave was out there and Mac had gone out that night to get some new pieces to sell, Rachel might have followed him. If she'd had a few drinks before following him, she might have simply slipped on the trail and fallen to her death without Mac even knowing she was there. Jessica guessed that now they'd never know, especially since the cave had not been found.

She had turned over Rachel's journal to the FBI and the information in it about a cave had fortified their theory, but it had not helped them to locate the gold. And now with Mac dead, it was pretty obvious the cave would never be found again.

At least, that was what everyone else thought, but not Jessica. That morning, she'd been watching "The Wizard of Oz" when she'd suddenly gotten an amazing idea. It came when the dog Toto climbed over some rocks, trying to lead Dorothy's friends to the bad witch's castle. It reminded her of when Chili had gone down into the hole in the floor of the ruin out on Blue Moon Bench. Something had bothered Jessica then, but she'd been too busy to dwell on it. What had bothered her was that the hole had looked shallow, but Chili had actually disappeared into it for several seconds before coming out. And she hadn't backed out as if the hole was small, but came out forward looking as if she'd had plenty of room to turn around in there. Jessica wasn't sure, but she had a sneaking suspicion that the hole might be bigger than it looked, and might even be the entrance to the cave. And remembering the climbing equipment down in the small cave she'd explored the day Mac died, she brought some climbing equipment of her own, with a headlamp, just in case she got lucky.

She'd decided that if the climb looked too terrible for her shoulder to bear, she'd just confirm her suspicions about it being a cave and then return to the ranch to tell Alex. But what she was really hoping for was to get closer to knowing how Rachel had died, and the cave's discovery might help with that.

When she'd left the ranch, she'd written a note for Alex, just in case. She didn't want to tell anyone else what she was up to, but she did want Alex to join her if he got back early enough. Her note had been a little cryptic, but she knew he'd understand. She said something like, once in a blue moon you could find what you were looking for, but you had to look carefully. The thing they had lost, the note said, was found. It was in the hold of the boat, hinting at the boat-like shape of the plateau where the ruins rested. Let anyone else read it and she was pretty sure they'd never figure it out. But Alex would know what she was talking about.

When she arrived at the ruins, it was only just after one o'clock. A crisp, sunny day with a small November breeze out of the south that left the air so clear Jessica could see the Desert Tower perched on the National Park side of the Grand Canyon.

She parked her truck where it could be seen from the road in case Alex did come out looking for her and closer to the Manygoats hogan than the ruins. She was sure no one else would care that she was visiting the ruins on a quiet Thursday. She brought her pack with the climbing gear inside all the way to the room with the hole in the floor.

It was just as she suspected. The hole was quite deep; it just wasn't evident from the side where she'd been standing on her first visit. Rubble from a fallen wall blocked the entrance, but from the other side, you could see a dark chimney that angled toward the plateau rim, and opened to daylight about fifty feet down. The descent was gentle and not a problem for Jessica with her bad shoulder. She didn't even need her ropes.

Gently lowering herself down with her climbing gloves protecting her from the cold rock, she came to an end and looked out with fear to a dead drop into the Grand Canyon, where both Rachel and Mac had died. Closing her eyes and taking a deep breath, she slowed her heart. She had to block the imprinted image of Mac as he dropped out of sight over the edge.

She almost climbed back out of the cave, thinking she needed to forget being a hero, and let someone else actually find the cave. But her sense of curiosity overcame her fear.

She tied off right there in the cave and slowly scooted on her butt to the end of the opening, and her efforts were rewarded. She saw directly beneath the mouth of the cave... a trail. It was a good five feet wide so she rolled over on her tummy and lowered herself onto the ground, keeping her face to the wall, her pack scraping the rock above her. She was relieved to find the trail solid and wide, a wall of rocks shooting up on the left side of the trail, putting the path between the canyon wall and the rocks, making it a safe traverse and impossible to see from the rim. She also noticed a small outcropping of bushes shielded the mouth of the smaller cave from eyes on the rim. As she lowered herself down, a colorful lizard darted into view and then dashed away. It made her feel happy.

She stood a few moments catching her breath, and trying valiantly not to look out over the edge. Instead, she looked at the trail as it snaked away from her, and turning around, she had a good view of the Manygoats family hogans. She looked at the trail and back to the hogans, and suddenly understood what the 'spirit lights' were that Billy had talked about. They probably were the headlamps that Mac, and anyone with him, would have worn when he'd been visiting the cave at night. Walking along the trail in the dark, the light would have created eerie, ghostly reflections on the walls making Billy's spirit lights real instead of fantasy.

Kenneth had said Billy had seen the lights one night, and the next day found a sheepdog dead, and he'd thought it was a skinwalker 'looking for its own'. Mac had probably poisoned the dog because he would bark when Mac didn't want to be discovered, and perhaps he'd been afraid someone would investigate and find the cave.

And he also said he'd seen lights the night before he found Rachel's body. That would mean someone had indeed been out here the night

Rachel died. Maybe Rachel had been out here alone, and slipped and fell. In the journal she talked about the cave but not it's location, but there seemed to be missing pages that were torn out by someone. Maybe Rachel wanted the cave's whereabouts to be kept secret. Poor Rachel.

Jessica wiped a line of sweat off her forehead and tried not to think of how she'd almost fallen to her own death the day Mac died.

She adjusted her pack, unhooked the rope and began to walk the trail, which traveled around the 'boat' to what would be the bow. By the time she reached the point, the ridge of rock next to the trail had risen about four feet high, but when she came around the last bend, the entrance to the cave she'd been looking for loomed before her, and there was no wall between the mouth and the drop into the Grand Canyon. The view was majestic. Looking north toward a bend in the river, tall pinnacles piercing the sky. The afternoon sun slanted rays of light through some high clouds, making the scene look almost divine in nature. For just a moment she was blown-away by the beauty of the view.

When she turned away from the view, she saw that the cave before her had a ceiling over fifty feet high, and looked to be about twenty feet deep, grey rock, massive and solid. There was evidence of a series of mud walls, buildings that once made up homes, now broken down and almost gone. She walked into the large cave with expectation and found at its deepest point a smaller arched entrance that she hadn't seen at first. It looked as if it was carved from the native rock, a rounded tunnel, smooth and beautifully polished. Complex, curly symbols had been engraved, intertwined one after another, around the rim of the arched doorway, making it look larger than it was. The symbols were at one time painted, but now the colors were mostly faded and worn away by time.

Jessica carefully stepped into the archway of the second cave and slipped on her headlamp, snapping on the light. The sun was shining at the right angle to add its own light, but there was so much to see, she was glad she'd brought it.

She stood frozen, stunned by what she saw. It was a long and narrow chamber, and all around her were large figures painted onto the walls of the cave, with long skirts and naked torsos. They were each carrying different kinds of vessels and containers, offerings of some kind, walking in procession toward an even smaller entrance with an arched doorway at the end of the chamber.

Jessica let out a quiet whistle as she realized that, to her, this cave had nothing to do with Spanish visitors. It was a cave that was very mysterious, and might be connected with the Anasazi (A Navajo word meaning "The Ancient Ones") whose culture is still unknown today. On the other hand, what she wasn't prepared for was its similarity to Tibet's art, or even Egypt's; the act of offering, the wearing of a topknot, and robe-like garments draped over one shoulder. This cave was something quite significant; there was no doubt of that. She wished Alex could be there with her to see it.

She was so amazed she almost tripped as she went into the last chamber and caught her breath. Her headlamp beam bounced off the murals that completely covered every wall, and the ceiling.

A beautiful blue sky with swirling clouds of rainbow colors on the arched ceiling gave it a feeling of space and fresh air. The room smelled beautiful and fresh, not like other caves that smelled of earth and dampness. She wondered if there was a fresh air hole to the surface somewhere. In this inner chamber, far from light, the colors were still quite vivid. Here all the figures painted on the walls were seated cross-legged, and each one was a little different, with elaborate crowns, topknots of hair, necklaces and bracelets. The floor was inlaid with a large circle made of stone with what looked like a lotus flower in the center. On both sides of the chamber were stone benches that ran along the wall. On the benches were hastily arranged gold and silver artifacts as if they were ready to be removed. There were beautiful, small statues, some standing and some sitting, all very intricate in workmanship, obviously well loved images for the inhabitants. They looked similar to the Tibetan Buddhist figures she was familiar with, but the crowns were taller and more like rays of light shooting upwards. Some items were intricately carved stone, while others looked to be of a metal - tarnished and ancient – the thing legends are made of. It was obvious even to her untrained eye, that the pieces looked to be ceremonial. Jessica stood in the center of the small cave quietly looking around her. It was a silent island of auspiciousness in the middle of a vast land of change.

This place must have been in existence for centuries, and stood the challenges of time and space. A feeling of sadness descended as she looked around, wishing it could have been left intact, unmoved and respected by all those who came before her.

Her headlamps' beam moved over the artifacts, each movement revealing yet another amazing find. Her eyes finally came to rest on what seemed to be the focal point of the room. There was an elaborately carved altar, the top holding a large, majestic gold figure, tarnished but still impressive, measuring at least four feet high, sitting in a crossed-legged position. It was more simply dressed than the others, quiet in its posture and wearing an almost Madonna-like smile. It looked as if someone might have attempted to move it, but abandoned the project, perhaps because of its weight.

She studied a large, amazing mask that was carved wood, sprouting hair around a face with large features. It was over four feet tall, about three feet wide, and carved so thin it weighed little. She moved closer to inspect the features. It was obviously a male, and had a face that looked almost like a skeleton with teeth bared, and empty, round eye sockets. He wore a large, square headdress that was sculpted of intricate geometric shapes and encircled the face. An elaborate breastplate was around his neck and was also covered in detailed shapes that looked like a necklace of small, human skulls. On the back of the mask were two handles for holding the mask in place and eye holes so the holder could see while carrying the mask.

Jessica looked down to where two open bags lay at her feet, filled with painted clay vessels, figures, chests and other artifacts she could not identify. Several large canvas bags lay folded to the side ready to carry more away. It was apparent the pieces had been moved and even sorted recently, but left in some disarray. She picked up one of the dusty bags almost as tall as she and wondered if Mac had been the one who had left them here.

Looking around her at all the wealth and history, Jessica wondered how Mac had kept such an amazing find a secret. She realized that his love for Rachel must have been very true to not reveal this cave to colleagues, and even more, to sell things from such a site just to keep Rachel's habit supported. It almost made her ill that pieces of this beautiful site were now somewhere in the world probably unappreciated.

In Rachel's diary, she had mentioned that for months Mac had been reluctant to show her the cave's location. She said he had been frightened that she might tell someone. There hadn't been a mention of the cave's location in the journal, only a couple of places where pages had been torn out that may have given that information. She now wondered again who might have removed them.

She decided that she needed to find Alex and show him the cave as soon as possible. It needed to be protected. Often these sacred sites on reservation land were still used by today's Native Americans as sacred ceremonial sites, which obviously wasn't the case here because of the recent looting. There were even sacred sites on BLM, or Bureau of Land Management land, still being used today by Natives with the government's permission. Maybe the entrance to the access cave here could be closed and with Alex's connections, that could be done before more of the cave disappeared through the hands of casual looters.

She was about to turn and leave when she heard the very distinct sound of voices. She froze as a shot of fear went through her, but she quieted it with the knowledge there were no signs saying she was trespassing, and she was after all, just looking. Still, Jessica quickly snapped off her headlamp and stepped away from the arched doorway so the casual eye couldn't see her from the first chamber. She held her breath. Who could be in the cave with her?

"I just don't think she'd find the entrance. She ain't smart enough," a man's voice said loudly.

"Shhh," a woman's voice answered. "Listen." The voices had sounded familiar to Jessica, but she couldn't quite place them. Was it possible they were talking about her?

A beam of light bounced on the walls around her as someone came from the next room with a light. She quickly crouched against the wall next to the bench, pulling the canvas bag over her, getting as small as possible in the corner, not daring to breathe. She instinctively knew she needed to be cautious until she figured out who was in the cave with her. Luckily the large facemask and the other bags next to her helped hide her body crouched under the canvas.

"See, I told you. Now come on, get the bags." It was the man's voice again; both apparently deciding no one was in the cave with them. Just as he spoke, he came into Jessica's view from her hiding spot. She could barely see him in the dim light, but suddenly he turned his face towards her so she could see his features. It was Ralph, her ex-ranch hand! Could the woman's voice be Dorothea, their ex-housekeeper and Ralph's wife? Her mind quickly tried to comprehend what they might be doing there. Weren't they in California? She squeezed her eyes shut and let out a quiet breath just as the woman's voice came to her, clear and loud.

"Alright, alright," she said. "Just let me catch my breath. That damn tunnel isn't easy to crawl down. Sit down for a second." It was definitely Dorothea, no doubt!

Jessica crouched in the dark, wondering what to do. The fact that they were here in the cave seemed out of place and disjointed in her mind. And Dorothea using curse words when she'd never used anything stronger than darn to Jessica's face. The deception made her uneasy, and what more could be behind that quiet exterior?

"I just wanna get the stuff and get the hell out," Ralph spoke again. "This place gives me the creeps."

"That's just because it reminds you of your precious Rachel," Dorothea said, her contempt obvious. "I thought the woman was useless when she wouldn't tell us where this damn cave was. If I hadn't found the journal with the location, we never would have found it."

"Yeah, but I thought you ripped out the pages that told where the cave was," Ralph's voice said. "Why did you try to get it back? That was a mistake. Now that woman is out here snooping around."

"I was afraid I might have missed an entry about the cave," Dorothea answered him with impatience. "Besides, I think she's visiting the Manygoats' family or she'd be here now. She doesn't know anything about the cave."

"But after Rachel died, Mac stayed away from here for a whole year! Why was he back here with Jessica on the day he died?" Ralph's voice got higher in pitch. "I don't like it. There's something screwy about it." His voice faded as he moved away from the room where Jessica hid.

"I know it, you idiot," Dorothea said with indignation. Suddenly Ralph let out loud, "Hey" right before the sound of a scuffle echoed around the walls, followed by a whimper.

There was dead silence after that, and then, "Quiet you fool. Her car is up there. She might be near enough to hear us. Get in there and start loading those bags. We need to get out before dark. I'm going up top to keep watch. Let me know when you're ready."

Jessica suddenly realized that he meant to come into the room where she was and pack up more artifacts in the bags. She held her breath and began to pray like she had never prayed before. She threw off the big canvas bag and pulled the large wooden mask to the wall and leaned it in a way that allowed her to crouch behind it, completely hiding her from view. She squeezed her eyes shut and tried to come up with a plan to save her own skin. She began to sweat and was stunned about what she'd just learned. Dorothea and Ralph had known about the cave! No doubt they had wanted the riches for themselves. So finding the cave had solved a mystery, but not completely. How did Rachael's death figure in all this?

Luckily, Ralph was going for small, easy to sell pieces and ignored the large mask in the corner with Jessica hiding behind it. She watched through one eye hole in the mask as Ralph began filling the half loaded bag she had held earlier. Dorothea joined him apparently after assuring herself that Jessica wasn't around, and they filled three bags altogether and then decided to head for their truck. Her shoulder had started to scream because of the cramped quarters about half way through the second bag, so she was relieved when they finally carried the third bag, filled and bulging, out the door. They had given the large mask a cursory look and turned away, probably because it was too big to carry.

She cautiously decided to stay where she was for at least another five minutes, holding her breath in the quiet of the cave. Then she quickly set the mask aside and slid out of her pack. Massaging her healing shoulder, she gave herself the luxury of stretching her legs and then slowly crouched back down to gather her thoughts.

She trembled slightly, thinking what might happen if they found her in the cave. She gave them enough time to reach their truck and then stood up from her crouch and made it back to the tunnel. It was quiet and she saw no signs of either Dorothea or Ralph at the top. She quickly scrambled up into the slanted passageway, her shoulder aching and stiff, and climbed out into the ruin, keeping low. The rope was now missing, so it was a little awkward and scary scaling it alone with a bad shoulder without any help, but she managed it with determination, relieved that she didn't meet them as she was coming out.

Just as she reached the top, she again heard their voices coming from the natural steps that led to the plateau. Slithering over the room's low wall, she crouched behind to keep out of sight.

"Alright, one more load, and then we're outta here. I just don't feel comfortable stayin' too much longer with her car out there," Ralph was saying. Another load, Jessica thought, she hadn't known. She'd gotten out just in time to hide.

"I hope we see her," Dorothea's cruel voice said. "I'd love to get that bitch alone out here. I'd throw her over the edge the same as I did Rachel. Would serve her ass right!"

Chapter 23: A Glint of Murder

Navajo Reservation, Northern Arizona

Jessica went cold with shock. Dorothea had killed Rachel! It took a moment before the realization sunk in all the way. Her husband wasn't a murderer! She was stunned beyond belief, and relieved at the same time as tears filled her eyes and spilled down her cheeks. Dorothea was the murderer, not Alex!

She didn't even give her own safety a moment's thought. She wanted them caught! She waited until she was sure they were deep in the tunnel. She quietly took out her cell phone, but this time she had no reception. She quickly went back over the wall and headed quietly for the exit of the plateau. She decided that as soon as she got reception on her phone, she'd call the sheriff in Tuba City, hoping they would get there before Dorothea and Ralph left.

Unfortunately, just as she reached the steps, she heard Dorothea's voice behind her. "There she is!" she shouted.

Jessica almost tripped, getting down the steps of the ancient city. As she ran to her truck she luckily had her car key still in her jacket pocket. In her hurry to get the door open, she dropped it from her sweaty hand and into the dirt. She quickly scooped it up and leaped into the truck, starting the engine with the gritty key even before she'd shut the door, pedal to the floor trying to leave them in the dust.

Dorothea and Ralph were sprinting to their truck, and had the engine running almost as soon. Their vehicle was parked for a fast getaway, and they were after her before she could get some distance between them. She gunned the Discovery, not known for its great pickup, and her first thought was to get to the highway in hopes of finding a Tuba City Sheriff on the prowl. But Dorothea and Ralph were so close; she feared they'd ram her before she'd make it there. Suddenly, when her back window exploded from a rifle shot that barely missed her, she knew she had more to worry about than being rammed.

With desperation, she saw a small two-track that suddenly took off to the right. She slammed on the brakes and jerked the wheel, sending the car into a skid, dirt and dust flying in the air behind her. She gunned the engine so the truck spurted down the side road and realized the importance of seat belts when she hit her head on the roof as the truck accelerated over a huge rut. She quickly grabbed the belt and slammed the thing into its latch just as she hit a second hole and went airborne. The Discovery dove back onto the road like a champ and kept moving.

In the rearview mirror, Jessica barely saw through the dust that the two were driving their big red truck with a camper shell, easy to see because of its color. She found it morosely humorous that it was the one Alex had given them for their years of good service.

They hadn't anticipated Jessica's move, but Dorothea was an aggressive driver, and she also slammed on her brakes, but late enough that she had to drive across the desert to intersect the road and follow Jessica. It gave Jessica several car lengths and she felt some satisfaction when she saw their truck's rear end leap into the air as they met deep cuts in the terrain before rejoining the two track road.

Now Jessica was far enough ahead to be out of their rifle range.

The next time she tried the same trick with the abrupt turn, Dorothea was on to her and it gained her nothing, so she headed to a hogan she'd seen in the distance. She thought the two wouldn't dare try to kill her before witnesses.

Unfortunately, there appeared to be no one home at the first hogan she found. In frustration, Jessica bounced through the yard and back to the main road, driving so fast the washboard pattern in the road had no effect on her airborne tires. She had lost them in the cloud of dust behind her and couldn't tell just how close they were. But in an act of desperation, she turned sharply to the left at the bottom of the next wash, pushing the Discovery down the sandy terrain, taxing even its four-wheel drive prowess. She switched it into high four-wheel assist and stomped on the pedal. Unfortunately, the high profile of the automobile became a disadvantage. With the tilt of the car, and her attempt to accelerate in the sand, the Discovery went up on two wheels, threatening to turn over.

Jessica immediately let off the gas, but it was too late. Like a dying elephant, the big SUV slowly rolled over on its right side and came to a stop in the deep sand. She hung sideways in the seatbelt, gasping and making small, fearful sounds. She fumbled with the seatbelt clasp, pulling herself out the shattered back window, trying to ignore the pain in her shoulder.

A huge cloud of dust was still all around her, preventing her from seeing if her assailants had stayed on the road or followed her into the wash. She stood up from the rolled truck, coughing and scrambled out of the dry creek bed, looking frantically around for cover.

"Don't even move," Jessica heard someone say above her. She looked up on the rim of the shallow canyon and standing right on the edge was Dorothea and she had the huge rifle trained on Jessica, the red truck idling just behind her, the door hanging open.

"On second thought, move," the woman shouted down to her. "It will give me a reason to shoot your ass!" She looked serious as she sighted down the barrel. Jessica felt terror well up inside of her chest. This lady had already killed Alex's first wife, what would stop her from pulling the trigger here on the reservation in such a remote place?

"Dot, I think someone's coming," Ralph's voice said somewhere beyond Jessica's sight. Dorothea glanced over her shoulder and obviously thought better of leaving a dead body where someone could find it so quickly. She motioned the rifle's barrel toward their truck to show she wanted Jessica to move in that direction, while keeping her in the rifle's sights. Jessica had no choice but to comply, and Dorothea followed her progress along the rim. The canyon got shallower and Ralph descended into the wash, grabbing Jessica's arm and leading her to their truck. Before putting her in the cab, they tied her hands behind her back, and she cried out with pain from the rough handling of her bad shoulder. They immediately stuffed a rag in her mouth, tying a dirty bandana over it to keep her quiet.

Jessica saw a billow of dust left behind by someone on the main graded road. She realized that her Discovery was too deep in the canyon for it to be seen by a casual passerby. The trail of dust was apparently left behind by someone on the way to a hogan and thought nothing of seeing Dorothea's old pickup parked down a two track.

Her two captives argued about what to do with her the whole way back to the cave. They decided to go back to get the rest of the artifacts, wanting to get all they could before they headed for the Mexico border. She knew that she was in real danger of losing her life when they talked without any concern of her knowing their plans. She also knew that if she were going to survive, she would have to escape from them before they finished loading the stolen artifacts. After that, disposal of her body was the only thing standing between them and a clean escape.

They hustled her back down into the cave, her injured shoulder screaming its resentment. Ralph tried to get her comfortable in a corner of the first chamber where she wasn't in the way and asked if she needed anything. Dorothea pushed him aside with impatience and shoved Jessica on the ground, banging her bad shoulder. She winced in pain and moaned behind the gag. "This witch is nothing but an inconvenience you idiot. Stop treating her like she matters. Now get in there and start loading the rest of the stuff. Hurry up." With no remorse or compassion, Dorothea tied Jessica's feet together and left her lying on her side. She then left the cave while leaving Ralph to his work.

Jessica struggled, trying to wiggle the bandana just a couple of inches down so she could speak around it, but the rag they had stuffed into her mouth made it impossible. Her tongue felt so swollen and dry, when she tried to swallow she almost gagged.

Ralph came out dragging two of the large masks with him. "I'm so sorry," he told Jessica, "Sometimes she's rougher than she means to be." He tilted Jessica back up so she was sitting upright against the wall. She lashed her feet out with a desperate attempt to trip him to the ground, her eyes stinging from her tears.

"Hey!" he shouted at her, jumping back just in time to escape her kick. "Stop that! I was tryin' ta help!" Jessica fell back over on her side, helpless with her hands and feet tied.

"I said, leave her alone you fool!" Dorothea came back into the cave in time to see Ralph standing over her. Dorothea cuffed him across the jaw and sent him reeling onto the cave floor. Ralph came up looking scared, holding a hand to his face to soothe the sting.

"If I find you messin' with her again, I'll toss you over the edge too!" That couldn't be good, Jessica thought. Throw him over the edge too?

"Are we gonna take the big statue?" Ralph asked Dorothea, carrying the masks to the cave entrance.

"Sure, honey, you go ahead and carry it up there," Dorothea sneered at him. "It probably only weighs two tons."

Ralph stood there for a couple of seconds, taking in her comment while Dorothea posed with her hands on her hips. He finally got that it was sarcasm and shrugged before turning away and continued with the masks onto the trail.

It was the first time that Ralph had left the cave, and the first time she had been alone with Dorothea. Jessica was certain the end was near and wondered how she could possibly defend herself. She tried the strength of the bonds she'd been pulling on and they seemed looser, but she still couldn't remove her hands. Her shoulder was so painful now that she was finding it hard to concentrate on what she should do. She badly needed to swallow, and was afraid she was going to throw-up into the gag.

Dorothea walked over, loomed over her and smiled. Jessica tried to push herself up to at least get her legs in a good position to defend herself as much as she could. But her injured shoulder had been put through more than it could stand and gave out, keeping her on her side and in pain. Dorothea pulled her upright by her hair and sneered into her face.

"Are you ready to go over? Won't it be interesting, three people dying all in the same place? Those idiot injuns will probably think some stupid superstitious shit again." She laughed pulling Jessica along the floor of the cave. She couldn't stop a scream of pain, muffled by the gag in her mouth.

Jessica's pain was so excruciating she was blinded by it until she opened her gritty eyes to look at her assailant and realized she was at the mouth of the cave with her body perpendicular to the edge of the canyon, only inches away. She was frozen with terror, helpless with her hands and feet tied, the gag over her mouth, dirt and dust caked on her from being dragged across the floor. A sudden calm descended over her. She felt sorry for Dorothea in her confusion.

Dorothea raised her foot and placed it on Jessica's body, still keeping her ponytail in her grasp, ready to push her over the edge. "Sorry honey, you know too much, you have to go." For the first time Dorothea actually displayed a little compassion. Jessica took advantage of it and looked up at her, pleading in her eyes. That moment of hesitation miraculously saved her life.

From above them, seemingly out of thin air, a figure swooped into the cave. A brilliant glint of the afternoon sunlight reflected and bounced around the walls, blinding Jessica only for a moment until she blinked three times. Dorothea had been knocked face down onto the ground. It was Alex! He had repelled in on a rope, slamming his feet into Dorothea's back as he swooped by. He now stood with his feet wide apart, hands raised, in a classic martial arts stance ready to take action. Jessica's relief was so enormous she felt a surge of gratitude and love for Alex and knew her prayers had been answered. She was safe.

Dorothea suddenly leaped up and pulled Jessica in front of her, using her like a shield. She grabbed one of her arms, got a better grip on her hair, and began backing closer to the rim. "I'll take her with me," she told Alex. "I don't stand a chance if you don't let me go. I'll bargain with you, but I won't go to jail." Alex said nothing and Jessica felt her head pounding as strands of her hair were painfully coming out one-by-one. How could he save her now?

"Ralph!" Dorothea screamed. "Ralph, where are you damn it!" She moved closer to the edge of the canyon, the two of them leaning backward, Jessica still and waiting.

"If you surrender now you can plea bargain," Alex told Dorothea. He was obviously trying to buy time. He slowly continued his progress, getting closer to them until Jessica could see the texture of the hair where his eyebrows grew together. Right at that moment she loved those tiny hairs, and now that she knew he wasn't a murderer, she yearned for the opportunity to live long enough to get to know each and every one of them intimately. She closed her eyes against her pain and fear, and prayed, "We haven't had enough time together yet, oh please don't let anyone die here…"

Without warning, Dorothea suddenly fell forward into Jessica, knocking them both to the ground; Dorothea landed on top of her. In the next instant Dorothea's weight was no longer smashing her down, and Alex was beside her.

"Are you alright?" Alex asked her while he untied the bandana and removed the gag from her mouth. She tried to sit up while gasping and spitting.

That was when she saw Agent Rand covered in dust and also in climbing gear, a rope dangling from the top of the cave attached to his belt. He had Dorothea in handcuffs and was standing over her with a gun and two-way radio, talking to someone quietly. She realized that he must have repelled into the cave after Alex, swinging into Dorothea from the back and shoving her away from the edge of the canyon, causing her to fall onto Jessica. That was the last thing she thought of as she passed out in Alex's arms.

Hours later, she woke up once again in the hospital. As she came to, the first thing she saw was Alex's loving face. She reached up and stroked his eyebrows, smiling with tears in her eyes.

"I lived?" she said in a small voice.

"Damn right," Alex answered her, brushing her hair from her face. "I wasn't about to let you go."

"What happened? The last I remember..."

"Shhhh," Alex told her in a gentle voice. "You're safe now. Dorothea will never give either one of us any trouble again. Now, get some sleep. I'll be right here." Jessica closed her eyes and smiled, the feel of Alex's warm lips against her forehead as he climbed onto the hospital bed next to her, spooning her close. Both fell asleep with a deeper understanding of what real love was about.

Chapter 24: The Magic Shaman

Colorado River, Grand Canyon, Arizona

The front end of the raft leapt up into the air and came down with a dizzying jerk. Everything in the boat would have ended up in the river had it not been tied down. The whitewater roiled around them, and their oarsman was skillfully using his oars to keep the raft from getting into trouble in the rapids.

Jessica was soaked and exhilarated by the cold water, cooling them from the July heat in the Canyon. She clung to the ropes on the side of the raft and braced her feet against some of the boxes in the middle. Alex sat behind her and had one arm around her waist to make sure she didn't go overboard. She would have been insulted by the insinuation that she wasn't able to take care of herself, because in truth, her shoulder was healed and strong. She just had to convince him of that.

The wild ride continued as the raft shot into the air once more, white foam spraying the occupants, and then came down into a hole. They came up out of the boiling water and headed directly toward a huge boulder, and the oarsman deftly steered the boat around it with one flick of the oar. After a few more minutes of whitewater, the large raft shot into the calmer waters of the Colorado River, and they continued at a more languid pace.

Jessica turned toward Alex, saw the smile on his tan face, and knew this trip was giving him the break he had needed. What she hadn't told him was that she'd agreed to go on the expedition because of Alex, not for herself, as he thought.

After Dorothea and Ralph had been apprehended, and they had gotten a confession out of Dorothea saying that she had actually murdered Rachel, Alex had gone into a quiet depression. Jessica was sure that he still blamed himself for what happened to his first wife. Now it seemed that this trip was helping him to get his mind off what had happened in his past, bringing him back to today.

Dorothea and Ralph were both in jail awaiting trial. Dorothea had told the FBI the story of the night Rachel died. She had overheard Rachel and Mac talking about the gold taken from a hidden cave to pay for drugs. When she and Ralph had no luck in finding the cave on their own, they tried to follow Mac, but he was too careful.

So the night of the party, Dorothea told Rachel that Mac was waiting for her out on Blue Moon Bench, and then told Mac Rachel was waiting for him. They picked the night of the party because they thought it would add confusion and act as cover to their plan, and hoped the two of them would lead them to the cave's entrance.

As Rachel drove to meet Mac, they followed her, but she didn't get to Blue Moon Bench until it was too late. Mac had already left, probably thinking Rachel wasn't coming, destroying any hope of him revealing the way to the cave of gold.

Dorothea and Ralph then surprised Rachel with their presence, and tried to force her to tell them where the gold was. Jessica didn't remember the details of what happened then, but apparently Rachel either didn't know where the cave was or wouldn't tell. But the final outcome was the same. Dorthea went into a rage and pushed Rachel over the edge to her final, lonely death at the bottom of the Grand Canyon that very night. If only Mac had stayed, if only Rachel hadn't gone out there. But now it was too late.

Later, one of the construction guys remodeling the stone building into a studio mentioned finding the cubby above the fireplace and that it had an old journal of Rachel's in it. Dorthea was sure it held the location of the cave, so she tried to find a time when no one was around to grab it, but unfortunately Jessica and Alex arrived home from their honeymoon, and the security system had been set, stopping her from entering without Jessica's permission.

Jessica had learned all this when she was released from the hospital. Alex told her the story and what had happened after Rachel's death. It seemed that almost a year later, Dorothea and Ralph still didn't know the cave's whereabouts. Mac no longer needed the artifacts to pay for Rachel's drug use and stopped visiting the cave altogether.

It wasn't until Dorthea found the security code in Jessica's misplaced iPhone that she thought she was finally going to be able to get to the journal.

That's what she had been doing the night Jessica caught her in the studio, standing before the tile on the fireplace. And when Jessica had gone to California the next day she took the journal with her. A few days later Dorothea got drunk, tearing the studio apart in her search for the missing book, the only evidence of the cave's existence.

After Alex fired them both, they made one trip to Blue Moon Bench, and this time they were successful. Mac had revealed to them the location of the cave when he was drunk, and so they started to make their plans. Ralph immediately went to California and created cover by looking for a job there, while Dorothea stayed in Arizona firming up arrangements with Heathcliff, giving him time to find a buyer for such a large and important group of ancient artifacts. Ralph came back from California to help Dorothea in her plan, which was to sell half the artifacts through Heathcliff and take the other half with them over the border into Mexico. But their plan failed when Jessica and Alex showed up at the cave.

Jessica looked back now and realized that she had learned

something from the experience she hadn't expected. She'd learned that she was a strong woman of faith, who could handle almost anything life handed her because of that strength. And she had also learned that she had made the right decision when she'd married Alex after only three months. For the first time in her life, she didn't run away as soon as things got tough. She'd stayed and fought, and overcame forces that would have left a weaker woman trembling. She knew now that she and Alex had the kind of love that most people dreamed of and never experienced. And she was glad she hadn't thrown it away in fear.

Will and Emma were on the river trip with them and now that the boat was out of the whitewater, they were all talking at once. It wasn't really necessary to towel off after the blast of water, because the temperatures were warm enough to make the cooldown feel good. Before long, they all settled back down into the boat, watching the passing panorama of spectacular canyon walls. Jessica knew the Grand Canyon, in its entire splendor from the bottom, would be hard to match in beauty.

Alex took out his camera and began shooting the late afternoon sunlight as it played off the water. Jessica laid her head back and began drifting off into a languorous doze. It felt so good to just let go of all the stress of the last few months, and know that the only concern was if she wore enough sunblock.

Seeping into her sleeping doze was the sound of Will and Emma talking quietly. Jessica smiled to herself. The two had been getting closer on this trip, and Will really seemed to be taken with the small Navajo woman. Emma had given birth to a healthy little girl two months ago, and the secret of the father was revealed only to Jessica and Alex. It had been her cousin who raped her just before she and Alex had rescued her. Jessica thought Will might make a great father, and couldn't think of anyone better for Emma to spend the rest of her life with. She hoped things would work out for them.

Jessica sat up in the raft and spoke to the boatman, asking where they were beaching for the evening. His name was Greg, and he was a friend of Ron's. Ron had made all the arrangements for this trip, and in fact, he and another couple were riding in the other raft that was with their group. Ron had suddenly given up river running, and decided to settle down with a new woman he'd met just a week earlier. After Ron realized that Jessica wasn't going to leave Alex, he confided to her that he'd decided to make a change in his life, and she was relieved and happy for him. He'd been offered the job of manager at The Edge and decided to take it, put in an offer on a house, and he kept talking about a dog. She knew these were big commitments for Ron.

Greg started steering the boat toward shore and before long, they were all involved in unloading for the evening. The camp was set up away from the river's edge, and the port-a-potty was discreetly placed behind a huge boulder at the end of the sandbar where they had put in. Jessica had been amazed and then impressed with the committed concern the crew had for conserving the beauty and ecological balance of the Grand Canyon. The group had been given a very detailed list of what to pack, and what not to pack, well before the trip. They were warned to never leave soda cans or even a tissue behind. Jessica had a plastic zip lock bag that carried all her trash, including wrappers from her granola bars, tissues, and any other personal trash, which she would take with her when leaving the canyon.

Every morning, when they left the area where they had camped, the beach looked exactly the same as when they arrived, except for their footprints. All this care and concern seemed to be echoed by all the other licensed river runners, because never did Jessica see one piece of trash, soda cans, baby diapers or any other garbage usually left behind by tourists. It gave the river a special feeling of pristine wilderness and helped to make the trip even more special. You could not camp or boat these days in the Canyon without a permit, which helps the forest service control the number of boats that enter the canyon each year, helping to preserve its environment.

It was the sixth day of the expedition, and the next day they'd be putting into Phantom Ranch, where they would spend their last night. Then it was a long nine-mile hike out of the canyon.

The crew had already begun the preparation of dinner, and the rest of the group occupied themselves with setting up the rest of camp. Alex had found a large flat ledge and pitched their tent on the top, facing the river.

After camp was set, and dinner cooked, they all sat down for another amazing meal cooked in the open air. For this last night, it was chicken cooked over their huge gas grill, green beans, baked sweet potatoes and pineapple upside-down cake. They had hot ginger tea with their dessert, and everyone moaned from being so full.

As the sun set in the Canyon, the ten of them were expected to chip in and help with the work, and clean up was done in no time.

They sat around a fire built in a container on the sand. The crew had brought along a small cache of wood and was using it sparingly throughout the trip. Tonight, they would use up what was left since they'd be at Phantom Ranch tomorrow before dark.

One of the crew pulled out a harmonica and began playing a quiet tune as everyone sat listening to the sound of the river and the crackle of the fire in the background. Alex lit his cigar, and pulled Jessica back against his chest so they sat close together. It got later, and the music dwindled, leaving silence to talk about the trip and a review of all the places they had seen and explored. After some laughter and more talk, there was a general feeling of sadness because it had to end.

Soon the group was down to just Alex, Jessica and Will. Everyone else had gone off to their respective tents, ready to sleep through their last night in a small piece of heaven on earth.

"Well, I guess we have to get back to the real world tomorrow," Alex was saying.

"We'll get to sleep in a real bed tomorrow night at Phantom Ranch," Will commented.

"I can't say that won't be a pleasure," Jessica said, "I never knew sand could be so hard."

"I wonder if they finally arrested Heathcliff and his group," Alex said. "I know they had the warrant when we left the ranch last week."

"You know, I remembered overhearing a conversation the night I went to the topless club," Jessica commented. "I think it was Heathcliff saying that an older couple had brought him an artifact to sell that was very impressive, and that he hadn't seen any pieces of such quality since Rachel died. It must have been a piece Rachel had been keeping at home."

"I guess Dorothea and Ralph wanted to test the black market waters," Will said.

"It sounded like Mac hadn't sold any artifacts after Rachel's death," Alex commented. "That just confirms the only reason he was fencing them was to pay for Rachel's drug habit." Jessica was thrilled because he still found it difficult to talk about Rachel, but among his friends, he'd begun to open up a bit more.

"Poor Mac," Jessica said almost to herself. "He really lost it after Rachel died. I'm just glad that I found the journal." She looked up at the others. "If I hadn't figured out where the cave was, all those priceless artifacts would be in Mexico by now."

"But you said the journal didn't tell you where the cave was," Alex said.

"It didn't," Jessica answered him. "But it did say there was a cave and that's what clued me into it even existing. Chili did the rest." They laughed and Jessica smiled as she thought of her faithful dog.

She was now healthy and back at the ranch, just a little worn and not so quick, but otherwise just as spunky.

"I'm just glad you showed up when you did," Jessica said once again.

"Well, the note you left behind wasn't the reason for that. I couldn't figure out what the heck you meant about 'boat hold.' What boat?" Alex asked her.

"Oh, Alex. I meant the plateau where the ruin was. It looked like a boat to me." Jessica looked at him in disgust.

"Well, maybe to you artists. But the damn thing looks like a plateau to me." Alex winked at Will.

"Very funny," Jessica conceded. "But at least you understood 'once in a blue moon.'"

"Well, that one was pretty obvious," Alex answered, smiling. He seemed almost younger to Jessica, and she hoped it was because he was happier. The group of businessmen who had been pushing him to run for State Representative had withdrawn their offer of support. They were afraid the bad press had been too negative. Jessica was glad because she knew it was better for Alex. He needed to be himself, not in a public position that would take him from what he loved.

They all stared into the dying fire for a few minutes, then Alex stood up and said, "Well, Will, I think I'm gonna take this good woman to bed." He reached down to Jessica, whose eyes had begun to grow heavy. "Can you take care of the fire?"

"I got it," Will said, giving Alex a mock salute.

Jessica and Alex made their way to the tent and they stripped down to the bare essentials and slid into the two bags that were zipped together. They gently made love, sealing their last night on the river, a kind of celebration of being alive and together. The taste and feel of Alex gave her the comfort of security she so badly needed after the fear she'd had when all arrows pointed to him as a murderer. He had forgiven her for her doubt almost immediately, but it had taken her a little longer to forgive herself. Now that it was behind her, she knew the trip had renewed the bond between them.

"Alex," Jessica said into the dark after a deep sigh, "I'm anxious to get back to the ranch. It will be so nice to go back to work with Gary, and I'd love to see you find some new projects. And I know Chili will be glad to see us when we get home."

"I'm sure she will," Alex said, and Jessica could tell he was smiling. He had become as attached to the puppy as she. "Actually, I didn't tell you but just before we left, I received a phone call from the Smithsonian again. Do you remember the site Mac and I found around the time we met?"

"Of course," Jessica said, propping herself up on an elbow and peering at him. Light from the distant campfire illuminated the inside of the tent just enough so she could see his face. "It was a burial site, wasn't it?"

"Exactly, and the site yielded one man who has caused real interest," Alex told her, turning on his side so he could see the outline of her curly hair in the dark. "The Forest Service has agreed to allow us to excavate the whole site. The burial site is in an ancient city ruin on a terraced hill. It has a couple of ball courts and a complex maze of buildings around it. There are area pit houses and other kinds of dwellings that mean this civilization was very powerful, and that this man was the center of that power. He was buried in a structure on the top of the hill with the most amazing collection of jewelry and magic medicine bags. At first we thought he might be from deep in Mesoamerica, but now it seems his origin is a real mystery."

"Why didn't you tell me this before?" Jessica asked.

"I wanted you to rest, to not have anything else on your mind except getting well," Alex told her, leaning over to give her a gentle kiss.

"But now that we're almost ready to go home, I thought you'd like to know."

"And you're so excited I'm surprised you're here," she kidded him. "It sounds fascinating."

"I was hoping you'd say that," Alex told her, pulling her down next to him. "Because the Smithsonian liked the illustrations you did for the Forest Service last year and they would like you to assist me on this project. We're getting funding from three sources, and it looks like this may turn into our very own King Tut's tomb. Admittedly there isn't any gold involved, but I think this site might yield some really exciting things."

"I don't care if I ever see any gold artifacts again, to tell the truth. So this guy was a powerful man?" Jessica asked him. "Exactly what does that mean?"

"He was a Shaman, a holy man. He did magic and healed the sick. I call him 'The Magic Shaman'. I think you'll love him; he's undeniably handsome." Alex's voice was very persuasive.

"Oh, Alex," Jessica laughed. "Go to sleep. We can talk about this tomorrow when we're rested."

"Okay, but please just say yes, you'll help. It'll be fun," Alex started nuzzling her ear. "Please."

"Alright, alright, so much for a quiet life back at the ranch. But I'll tell you this Alex Dawson, no more murders or crazy women. I don't think my body can take it!" she finished, referring to her wounds from Mac's stray bullet, and the scar on her cheek she would carry for life.

They kissed after Alex promised there would be no more craziness, and then they shifted into what had become their usual positions for serious sleep. Jessica smiled to herself in the dark just before she drifted off. She instinctively knew there would never be a dull moment while she was married to Alex Dawson, and she was grateful.

The End

ABOUT THE AUTHOR

Thank you for reading Blue Moon Bench.

D.L. Blanchard is a writer, single and living on the Western Slope of Colorado. She is a Tibetan Buddhist, fine artist and author who lived in northern Arizona for over 17 years and spent many days hiking the canyons and deserts in the southwest. She has written many articles for magazines such as Southwest Art Magazine, Tucson Lifsyle, as well as the paper "Shaman's and Master Artists: Understanding the Parallels in Rock Art" published by the American Rock Art Research Association. She has also published a small illustrated gift book, 'The Heart Sutra. The Perfection of Wisdom' This book is based on one of the most well known text in Buddhism, the premise that all phenomena is entirely empty of inherent existence

Blue Moon Bench is her first novel and highlights the love the author has for northern Arizona and its native culture and majestic beauty. She is currently writing the sequel, "The Magic Shaman."

Please visit **bluemoonbench.com**

www.ingramcontent.com/pod-product-compliance
Lightning Source LLC
LaVergne TN
LVHW030910080826
845145LV00010B/2836

* 9 7 8 1 9 6 9 6 4 4 0 1 6 *